Love Out of Focus

More from Phase Publishing
by

Rebecca Connolly

Agents of the Convent
Fortune Favors the Sparrow

The Arrangements
An Arrangement of Sorts
Married to the Marquess
Secrets of a Spinster

The London League
The Lady and the Gent
A Rogue About Town
A Tip of the Cap

The Spinster Chronicles
The Merry Lives of Spinsters
The Spinster and I
Spinster and Spice

Love Out of Focus

Rebecca Connolly

Phase Publishing, LLC
Seattle

Text copyright © 2017 by Rebecca Connolly
Cover art copyright © 2022 by Rebecca Connolly

Cover art by Tugboat Design
http://www.tugboatdesign.net

Phase Publishing, LLC second paperback edition
September 2022

ISBN 978-1-952103-44-5
Library of Congress Control Number 2022914358
Cataloging-in-Publication Data on file.

Acknowledgements

To Lake Lure, North Carolina for giving me this story almost from the first moment I set foot in it. For being the most beautiful place I have ever been in America, and for making this romance such an easy, captivating, and fun project all at once.

And to Sublime Lime Diet Coke. You're still my favorite. I'd come to the UK just for you.

Want to hear about future releases and upcoming events for Rebecca Connolly?

Sign up for the monthly Wit and Whimsy at:

www.rebeccaconnolly.com

Chapter One

"Freaking A!"

Mallory dropped the hammer and jerked her thumb to her mouth, sucking softly to deaden the throbbing pain. She slammed her free hand on the incomplete bookshelf that had caused her injury, wishing for the fifty-second time that she had hired someone to do the handiwork in her refurbished studio. At this rate, she wouldn't have any fingers left to actually take the pictures she was supposed to, let alone the ones she hoped to in the future.

"You know," drawled a surprisingly Western-twanged voice from nearby, "your inability to swear is really adorable."

Mal twisted her head to glare at the dark-complexioned, ponytailed young man leaning back in his chair, grinning at her. "Shut up, Dan," she said around her thumb.

His grin spread further, his dark eyes twinkling mischievously. "My grandfather would call you Terror with a Hammer."

Mal rolled her eyes and removed her thumb, shaking it. "Clever. What'd he call you, Brain of a Peacock?"

Dan chuckled and folded his hands behind his head, still leaning back. "Peacocks are the finest birds on the planet. I could go for that."

For a graduate assistant, Dan was fairly insolent, seeing as his graduation and future were conditional upon her reports. But considering she was not exactly demanding as far as mentoring was concerned, that was probably her fault.

She grumbled under her breath and returned to the impossible bookshelf at hand. Dr. Durango swore up and down that the two students he'd given her were the best in his class and would be promising photographers themselves in the future, and she believed him. But working with them, or anyone, was not quite in Mal's nature yet. At the moment, Taryn was working secondary camera shots and the front desk, while Dan handled editing and lighting. It wasn't ideal for them—or for Mal, as she preferred to have her hands on everything—but it was the best she could come up with.

Apparently, internships and assistantships for photography students were hard to come by. She'd never thought her old professor would actually consider her fit for mentoring, let alone guest lectures, but she was finally hitting her stride with that.

And the boost to her salary was pleasant enough.

"Don't you have some work to do?" she muttered, knowing Dan was still leaning back in his chair and watching her. "Or are you going to start talking about the ancestors now?"

Dan snorted and shook his head, his long hair whipping around a bit in his ponytail. "You really need to get your ethnicities straight. I've told you before. It's not Mulan, it's Pocahontas."

She looked up at him with a raised brow. "You're a Disney princess?"

He opened his mouth to retort something that probably would have been brilliant, but they were both distracted by the appearance of Taryn, looking like the trendy fashionista she was, if a bit sloppy. She gaped at Mal with wide eyes, her Trident gum threatening to fall out of her mouth.

"What?" Mal asked when it was clear her assistant was beyond words.

Taryn's blue eyes blinked once. "You never told me Jenna Hudson was your cousin."

Dan's chair crashed backward, and Mal exhaled in a slow, measured breath. She'd gone her whole life without anyone making that connection. And she'd enjoyed every minute of it.

"She is," Mal finally said. "So?"

"So?" Dan echoed in disbelief, picking himself up, finding his discarded baseball cap, and plopping it backward on his head. "So, it's Jenna Hudson."

"Who is in the front of the studio," Taryn said, folding her arms, "and asking to speak with you."

"Shasta," Mal muttered, making Taryn and Dan grin at each other.

She put the hammer on the floor and got to her feet, wiping at the bit of sawdust that had settled on her black denim pants. She glanced down at the emerald green V-neck she wore and remembered the mustard stain from lunch. There wasn't much she could do about that now. Then she remembered the old button-ups she kept for little-kid shoots. The parents loved the dressed-like-dad look, so she kept a few on hand. She never thought she'd wear them herself. Still, there was no way she was going to face her Saks Fifth Avenue cousin looking like she did now.

She grabbed an off-white pinstripe and tossed it on, rolling the sleeves to her elbows. Then she twisted her hair back into a messy, hopefully artistic bun and fastened it with the hair tie that lived on her wrist. It would have to do, but for the first time ever, she wished she kept a mirror back here.

Her assistants still stared at her, Taryn's arms folded across her chest and Dan's hands on his hips, both looking expectant.

"What?" she asked, wiping under her eyes in case her mascara had smudged.

Taryn pushed a strand of her currently Ariel-red hair behind her ears. "Your famous Southern socialite cousin comes to visit you in Denver, and you expect us to pretend it's cool?"

Dan shifted and looked at her. "It is cool," he pointed out.

Taryn twisted her lips. "Truth. But we need the story."

Mal ignored that. "What does she want?"

Taryn made a disgruntled noise. "Come on, boss! Tell us!"

"You want me to keep her waiting?" Mal asked with a quirked brow.

That seemed to shake Taryn. "Why are you still standing here, woman? Go! Go, go, go!"

Mal shook her head and passed both of them on the way to the front, knowing they would listen at the door. There was only one thing that her cousin could possibly want with her at this point, enough to make her take the trip from Tennessee to Denver without some massive social event taking place. Despite what her assistants and pretty much everyone else thought, Mal did follow some of the celebrity gossip. And what was being dubbed "America's Royal Wedding" was destined to be the most sought-after event since the actual Royal Wedding.

Wealth and consequence could get people pretty far, but when Southern charm and family values came into play, everything was a whole new ball game. No one got invitations to these things. No one. When Tennessee's favorite daughter married North Carolina's pride and joy, the very few people with invitations would be witness to one of the rarest and most elite spectacles in recent history.

Mal had wondered faintly if she would receive an invitation. She might not have been close with her father's side of the family anymore, but they had been as thick as thieves back in the day. Besides, family meant something to the Hudsons. Always had, always would.

The question remained whether or not Mal would have accepted the hypothetical invitation.

She glanced into the waiting area and saw Jenna sitting in one of the straight-backed chairs, looking every bit like Carrie Underwood's doppelganger. Her unnaturally perfect, but shockingly natural, blonde hair was pulled back into a ponytail, and her long, lean legs were crossed, bouncing anxiously. Just as they had when she was a kid.

Mal smirked at that. Despite what people said about Jenna Hudson—mainly accusations that she was a fake—Mal knew that Jenna's perfection was genuine. She was rare that way. Or, at least, she used to be. She could be anybody now.

"Jenna?" Mal said softly as she entered the room fully.

Jenna turned to face her, her smile revealing blindingly white teeth. "Mal!" she squealed, getting to her feet. "Oh my gosh, you look so good!" Her twang sounded heavy to Mal's ears, reminding her yet again how long it had been since she'd been down to Tennessee.

It was clear that Jenna was going for a hug, but Mal wasn't ready for that yet. "So do you," Mal replied with a smile, intentionally not approaching. "Nice to know they don't photoshop you."

Jenna's smile faded, and Mal wanted to kick herself. It wasn't Jenna's fault she was a celebrity. All she had done was date a guy from high school who went on to become a country star. She'd been on his arm at events, and he hadn't liked the fact that she had become more popular than he had. Even after he broke it off, Jenna had attracted the media instead of him. That was probably one of the reasons he was in rehab now.

Mal gestured to the chairs, and she and Jenna sat.

"It's good to see you," Jenna said softly, her smile just as soft. "What's it been, ten years?"

"Roughly," Mal replied. She'd visited after graduating high school, considering that her Uncle Drake, Jenna's father, had been intent on funding college for her. Checking in with her godfather had seemed appropriate at the time, even if she didn't know him as well as she used to.

Jenna looked at her for a long moment. She shifted, crossed and uncrossed her legs, and sighed. "Okay, I know you want to know why I'm here."

Mal smirked. For all her blonde hair, Jenna wasn't an idiot. "True."

"I'm sure you've heard about my wedding in May," Jenna said, pushing back an invisible strand of hair, her extraordinary diamond solitaire glinting briefly.

"I have," Mal replied slowly, shifting herself. "But the details are under wraps."

A thin smile appeared on Jenna's face. "That's on purpose. We're going even smaller than people think. Tom and I have lots of friends, but most of them are 'friends,'" she said as she rolled her eyes and used her fingers to quote the word. "And we're tired of pretending. I can't get away from it completely, but we can cut down on it. So, the location is top secret, and the invitations are strictly family, close friends, and significant people in our lives."

"And the press is gonna go for that?" Mal asked in disbelief. With how many tabloids and magazine covers that plastered pictures of Jenna whenever they could, Mal had a hard time believing that they would go along with that. Jenna was worth a mint every time they could snag a picture or story about her. No sane person in the media world would bypass the chance to sneak a glimpse of her wedding.

Jenna shrugged. "They'd better. None of them are coming."

Mal's jaw dropped, and her Rocketdogs skidded on the tile floor. "No press?"

Jenna smirked and shook her head. "Not a single reporter. No magazine access, no TV coverage, and no famous people." She rolled her eyes. "Except for us."

Mal sat back heavily against her chair, impressed by the implications, if it worked. "How'd you manage that?"

"I know people now," Jenna said with a grin. "But we also promised the press something they can report on for a while."

Something in her cousin's voice sent a warning signal to Mal's brain. "What's that?" she asked suspiciously.

Jenna tapped the table between them lightly in an absent rhythm. "Post-wedding access to a week-long prewedding extravaganza involving the wedding party and immediate family. Exclusive photos from one official camera approved by me. If they agree, and there are no paparazzi, they get the photos and interviews with guests after the wedding. If they don't, they get the secondhand version and the blurry selfies that Aunt Joni posts on her blog."

Mal snorted and covered her mouth, squeezing her eyes shut. That image would be her happy place for months. Aunt Joni loved nothing in the world but her niece's fame and her cats and thought every family event was actually a tribute to her. She was tolerable in large family gatherings, but lethal if she cornered you. Anybody restricted to her version of things would get far more than they bargained for.

Jenna bit her lip and shrugged. "We'll see if they agree to it. We have contract agreements with the major networks, so it looks good so far. We just want our wedding to be like anybody else's, you know?"

Mal gave her a look that clearly told her what she was thinking. Thomas Gregory Yardley the Third and Jenna Charlotte Hudson were not just anybody, and there was no way they could have an event that would remotely resemble "anybody else's."

"I know," Jenna said, answering the look. "But we can try."

Mal would give her that one. If anybody could pull it off, it would be these two. Tom came from money and power, and Jenna could charm anyone to do anything, and Uncle Drake wasn't exactly hurting for money either.

"Who's taking the exclusive photos?" Mal asked, thinking up a dozen names of people who would love to get their hands on it. "You've got that all decided, right?"

"Oh, I've decided," Jenna said slowly, "and Tom thinks it's a great idea. I haven't settled it yet."

Mal nodded, not quite sure why she was doing so, but it felt natural. "Better take care of that. You've got, what, two months? It's going to be tight, usually high-end photographers book a year out." She shrugged. "But it's you, so I don't think you'll have a problem getting anyone you want."

Jenna smiled. "That's good. Because I want you to do it."

Mal blinked once, then again. "Say what?"

"I want you to take the pictures at the wedding party, the whole week, and the ceremony and reception," Jenna said, leaning forward. "But more than that, I want you there, Mal. I want you to be a part of this."

"I don't do celebrity," Mal said faintly, ignoring the family plea. "I'm not that sort of photographer."

"I know exactly what sort of photographer you are." Jenna raised a brow and sat back, crossing her legs again. "You're the best. And I am not just saying that because you're my cousin. I went to the galleries in Colorado Springs and Des Moines. I saw your graduate project. Rustic Americana. It was the most amazing thing I've ever seen."

Mal could have been knocked unconscious by a breeze. Never in a million years would she have pegged Jenna to have an interest in her work. And to go to the galleries? It was impossible.

"It was so touching that you put on a show in Iowa so your aunt and uncle could see it," Jenna said with a smile. "I bet they loved that. And their neighbors too. That one of the old man with the scruff and the prairie grass in his mouth? Was that your grandpa?"

Mal slowly and shakily nodded.

Jenna put a hand over her heart. "I loved that one, Mal. Loved. So poignant and moving. It's his farm y'all lived on, right?"

Again, Mal could only nod. Jenna had seen the pictures. And that one of Grandpa Ned was Mal's favorite too. He'd thought it silly she wanted a picture of him, but she insisted. He died a month later, and it meant more to her now than ever.

"And your Aunt Nancy with the cow," Jenna continued, shaking her head. "She looks just like your mama, Lord bless her soul. It made me miss Aunt Tess like nobody's business."

"You did see them," Mal said in surprise.

Jenna nodded, still smiling. "Told ya. And I want you to take the pictures, Mal. I know it's not your thing, but I don't want regular pictures. This is my wedding, and we are going to be in a beautiful place. Heaven on earth. I want your type of photos to capture it all."

Well, now, that was a tempting offer. Someone who actually knew her work and wanted her style, even if it wasn't her usual sort of setting and theme… That sounded like a challenge she liked. Granted, at the moment, her most popular clients were stay-at-home moms who wanted to test out Pinterest ideas, but sometimes she scored good projects she could actually put in her portfolio.

"And if that's not enough," Jenna said, her voice growing more excited, as if she knew she was winning, "I scored you something else too. The resort we're staying at? They need some new photos taken, something to get more publicity, and they want high-class. The very best. Conveniently, I know the very best, so it works out well. Mountains, vistas, cabins, lakeside docks, old houses, and really bad cell reception… Mal, it's perfect for you. You would have a field day."

Mal looked at her cousin, impressed again. She was actually quite brilliant. "You've thought of everything, haven't you?"

Jenna grinned. "I couldn't take a chance you'd say no."

"I haven't said yes yet," she reminded her. "I won't do it for free, Jenna, not even for you."

Jenna snorted. "I would never ask you to, especially not with what we have in store. And the contract for the resort is all you, no favors here and no deals." She reached into her purse and pulled out a slip of paper, folded it, and slid it across the table to her. "This is what we're thinking for the wedding. I have no idea what your contract is, that's up to you and the resort. But it'll be good, Mal. Promise."

Mal felt a little cheap taking that slip of paper, demanding money from her family when they already took care of her more than she'd admit to anyone. But opening that paper, seeing the astronomical number written there, and reading it twelve more times to make sure she hadn't imagined the number of zeros, she suddenly didn't feel that cheap.

"Done," she said simply, tucking the paper into the pocket of her shirt.

Jenna grinned brilliantly. "Thank you, Mal! I promise you will love it. We've got a spa and fashion designers coming to spruce us up and a schedule for the entire week. I have a copy here for you, that way you can plan out what you need to bring. Now, you ever been to Lake Lure in North Carolina? 'Course not, you've never even heard of it. You've been in Iowa and Denver, and didn't you travel Europe after college? Someone said you had amazing shots of the Eiffel Tower in a snowstorm. Anyway, bring whoever you need, all paid for. Just let me know, and we'll get it."

Mal's head started to swim the longer Jenna talked, and she wondered what in the world she'd gotten herself into. Her father's side of the family was nuts, utterly and completely, but the kind of nuts you talk about with a smile.

At least, she thought they were.

It had been a long time.

She had no problems bringing Taryn and Dan with her, assuming they could keep their traps shut about whatever family secrets were unearthed. But if the muffled squeals and sounds of high fives behind the studio door were any indication, she'd need to figure out some pretty specific contracts for them.

There was no telling what sort of crazy her family would unleash—particularly at a secluded resort with no one to witness any of it.

Chapter Two

Two months later.

"Right, so Kids' Day is tomorrow. What kids are even going to be there? This isn't the wedding, it's the prewedding shindig!" Taryn snorted and shook her head. "But, to be fair, tomorrow is also Designer Day. What does that even mean? Do you think Gucci is coming? Then makeup and hair tests the next day, that should be fun. And Wednesday is a live band and karaoke at the resort. Maybe I'll get to sing Celine Dion–"

"Holy crap, Taryn." Dan snorted from his seat, looking over at her from where he rode backward in the limo. "Did you memorize the entire itinerary?"

Taryn glared at him and adjusted the vest over her burgundy peasant top. "Shut up, Dan. This is a once-in-a-lifetime opportunity."

"To take pictures of your idols?" he asked innocently, crossing his ankle over his knee. "You always wanted to be a paparazzo, didn't you?"

Taryn actually snarled a little as she smiled. "Don't be petty, Dan. If you're nice, I'll have the girls bring you some crackers and talk to you for a bit. That way you can have the most action you've had since fifth grade."

"Good year, fifth grade."

Mal watched her assistants with a small smile, trying hard not to think about the week ahead of her. She'd debated the wisdom of her decision multiple times a day ever since Jenna had asked her to do this ridiculous thing—taking pictures of all those high-class people and snobs, most of them wanting her to shrink the size of their nose and trim their waists in editing. There was hardly anything artistic about this venture.

But she was getting paid, and paid well, and there was simply no refusing Jenna, even now. And if Mal were being honest, she did want to see the rest of the family. It had been too long since she had seen any of them—too long in Lorimor, too long in Europe, too long in Colorado. She'd been avoiding them. She'd wanted to make her own name without them.

Which was ironic, since now she might just make her name because of them. Jenna's popularity and strict media contracts pretty much ensured that Mal's work would be in high demand. Yes, by companies and people who wouldn't treat them with the same appreciation that Mal was going to take with them, but it just might be what got her name out. She would give Jenna her best work, despite what she felt about it. She could never take a project and do it half-heartedly, even if it wasn't what she wanted to spend her time and effort on.

Taking pictures at Rambling Ridge Resort on Lake Lure might give her some notoriety as well, and in the fields where she wished to thrive. She'd analyzed the same itinerary that Taryn had memorized, and she found several gaps where she could take the time she needed to explore. The contract with the resort was straightforward: she was to take pictures they could use in brochures, on websites, for artwork. She had absolute freedom, free rein of the place, and any additional help she needed would be provided upon request. She'd had enough with the lawyers, who really couldn't answer her questions about the artistic details, but they knew enough about her contract and requirements that she didn't mind that much.

She just wanted to work now.

"Taryn," she finally said, as the two continued bickering, "you do realize that we're not actually part of the group, right?"

That shut the two of them up. Taryn gawked, her gum threatening to tumble out, and Dan's eyes were wide.

"We're…" Taryn started, apparently unable to fathom such a shocking thought.

"We are the photographers, Taryn," Mal reminded her, reminded them both.

"You're her cousin," Dan said faintly, which made her want to laugh. He'd been so blasé about the whole thing, seeming not to care one way or the other, but he looked as devastated as Taryn right now, and it was hilarious.

Mal shrugged. "I'm her cousin, but I'm the photographer. The only one, remember. And I'm the photographer this week, not her cousin. I'm not her cousin until Saturday at the family breakfast before the wedding. We might get some bits and pieces of what everybody else gets, but if you think we're going to be decked out in designer clothes and having our pictures taken, I think you'd better check that now."

Taryn and Dan looked at each other and frowned in unison.

Mal snorted. "Wanna get out? We're not there yet; if being only a photographer isn't good enough for you…"

The limo stopped then, and Jerry, the cheerful driver who had joked with them all the way from the airport, turned to face them with a grin. "Too late now, folks. We're here."

For a second, all three of them looked at each other in a sort of bewildered horror.

Mal swallowed quickly. "Remember, guys, we're professionals."

"Right," they said together as they clambered from the limo, one saying it with determination, the other with sarcasm.

Mal felt a whole lot of both.

The first steps out of the limo told her everything she needed to know about this place. The trees were tall and stately, the pavement beneath her feet worn and dusty, and the air was so fresh she might have been at the top of a mountain in Colorado—except there was something very earthy about this place, a sort of flowery-pine scent that bore a hint of fresh water. And yet it was the most unearthly place she had ever been. She inhaled a few times, then found herself smiling.

"Mal!" a familiar twanged voice called.

She looked up the road to see Jenna with six other girls coming toward her. Jenna was grinning and waving and skipping to hurry up. She was wearing pristine white capris and a sleeveless yellow top, with her hair down and flowing in the wind. She was a picture in and of herself.

To her right was another perfectly blonde girl, a bit shorter than her, but just as unnervingly gorgeous, with a brilliant and perfect grin. Her hair was pulled back in a high ponytail, and she was more casually dressed in denim cutoffs, revealing muscular legs, and an oversized boatneck shirt. She was waving, too.

Most people knew Jenna had a sister. Not many knew they were twins.

"Hi, Jenna," Mal said, adjusting her black denim skinny jeans and her too-expensive white blazer. Impressions were important, and she was here as a professional. "Hi, Caroline."

The sisters hugged her tightly and asked if the trip was all right, if she was exhausted, and telling her how cute she looked. Normally, she hated this sort of stuff, but from her cousins, it was tolerable, and she couldn't help but smile. They got it from their mom, so it was second nature.

She introduced Taryn and Dan, who had come around from the back of the limo, where they'd been helping Jerry with their bags. Taryn was starstruck but managed to not look like an idiot. Dan couldn't stop grinning like a mad fool.

Men.

Jenna turned and waved the other girls over. "I want you to meet my girls. Ladies! Come meet our photographer!"

The other five girls came over, and Mal finally got a good look at them.

"I feel like I just stepped into the Real Housewives of Nashville," Dan muttered behind her with a low whistle.

Mal nearly burst out laughing. It was a perfect description for them. Two were multi-highlighted blonde and had used so much hairspray that their mountainous curls didn't even twitch in the breeze and wore sunglasses so large it reminded her of forties starlets. They wore heels and had bags that screamed money, not that the additional advertisement was needed. Their noses were so high in the air that the trees had competition.

Two were brunettes, one fake and one not, and their hair was equally stiff, their clothing too fancy for this natural setting. One had bangles that jingled loudly as she walked, and heels so tall all she was missing was a pole. The other was surprisingly natural in complexion and makeup and pushed her normal-sized sunglasses up on her head, which only made her hair more perfect.

The last one had a sharp, bold pixie cut that highlighted what had to be the most perfect bone structure on the planet. If she didn't have modeling contracts, someone was missing something. And the sheer platinum blonde of her hair could have been white in the sunshine, though a dark, bold liner on her thin lips offset it. She wore all white, as if she were the bride, and Mal could have sworn she wore the jacket on her shoulders so it could double as a cape.

Only two of them smiled as they approached; the other three analyzed her. Fair enough. She'd just done the same thing and made snap judgments. She was so glad she was the help this week and not one of them. That might have killed her.

"Girls, this is Mal. She is absolutely the best photographer ever, and we are so blessed to have her." Jenna gave her a brilliant smile, and Mal returned it with a small one of her own. "Mal, these are my best girlfriends."

She gestured to the two highlighted blondes. "Brittany and Bethany."

Mal had no idea who was who, and it didn't matter; they weren't looking at her either.

Jenna indicated the brunettes. "Alexis and Grace."

The normal-looking one, Grace, smiled and waved. The other was staring wide-eyed at her nail as if it had sprouted fangs.

Jenna pointed at the platinum bob. "And Sophie."

Sophie sniffed.

"Charmed," Taryn muttered behind Mal with a bit of a cough.

Mal bit back a grin. "These are my assistants, Taryn Chase and Daniel Brogada."

No one except her cousins cared, but the polite thing was done. Jenna turned back to Mal with a smile. "Well, let's get your things and let y'all get settled. Dinner's at six thirty, and we're havin' barbecue. Totally casual, just relaxed so we can all get introduced and stuff."

Mal nodded once, then turned to collect their equipment when a sharp, blatantly suggestive whistle hit the air. Everyone turned to see three golf carts racing toward the group, each bearing men, and from the looks of things, they were all fairly young. And fairly attractive.

Intrigued, Mal migrated with the rest of the group toward them, and she heard, and felt, Taryn and Dan behind her. Catching herself in the act, she stopped suddenly, and both slammed into her back. They snickered and tried not to topple over, and Mal finally felt more comfortable. It didn't matter if everyone around her was fancy, she was always going to be her awkward self, and that worked for her.

One of the guys got out of the golf cart and went over to Jenna, kissing her cheek. Tabloids and Google searches told Mal that it was Jenna's fiancé, Tom, and she could quite safely say that no photo did him justice. The man was tall, dark, and just the right mixture of heaven and earth to make toes tingle and mouths water.

As the rest of the men got out of the carts and came over, the wave of tingles intensified into a monsoon. Fairly attractive was a blatant lie.

There were six of them, all told, and it looked like a spread for GQ, except they all wore jeans—expensive, perfectly fitting jeans. They were old-money Southern royalty in every respect. Her cousin Lucas was among them, and where his sisters were blonde, his hair was dark, but he bore the same tan, the same twinkling eyes, and the same dimple, which, when combined with his crooked grin, made him dangerous. He saw her and grinned, winking boldly and shoving his hands into his pockets.

One of them was hanging back by the golf cart, leaning on it and surveying the group with a hint of amusement in the quirk of his perfect lips. Stonewashed jeans, pale green button-up open at the throat, sleeves rolled, dark, tousled hair, the ideal amount of scruff, and intense eyes that were indistinguishable in color from this distance… Mal knew full well she was openly gaping at him, and she didn't care. Every breath felt like a hiccup in her chest, and she was afraid to blink.

The other three men came over to the group and might have been male models with their perfect features, perfect clothing, perfect bodies. One looked too much like Tom to be anything other than his brother, and the other two had something of an "aw, shucks" air about them that made any sentient, red-blooded female smile and sigh at the same time. Something about the group of men looked posed, but perfectly so. And the combination of all of them together made one feel somehow both insignificant and on fire.

"Ooh," Taryn whispered in a guttural tone. "Pretty."

Mal gave a breathy uh-huh of assent, then murmured, "You know the… the thing about unrealistic expectations in men? This is… this is exactly what they mean."

Dan cleared his throat. "I'm feeling surprisingly insecure about my masculinity right now."

"Me too," Taryn echoed, starting to fan herself with a hand.

They gawked together for a long moment, and Mal felt a bit like a kid at Disney World for the first time and had no idea what to do next.

So, she did what came naturally to her.

She laughed.

And not delicately, of course. She snorted and wheezed and covered her mouth instantly, squeezing her eyes shut. Taryn ducked her head against Mal, giggling softly. Dan chuckled and put a hand on Mal's shoulder.

"Easy, boss. Breathe…" he teased.

"It's not real," Mal gasped between laughs. "This is so not real."

She opened her eyes again and tried to find calm, but it was impossible. How could she be serious when there was a display of eye candy that had to be the envy of the earth right in front of her? She wasn't normally the giggly type, but something about this whole situation was downright hilarious.

"Mal, Mal," Taryn tried, still giggling, "who are they?"

"That's Tom, he's the groom," Mal said, indicating with her head. "And that's my cousin Lucas. Jenna and Caroline's little brother."

Dan snorted. "Little brother? The guy is all perfect proportions—"

"I'd like a portion," Taryn interrupted in a low voice.

Mal snickered and covered her mouth again. "That's my cousin," she reminded her.

Taryn gave her a sharp look. "Mal, you have got to invite me to a family reunion. I will pay you. A lot."

"We're already here, Taryn," Dan pointed out wryly. "Need a

drop cloth?"

"Among other things," Taryn replied in the same low, breathy tones as she looked back at the men.

"Real people don't look like that," Mal said as she took in the entire group as a whole. Really, it was eerie how many beautiful people were standing in front of them. Lightning was going to strike them, or the earth would open up and swallow them whole or something. Things like this didn't happen.

"Those are real people," Dan quipped, his voice hitching as one of the girls tossed her hair, smiling brilliantly at one of the guys.

Mal felt herself sigh when Mr. Stonewashed Jeans looked at her and bit her lip to keep from making it audible.

"Really, really real." Taryn sighed again.

Mal and Taryn burst out laughing and stifled it as quickly as they could, as some of the group finally looked at them in confusion, which only made them laugh more, and breathing was suddenly too hard. Mal gripped her assistants for balance, though it was hard to do with Taryn leaning on her for support, gasping and wheezing for air. Dan was the only one moderately composed, but even he had to clamp down on his lips hard.

"This is, without a doubt," Mal managed, "the most bizarre thing I have ever done."

"Best assistantship ever," Taryn said as she stood upright, wiping her tears of mirth away. "Oh, man, sorry, boss. I just embarrassed all of us."

Mal shook her head, smiling broadly. "No worries. At least I can laugh with you guys. Who knows what the rest of the week will be like."

"Very well dressed," Dan said dryly, which made her grin spread even further.

"Mal!" Jenna called, linking her arm with Tom. "The boys just finished a tour of the place, but we want to see it too. Wanna go? You can get ideas for your shoot."

That was an idea Mal could certainly get behind. She nodded and turned to the others. "Let's get just primary shots for now, one camera. We can use phones for the others just for landmarking. Anything good we can come back and get."

All business now, the other two nodded and went to the trunk of the limo to finish unloading. Mal took off her blazer and tucked it under her arm, then grabbed the hair tie on her wrist and twisted her hair back. It was too hot for the jacket if she was going to work, and she needed her arms free. The sheer color-block shell she was wearing wasn't exactly what she was used to working in, but it would do. She was even more grateful she'd worn a black tank beneath it. With the flock of females parading around here, there was too much being revealed as it was.

"The resort concierge will take your stuff to the houses," Jenna called as she and Tom headed for the golf cart with Caroline. "Just pull it out of the limo and set it aside. No, wait, Mal!"

Mal turned as she had begun hauling her stuff toward where Taryn and Dan had set theirs. "What?" she called back.

"Silly girl, you're not staying with them." Jenna laughed as she got into her cart. "They'll have their own place. You're staying with us girls, won't that be fun?"

"What?" Mal bleated in shock, dropping her blazer on the ground. She glanced back at Taryn and Dan, who mirrored her horrified expression.

Jenna was too busy laughing with her fiancé and sister as they backed up and took off to notice her.

"Mal-Mal!" Lucas yelled as he settled himself into a driver's seat. "Come on! I called y'all for my cart. Let's go, heifer!"

Mal swallowed the wave of nausea that rolled over her and picked up her jacket, setting it with the rest of her equipment. Then she took the camera Taryn held out to her and, blinking hard to erase the sudden blurriness, wandered over to her cousin.

Hunter had never seen any woman turn that shade of greenish pale before, particularly over something as basic as staying with a bunch of girls before a wedding. She was the photographer. Why wouldn't she stay with the bridal party during something like this? And when it was a girl like Jenna, it should have been a natural assumption. But she looked as though she'd rather eat the dirt beneath her ballet flats.

She blinked as she finally seemed to come alert, thanks to Lucas's annoying honking. It was nice to see her look less zombie-like—and for her to be toned down a bit.

He'd really not been paying any attention to anybody when they'd come back from driving around. Tom and Lucas and the rest of the guys had gone over to mingle and talk, and no doubt flirt, but Hunter didn't care about any of that. He wasn't a particularly social person unless he had to be. He was here for Tom and for the years of friendship they'd had, and for Jenna, because he couldn't help but like her. But as for the rest, he really couldn't have cared less.

He had noticed enough to wonder why the small brunette and her two friends kept their distance, but it wasn't until he heard an unmistakable snort that he'd taken a good look.

She was cute, he was honest enough to admit, and he couldn't have even said if she was wearing makeup, which was an interesting thing to see in a crowd like this. Her assistant wore enough for both of them, but she seemed to be the sort of character that collected attention the way others collected stamps or keychains. The three of them had been huddled together, talking so quietly he couldn't catch any of it.

Then the photographer laughed.

There was nothing unusual or magical about her laugh. It held no musical qualities. It wasn't infectious or adorable. It was absolutely nothing out of the ordinary. Except it was. It absolutely was extraordinary.

It had completely transformed her from being merely cute into something incomprehensible. It lit her eyes and brightened her cheeks and made her hair dance in a way that clawed at him somehow. She radiated light when she laughed, and her smile afterward held glimmers of the same. And from then on, he couldn't not notice her. It was as if a magnet had suddenly been held up and something, somewhere between the pit of his stomach and the beating of his heart, had caught fire and been tugged toward it. How he'd stayed in place by the golf cart was a mystery, but he was grateful for it.

He was a man of calm and control, usually, and this tiny, strange, confusing photographer was not going to make him a man of impulses and instinct. Not to mention the fact that this was one week of wedding madness, and he was not about to become one of those guys who took it as an opportunity for a free hookup.

That wasn't him.

She started to get into the cart when her assistant cleared her throat, hands on her hips, tilting her head so that the chopsticks she wore in her two-toned chocolate and maroon hair looked ready to puncture her shoulders. "Uh, boss? You forgetting something?" the assistant called.

Mal—he thought that was her name, at least—turned in confusion. "Huh?"

Her assistant, dragging her stuff to a pile, pointed at a lone suitcase.

Mal's brows snapped down. "Shasta," she hissed, marching toward it.

Hunter looked at the other assistant, who was about five feet from him now, getting onto Lucas's cart. "What did she say?" he asked him.

The young man grinned, loosening his tie. "Mal makes up her own swear words. You get used to it."

Hunter opened his mouth to respond, then thought better of it. He sat down in his own cart and waited for the other girls to decide who was going to ride and who was going to stay. Meanwhile, he kept an eye on Mal. Apparently, she only had the one suitcase, which was absurdly small by comparison with everyone else's. He'd seen what the other girls had brought, and he had seen what his sister packed for trips of this length. There couldn't be much in Mal's suitcase at all, except for bare essentials, and she had been ready to forget it.

This was the photographer he'd been convinced to hire for the resort? He hoped she was far more organized in other respects than she was with her own stuff.

Lucas grinned at Mal as she came back and threw an arm around her shoulder as she sat next to him. He pulled her in tight against his shoulder and said something that made her roll her eyes, but she smiled and didn't push him away.

Something about that made Hunter frown. He didn't know Jenna's brother well, but he seemed to be a pretty good guy. That didn't explain why he was so familiar with Mal, or why he'd called her a heifer, and that set Hunter's teeth on edge.

"Ready to go?" Bethany asked in a too-chipper voice as she sat beside him. "Oh… are you supposed to hold the steering wheel that tight?"

Hunter looked down and saw his white knuckles blaring back up at him. "Precautionary," he said as he forced them to relax. "Brakes don't always work."

Bethany nodded, eyes wide, not intelligent enough to know he was lying.

He exhaled and shook himself, then turned on the cart and followed the trail Tom had taken, frustrated by the sudden tension in his chest. That wasn't a good sign at all.

They caught up to Tom quickly, and Lucas slid up beside him, joking loudly with the people in his cart and making them laugh just as loud. Above all of them, he heard her laugh, and it jolted his senses.

Tom, Jenna, and Caroline got out of their cart as Tom talked about the house in front of them. It was one of Hunter's favorites, which was why he had given it to Tom and his family for their regular visits. No one else stayed there but the Yardleys, and at the moment, it was empty. Tom's parents and siblings were arriving in a few hours, so this brief window was all they would have to see it.

He had to admit, though he had seen this house time and time again over the years, he was still impressed with it. The view was one of the best from any of the houses on or around the resort, and the layout was one of the most natural he'd ever seen. The architect who had designed it was retired now, but he still consulted with Hunter and his family over new projects and renovations as a favor. That and he had the prime piece of property he'd always wanted on the other side of the lake.

Tom was saying something now, and everybody had gathered around and was listening. Tom had that effect on people. It explained why he was so good at his job; the business world was falling to its knees for him.

The group moved like an awkward museum pack around the house, toward the vista. Hunter hung back and walked slowly, hands in his pockets, letting everyone else see what he had memorized.

"I thought they said we were going to a resort," Alexis whispered to Bethany in front of him.

"I know, right?" Bethany whispered in her bizarre twist of Valley Girl meets Southern Belle accent. "All they've got here is… nature."

"Yeah. Is there always so much wood?"

A faint snort behind him echoed the thoughts in his head perfectly. He glanced behind him to see Mal shaking her head as she shifted around, camera raised. If she moved too far to her left, she would—

She lost her footing, and he heard her small gasp as if she had screamed it.

Impulsively, he lunged for her and seized her arm hard, pulling her back over to safety. He should tell her that the ground near the edges of the ravine wasn't as firm as it looked. He should tell her that it had rained last night so it was going to be slicker than normal. He should tell her… something.

She exhaled heavily and flashed him a wild grin. "Thanks for that. Guess I should watch my footing, huh?"

He swallowed roughly and let go of her arm as if he'd been burned. "Yeah," he managed, shifting away to collect what remained of his thoughts.

How did he know she was going to do that? How had he been moving before she actually slipped? How… how had getting to her become so important when he didn't know a thing about her?

He heard the camera clicking behind him, and it might as well have been the beat of his heart.

This was not good.

Chapter Three

"I thought she said casual dress."

Mal sighed, pushed her loose braid off her shoulder, and shrugged as she put her camera down and looked at Taryn and Dan, who had just arrived. "So did I. Here I thought I was going to look cute in my flannel and skinnies, so I dressed quickly and told Jenna I'd come up to the lodge and take some pictures while everyone else was getting ready. Then, when they showed up…" She trailed off, gesturing faintly.

Really, no explanation was needed. Every single one of the girls, including Jenna and Caroline, were in designer clothing. It might have been casual for the red carpet, but beyond that, it was anything but.

"Do I have time to change?" Taryn asked softly, adjusting her thrifty TJ Maxx combo uncertainly.

"Doesn't look like it," Dan muttered as he buttoned his shirt and tucked it in, tossing his hat into a corner of the room.

Mal looked over to see her aunt and uncle come into the room just ahead of Tom and his parents. They were all smiles, and they, too, could only be considered casually dressed if this was a five-star hotel in New York.

She sighed and shook her head. No matter how deep her family blood ran, she was never going to be like these people.

"There you are!" Jenna said loudly, pretending at exasperation. She went to her fiancé and planted a kiss on him that earned a few very Southern whoops and hollers. Then the smiling couple turned to face everyone.

"We want to thank you all for coming to this wedding extravaganza," Tom said in his smooth and carrying voice. "And to this introductory dinner. I know it's cheesy, but we're gonna go around the room and make sure we all know each other. It's a long week ahead, and we gotta get real comfortable."

That earned him a few good-natured chuckles.

One by one, they went around, and Jenna or Tom made sure to give full introductions for their respective families or friends. Aunt Cady and Uncle Drake got their sugarcoated introduction and praise, complete with applause and whistles from all. Tom's parents, who looked like stiff portraits on oil canvas, got a similarly warm introduction and said some very nice things, though they had no hint of North Carolina accents. Thomas Jr. and Corinne Yardley apparently had more money than some governments, and they looked like it. Aunt Cady and Uncle Drake at least looked like they were from the South. The Yardleys might have been Russians—very nice Russians, but still.

The bridesmaids came next, all of them looking plastic except for Caroline, whose pale peach forties-style dress made her look like a natural starlet off the screen. She got a very sweet introduction and blew a kiss to her twin. The rest of the introductions followed without too much extra fluff. Alexis and Grace were friends of Jenna's from high school, Brittany and Bethany she met in college, and Sophie she met during a music video shoot for Kenny Chesney that Jenna starred in. Mal was confused by that, as Sophie looked like any proximity to pickup trucks and cowboy boots would give her hives, but she went with it. No doubt she'd learn more about the girls, as she would be forced to be cooped up with them the entire week.

Lucas took the trouble to introduce himself, with much flair, which made her roll her eyes, and then it was time for the groomsmen.

She'd been snapping candid shots, with Taryn on second camera, when she saw the guy from this morning. Her throat shuddered under his potent gaze as his eyes were suddenly on her. The man was a magnet for sensation and appeal, and it was the most natural thing in the world to stare at him and lose breath control. Yet he was so unaffected by everyone and everything. He was achingly gorgeous in crisp, black trousers and a silvery gray button-up, which was open at the collar, exposing a tanned and muscular throat.

Who knew throats could be muscular?

She was faintly relieved that his shirt wasn't that tacky, shiny, metallic sort of gray. He was attractive enough to pull off a garbage bag and make people want him, but good taste was a huge advantage, and this was no high school prom or late nineties dating show.

Taryn made a throaty humming sound from beside her, and Mal glanced over to find her looking at him as well. "He looks like Fifty Shades of Yes Please," Taryn murmured.

Mal snorted in surprise and covered her mouth, but she could not say she entirely disagreed.

"You are a vulgar chick, you know that?" Dan muttered with a look of disgust. "This isn't a meat market."

"Speak for yourself," Taryn shot back, lifting her camera once more.

Mal went back to introductions, knowing she'd have to remember names and faces for later. Tom's brother she'd seen earlier was Dave, and a second, nearly identical brother, Trent, now joined him. One friend from this morning, Paul, was from Tom's college frat, which explained a lot. Paul had decided, most unfortunately, to wear a pale pink polo shirt to the event.

Taryn grunted beside Mal, shaking her head. "What, is he golfing after this?"

This time, Dan did not disagree. "Nope, definitely not golfing. He's wearing loafers. Ponce."

Mal bit her lip to keep from laughing out loud. The next friend was…

"O… M… G…" Taryn breathed with a hiccup, suddenly twirling a chocolate and maroon strand of hair around her finger.

"What?" Mal asked out of the side of her mouth, still looking at the friend with the dark hair and shockingly blue eyes.

"That's… That's Reed Summerfield."

Dan choked on something, and Mal was confused. "Summerfield? As in…"

"As in the Hollywood Summerfields!" Taryn squeaked, biting her bright red lips.

"You sure?" Dan asked, leaning closer.

Taryn sighed breathily. "Positive. Hollywood's Heartthrob is here. With me. Someone gimme a fan."

Dan snorted. "How about a bucket instead?"

"Whatever. I need something."

Mal gave up trying to make sense of her assistants and frowned, wondering how Tom and his business world clashed with a silver-spoon, Hollywood-dynasty producer.

Apparently, it was a humanitarian trip in college, which seemed out of character for him. Reed seemed way too much like a playboy for that.

If she was any judge.

He was… really pretty.

She swallowed and took some pictures that would probably be crap, but she didn't care. Pretty people were everywhere, and that was scary.

Then Tom got to *him* and paused. "And that is my best friend, and consequently best man, Hunter, whom I've known since high school, through rowing and rugby in college, and into our business lives, and beyond. The greatest guy I know, and the most generous, and the single reason I didn't fail out of the business program at UNC. I am who I am because of him."

Hunter raised one dark brow, and his mouth curved. "This is your wedding, Tom. I'm supposed to flatter you."

The room chuckled, and Tom grinned at his friend warmly.

"His name is Hunter?" Taryn murmured out of the corner of her mouth. "I volunteer as tribute."

"Stop that!" Dan hissed, though he grinned as well.

Tom's two sisters and their families were introduced, with a surprising number of kids. Mal would never keep them straight, but tomorrow was Kids' Day, and she was supposed to do a shoot with them on the playground in the afternoon. They were all really adorable, so that could be a lot of fun. They, at least, were fairly casual.

It suddenly occurred to her that the room was silent and everyone was staring at her. She and Taryn and Dan had been close to a corner, intentionally out of the way and unobtrusive, trying to blend in and be invisible. Apparently, that wasn't going to work.

Jenna grinned at her warmly, as did her cousins and aunt and uncle. "And this is our fantastically talented photographer for this entire shindig and my very favorite cousin, Mallory Hudson.”

Mal felt her cheeks heat, but she smiled all the same. “Come on, Jenna,” she said bashfully. “I’m your only cousin.”

Jenna giggled and winked. “Makes you even more special then, Mal. She’s doing us all a massive favor by being here, y’all. Can’t believe we got her. So, if you see her around, smile pretty and be nice.”

Everyone laughed and there was faint applause, while Lucas whistled loudly and yelled, “Yeah, Mal-Mal!”

Mal cleared her throat. “Actually, pretending I’m not here would be best. If I need you to look at me or do something particular, I’ll let you know. Otherwise, just act natural—except for Lucas.”

They all laughed again, and Lucas saluted her with a grin and loosened his tie. She gave him a bold warning look, which only made everyone laugh more, and he raised his hands in surrender. She smiled and looked around the room, fiddling with her camera involuntarily. She hated being the center of attention, so the sooner they could move on to the others, the better she’d feel.

Hunter was looking at her again, and his expression was hard to read, but he seemed almost impressed. Or intrigued. Or unsettled.

Or maybe that was just her being impressed and intrigued and unsettled by him. And very, very uncomfortable. The tingly sort of uncomfortable that makes you fidget and fuss with your hair and freak out about imaginary things between your teeth. And your neck is suddenly sunburned, your toes ache, and your skin is too tight.

Yeah, she was uncomfortable, to say the least.

She retreated back to the safety of her camera, her only shield from his intensity, and tried to remember the right way to breathe.

“And bonus, we got her assistants, Taryn and Dan, as well,” Jenna continued, making both of their days, if not lives. “So, again, be nice and smile pretty, or they might edit the pictures of you a bit wonky.”

That seemed to terrify the girls, who all looked at each other with wide eyes.

A warning. That was good. Hopefully, they wouldn’t need more.

“Is that everyone?” Tom asked, looking around quickly. “Yep. Okay, dinner is served!”

At that, the catering staff of the lodge came out of the kitchen with steaming trays of the most incredible barbecue and classic Southern comfort foods Mal had ever seen or smelled. And then she looked again and saw that one of the catering staff wasn't local to the lodge; he was a familiar face from Tennessee. Which meant the food was—

"My baby, Mallory Jo!" Aunt Cady broke through her thoughts, suddenly in front of her and pulling her tightly against her. She smelled exactly the same, like a mixture of Victoria's Secret perfume and Tide with a splash of honey. Her miraculously still naturally blonde hair had been teased to proper Southern height, and it wasn't moving from it, but she was just as warm and adorable as Mal remembered.

She hugged her back just as tightly. "Hi, Aunt Cady," she said into her shoulder. She laughed. "You're really tall tonight. What shoes are you wearing?"

Aunt Cady laughed merrily and stepped back, pointing her coral heels for Mal to see. "This darling designer Jenna told me about. You ever heard of a cat named Jimmy Choo? Fancy stuff, but I like it."

Taryn choked on hearing Jimmy Choo referred to as a cat, but Mal just grinned. That was Aunt Cady to a T.

"They look great," Mal told her.

"Baby, I haven't seen you in ages," Cady scolded, looking her over. "You are so skinny. You'd better eat some of that grub over there."

Mal smiled. "I wanted to ask you about that. How did you get Hal Barney's to come up here?"

"Do you think Hal would ever refuse your aunt?" Uncle Drake asked as he came over and looped his arm around his wife's waist. "I think he'd give her the recipes if she asked with a smile. Pretty woman like her is just dangerous to a man."

"Oh, stop it," Cady said with a smile, pushing at his chest.

Uncle Drake smiled back, then pulled Mal in for a hug and a kiss on her cheek. "Hi, baby."

"Hi, Uncle Drake," Mal replied, catching the familiar whiff of Old Spice and peppermint. "You're grayer than I remember."

"It's dashing. Or so your aunt tells me."

Her uncle held her close for longer than she expected, and when he released her, she looked up at him with a smile. He returned it with a grin, his eyes crinkling. "Missed you, kiddo," he said, as if that explained everything.

She suddenly had trouble swallowing. "I've missed you, too," she finally replied, her voice raw, and she was surprised at how sincerely she meant what she said.

He touched her cheek fondly. "Smile, hon. We got Hal Barney's, and Lucas got us a keg of Doc Porter's root beer. If that's not a happy thought, nothin' is."

Mal laughed and hugged her uncle again, then made her way to the line.

"Your uncle is the most attractive man over fifty I have ever seen," Taryn whispered as they each took a plate. "What is it with those bloodlines and how do I dip my toe in the gene pool?"

"Are your hormones always this raging?" Dan asked in exasperation as Mal barked a laugh.

"Yes," Taryn said simply. "It's exhausting." She looked at Mal again. "Mallory Jo? I thought your middle initial was S."

"It is," Mal said softly as she picked up a warm buttered roll. "But Aunt Cady has called me Mallory Jo since I was four, so it stuck."

Taryn smiled. "Cute! Little Mallory Jo running around and eating… what is this, anyway?"

Mal grinned broadly. "This is Hal Barney's barbecue. The best food in the entire world, and it's from this little place almost smack-dab in the middle of Knoxville and Nashville, and we used to get it all the time, isn't that right, Tucker?" she said, turning to smile at the familiar face standing by the meat.

The big man smiled, his gold tooth glinting in the light. "Sure did, Miss Mallory. Best part of the year was seeing all y'all come in and eat us out of house and home."

"We did not!" she laughed, spooning more sides onto her plate.

Tucker raised a thick brow. "Oh, really?"

She rolled her eyes. "Oh, fine, so we did. But only because it's so good."

He chuckled warmly. "Sure is, Miss Mallory. Sure is. What can I get you?"

Mal opened her mouth to reply when she heard some of the girls whispering nearby.

"Don't they have any idea how bad this food is for you?" Bethany was saying to Brittany and Sophie. "The calories alone are shocking."

"Oh, what do you expect?" Sophie said with a sneer. "This is a very backwoods, country-loving hick group, despite their money and fame. I'm surprised we don't have checkered tablecloths and plastic silverware."

Bethany whimpered. "There's not even a salad. What am I supposed to eat?"

"Just say you're not hungry. You can have a salad when we get back to the house."

"I wish they would have considered this. We have dresses to fit into, and I'm not about to have a food baby."

"Is it going to be like this all week?"

Mal's jaw tightened, and her grip on her plate became more of a clench. She met Caroline's eyes and saw that her cousin had heard and was just as furious. The girls had been speaking in low voices, but not low enough. She didn't know who else had heard, but she knew how mortified Aunt Cady would be if she found out. Mal lowered her chin just enough to assure Caroline she would do something, then turned back to Tucker.

"Brisket, please, Tucker," she said in a calm, but carrying voice. "A bit extra, if you don't mind. I'm starving. And lots of sauce."

She picked up the spoon for the baked beans she'd just loaded on her plate, looked over at the girls standing nearby, who were watching now, and pointedly spooned another helping on top of the rest. Then got extra potato salad as well.

"And a half rack, please," she added to Tucker. "You know how I love ribs."

Tucker was grinning in all-out delight. "Sure do, Miss Mallory. And they've got that honey barbecue glaze on them that you love."

Mal smiled and tilted her head. "Make it a full, then," she said. "I never pass up the honey barbecue glaze."

Tucker winked at her and did as she asked.

It was a ton of food, but she would make herself sick if she had to. And she would really enjoy doing so.

The girls looked absolutely disgusted with her, but she met their gazes calmly and walked over to an open table. Caroline squeezed her hand as she walked by, and Mal smiled tightly, then set her stuff at the table and sat down.

Taryn and Dan joined her, their plates just as loaded down as hers was. She looked at them in surprise.

Taryn shrugged, though her cheeks were pink. "I like barbecue, and I hate mean girls. We're pigging out tonight."

Dan looked unapologetic. "I always eat like this. I'm already looking forward to seconds."

Mal grinned at her assistants. "You guys already get bonus points."

"Yes!" they said in unison, giving each other high fives.

Lucas was suddenly there with frosted tankards of root beer for each of them. "For my absolute favorite table, I will also tell you that there is a hidden stash of peach cobbler in the back, and when we're done here, you signal me, and we'll go."

Mal groaned in half delight, half agony. "Food coma is coming," she moaned, looking up at her cousin.

He smiled in one of his rare, sincere ways. "You deserve it," he murmured, pressing a quick kiss to the top of her head. Then the roguish air was back, and he adjusted his checkered collar. "Now, if you'll excuse me, I must feed this glorious body of mine."

He left before Mal could reply.

"If only he were lying." Taryn sighed as she picked up a piece of fried chicken.

"Shut up," Dan ordered around a mouthful of potato salad.

Hunter stared, knowing it was blatant, but he couldn't help it. There was just something about that girl that drew his gaze and his attention like nothing else. She looked like a farm girl who'd been pitied by a rich family and brought in for a warm meal, but she was so natural and easy. She wasn't intimidated by any of this. Her actions just now had proven that.

Could she really eat all that food?

He'd always appreciated girls who could eat without shame. But she was a hundred pounds, if that; there was absolutely nowhere for that food to go.

She was talking with her assistants now, laughing again. He loved her laugh. She threw her head back with all that she was, thrilling in the joy of whatever had made her laugh. She didn't try to be delicate or reserved; she wasn't fake or boisterous; she wasn't anything but what she was. Warm and natural. And ridiculously adorable. It stirred something in him, and he wasn't sure he liked it very much.

Except he did like it.

A lot.

He shifted uncomfortably against the windowsill, unsure if he were frowning or smiling at the moment.

Mallory Hudson. He should have made the connection when he'd seen her name on the contract, but he'd somehow missed it. Jenna's cousin was the photographer. She would be everywhere in this wedding and everywhere in his resort. And she wasn't just the photographer, she was family.

Did that make this better or worse?

"Stop gawking," Tom's friend Reed said as he came over.

Hunter gave him a look. He'd never been especially fond of Reed, but he was better than Paul, and he wasn't exactly a bad sort of guy. He'd just never grown up.

"Gawking?" Hunter repeated. "At what?"

Reed quirked a brow. "I'm not stupid, McIntyre. You're staring at that chick over there. The cute one."

Hunter silently thanked his father for teaching him how to be stone-faced. His expression did not change. "Was I?"

Reed snorted and leaned against the wall, looking at the table now. "Yep. You were. You think that skirt of hers is a real tartan?"

Stone-faced wouldn't work now. He frowned and looked over at the table again, 99.7 percent sure that Mallory hadn't been wearing a skirt. And he was right. Her assistant—Taryn, if he remembered—was wearing a skirt, and it certainly could have been a tartan, but he failed to see why that was an interesting point.

Reed thought Taryn was the cute one? Moron.

She wasn't unattractive, he would admit, but if there was only one cute girl at that table, it could not be her.

Reed was talking again, but it sounded more like the buzzing of a particularly loud dishwasher, and Hunter stopped listening. He was so grateful that Tom hadn't forced him to stay in the house with the rest of the guys. He liked Tom and his brothers a great deal and wouldn't have minded spending time with them, but a house filled with the eternal frat boys and Lucas Hudson would be too much. He'd stay up at his place where he could think and be, without reference to anyone else.

Mallory gnawed on a rib, sauce on one cheek, loose hair at her ear, giggling at something her assistant had said, and his heart and stomach lurched to opposite sides.

"I'm getting food," he muttered to the still-talking Reed and pushed off the wall.

He was suddenly starving for ribs.

Chapter Four

Hunter woke up before the sunrise the next morning, which wasn't unusual for him, even if it was annoying. It didn't matter. He'd just drive down to the lake and take a single scull out for a chilly morning row. He could use the workout.

He put on his sweats and a hoodie, as well as a knit cap, and called the morning desk clerk to ask for breakfast at the lodge later. He might as well check in with them after he was done to see if he needed to calm any fussy guests or locals, as they hadn't completely shut down the resort for the wedding. Or he could check on any repairs, or do them himself, or… give a lengthy resort tour to a certain photographer.

He made an impatient noise and grabbed his shoes, tying them frantically. He really needed this workout—anything to clear his head.

The air was even colder than he thought it would be, and he shivered as he got into his truck. It would have to be a really good row to warm him up, and the sun wouldn't come over the mountains for a while, even as the morning lightened. But once it did, the day would be just as warm as it had been lately. He loved these mornings and had spent a fair number of predawn hours on the lake with his father and grandfather and, lately, by himself.

There was nothing quite like it.

The pavement was wet with the heavy morning dew, and the usual winding curves had less traction than normal. It wasn't a particularly easy drive normally, but on mornings like this… He predicted he'd have at least two calls about tourists who had been driving too fast and not known about the sharp curves or incline. Once things dried out later, it would be fine. But right now—

Something white and bright appeared around the curve, and he gasped and slammed on the brakes, the wheels screaming against the wet pavement. He stared out of the windshield in surprise and fear, adrenaline racing through him.

Mallory was on the edge of the road, white coat and black leggings contrasting starkly, worn-out tennis shoes on her feet, and fleece earmuffs around her head. She had two cameras around her neck, a satchel across her body, and a thermos in her hand. She stared at him with wide eyes, a good twenty-five yards from him, if not more. But the way the truck lights had caught her…

He could have killed her.

He rubbed his hands over his face and got out of the truck, his fear turning into rage the moment his feet hit the pavement.

"Nice braking," she said with a smile as he approached, oblivious to his fury. "New tires?"

"What were you thinking?" he barked, shoving his hood back and coming to stand directly in front of her. "What, exactly, possessed you to wander around in the woods in the dark? I could have killed you!"

Her brows snapped together. "Yeah, your tank there would have made roadkill out of me," she drawled sarcastically. "Speed limits mean anything to you?"

"I was going the speed limit," he retorted. "The roads are terrible in wet weather, no matter how fast you go, but I'm a lot smarter than that. And it's a Dodge Ram, not a tank, and you being roadkill is not funny."

"Who's laughing?" she asked with an impertinent tilt of her head.

He exhaled rapidly, his breath coming out like fog and his irritation melting away under her influence. "Look," he said slowly, deciding to try for calm, "it's not safe for you to be wandering around in the dark, especially with drivers who don't know these roads. Luckily, I do, but this isn't a good idea."

Mallory sighed and adjusted her weight on her tiny feet. "I'm wearing a white jacket with reflector strips, and I'm sticking to main trails. What is the problem?"

Hunter groaned and put a hand to his suddenly aching head. She just didn't get it, and he didn't have the energy to educate her. Plus, she was looking especially cute right now. He should have shaved. He shook his head with a sigh. "What are you doing up here this early anyway?"

She held up her camera with a shrug. "Photographer. I wanted to catch the sunrise, and views are limited at the Hen House."

He coughed a surprise burst of laughter at her calling it that, though the term was perfect. She grinned broadly at the sound.

That was quite enough of that.

"You're not dressed warmly enough," he pointed out in what was supposed to be a bossy, scolding tone.

"Thank you," she said, giving him a sardonic look. "I figured that out about thirty minutes ago. Tomorrow, I'll be better."

"You're doing this more?" he asked, torn between horrified, impressed, and shocked.

She nodded and pushed her ponytail behind her. "Probably every morning. Every sunrise is different, and I can find dozens of places to get shots."

He slowly shook his head. "If you manage not to die, it will be a miracle," he muttered.

She only shrugged. "Well, then I'll be a martyr for my art, and my pictures will be published to wide acclaim, so that works, too."

He stared at her for a second, hands on his hips. She was the most unusual woman he had ever met. And it was obvious she wasn't going to listen to him, which meant there was only one thing to do. He exhaled loudly and started back for the truck. "Come on," he called over his shoulder. "I'll drive you."

She barked a short laugh. "You don't know where I'm going."

He turned and gave her a look. "Neither do you."

That brought a half smile to her face. "Point taken. But you don't know what I'm looking for."

He shrugged and opened the passenger door. "Tell me what you want, and I'll get you there. I've been coming here since I was a kid. I know all the best places."

She frowned at him and his truck, looking somehow grumpy and uncertain at the same time.

"It'll be warmer and safer, not to mention faster, if you come with me," he said with infinite patience.

She bit her lip. "I really like hiking to my site."

He sighed and resisted the urge to roll his eyes. "So join National Geographic and come out again when you can see. For my sanity, and to save your fingers and toes, get in the truck."

She still hesitated, chewing her lip, which drove him crazy.

He cleared his throat, breaking the silence. "You're running out of time, and it's getting lighter by the minute. Your choice."

She huffed and came over to the truck, handing him her thermos and bag. She avoided his eyes as she grabbed the handle, stepped on the running board, and climbed in, then quickly took her things back.

He tried not to smile as he closed the door for her. He had no idea why he was so pleased right now, only that he was, but he was willing to roll with it. He got in on his side, buckled up, and looked at her expectantly.

She wasn't looking at him and therefore couldn't see his expression. She actually looked like a pouty child who'd just been scolded, and that intrigued him. He didn't want to be her boss or disciplinarian. He just wanted to figure out what made her tick, and why she made him tick. And keep her from breaking a limb or her neck.

"Where to?" he asked politely after a moment.

She shrugged. "You're the expert. Take me somewhere I can get a good shot. Nice view, morning light. Just go with it."

Still trying not to smile, he nodded and started driving. He looked at her, eyes flicking between her face and the road. He couldn't help himself. She was looking out the window the entire time, eyes everywhere, trying to catch everything, even though it was still fairly dark. Her hands clutched her thermos, but she never took a sip of it. Was it a hand warmer or a beverage?

He cleared his throat again. "You don't bring warm enough clothes, but you remember your coffee?"

"Cocoa."

"Excuse me?"

"I don't drink coffee," she said a bit louder, still looking out of the window, "and tea just doesn't cut it in the mornings. Cocoa is good all the time."

He smiled, but tried to hide it. "Duly noted. So, are you

fascinated by nature or are you mad at me?"

She glanced over with a brow raised. "I don't know you well enough to be mad at you, and this place is gorgeous."

He shrugged, ignoring the twinge of relief. "True. This is my favorite place on earth."

She looked back out the window, tilting her head back to try to see the lightening sky between the trees. "I can see why. It's amazing."

Hunter chuckled at her enthusiasm. "City girl?"

"Sort of. I spent my teenage years on a farm, and now I'm in Denver—the city part, not the nature part. For now, anyway. I used to take vacations with my parents to Eagle Lake in Michigan when I was a kid, but it's been years and years."

He stiffened in his seat and his hold on the steering wheel became tight. "Eagle Lake?" he repeated faintly.

She nodded. "It's up near–"

"PawPaw, I know."

She looked at him in surprise, and he met her eyes, just as stunned. His family had a house on another lake near there, closer to Decatur, but he'd become familiar enough with all the smaller lakes and towns. They'd been going there for years, almost as often as they came here. His cousin lived close enough to look after that place, and he had this one. Had they ever been at that lake at the same time? It wasn't as formally set up as the resort where guests mingled and events were held; it was a much quieter, simpler setting, but still one of his fondest childhood memories.

He broke eye contact and focused on the road, exhaling silently. They were almost to the spot he had in mind, and he needed out of this truck. They didn't talk again until they reached the summit, and he pointed her in the direction of the best spot. She nodded, suddenly all business, got out of the truck, and started for it.

"Watch your footing," he blurted out, leaving the truck himself, his eyes tracking her footsteps and the slick spots on the ground.

She looked over her shoulder at him with a crooked smile that sent his pulse skittering. "I remember. Thanks." She purposefully tiptoed around a puddle, then stepped out on the stone ledge, camera raised.

Hunter watched her for a while, bewildered by the amount of

clicks he heard. He came closer, trying to see whatever magic Mallory saw. It was a gorgeous view, but the sun had yet to come over the mountains, so the light wasn't very good. Apparently, that didn't matter to Mallory. She kept saying things to herself, directions and corrections and hushed praises of the view and the mountains.

He was smiling again before he knew it.

She leaned forward, getting more excited about the increasing light.

"Whoa, whoa," he murmured, coming forward and grabbing the back of her jacket. "No cliff diving. You're not close enough to the lake."

"So hold tight," she replied without concern, leaning even farther.

He chuckled and grabbed hold with both hands.

"This is incredible," she said, speaking to him this time. "I haven't seen nature like this since… maybe never!"

"It is one of a kind, isn't it?" he replied, looking around and finally feeling that wonder and awe she seemed to have. "There's no place like it. And I've been a lot of places."

She leaned back and lowered her camera, but he still held on to her jacket. She turned to look at him. "What are you doing with this crowd, Hunter?"

He reared back, smiling a touch at how perfectly she said his name. "What do you mean?"

She gave him a curious smile. "You're floating around with the likes of Jenna and Tom and Sophie–"

"Don't include her," he interrupted with a slashing motion.

She clamped her lips together on a laugh, then continued, "But you're so… normal. What gives?"

He'd never been called normal a day in his life. He'd always thought normal a fairly boring thing to be. It had never occurred to him that it could be a compliment. He shrugged. "What can I say? I know people."

Mallory grinned. "I know people. And they don't give me speeches like you got last night."

He rubbed at his forehead, where his beanie suddenly itched. "Tom's a good guy. Doesn't see the bad in anyone."

"Is there bad in you?"

He looked back at her and could see she was surprised by her words too. He held her eyes as steady as he could, his chest suddenly somehow warm and tight.

"Could be," he finally said. "Depending on who's looking and how deep."

She swallowed and looked down at her camera again, fiddling with something. "Philosopher too, Hunter? Impressive repertoire of skills."

"I gots lots of skills, Mallory," he said slowly, exaggerating the tone and grinning so she would know he was playing, which was strange. He was not normally playful, but it was natural with her. Maybe he needed to watch his footing, too.

She snorted and gave him a look. "Now that is not a skill. Don't ever do that again. And it's Mal," she added with a sly smile.

Screw footing.

He softened his smile. "Mal, then." He nodded at her camera. "Are you getting the shots you need?"

She nodded rapidly. "Tons. This is awesome. I can't wait for the sun to come up."

He looked around for a second, gauging where they were. There wasn't going to be too much more to offer when the sun did come up. It wouldn't have the same magic she was looking for, but something else might.

"I think you'll be disappointed when it does," he said slowly, thinking fast. "But I have an idea."

She lowered her camera. "Do I want to know?"

He smirked. "What would you say to a sunrise view from the shore? You could get tons of shots where the rowers dock and launch, and no one is out this morning."

She glanced over to where he had suggested, and then whirled back, dislodging his hold on the jacket in her excitement. "Yes."

He grinned and waved her back to the truck. "Let's go! We gotta hurry."

Moments later, they were racing down the winding roads again, this time with far less care and caution. Mal clutched the handle for dear life, her other hand braced on the dash. "We're not gonna make it," she muttered, her eyes wide open. "We're not gonna make it."

"We will make it," he insisted, grinning as the tires squealed again. "I'll get you there before the sun comes over the ridge."

"That's not what I mean," she hissed between her clenched teeth. "I'm going to die in your freaking Dodge Ram before we get anywhere. In a ravine."

He laughed. "You will not. I'll get you there in one piece—no ravines. Trust me."

"Trust you? I've known you for like three seconds. How's that supposed to work?" Her voice was getting higher, and he wished he could stare at her to see the play of emotions on her face.

He risked a glance at her. "Want me to hold your hand?"

"No!" she shrieked, laughing. "Two hands on the wheel, moron! Shut up and drive!"

He laughed out loud and took a few more curves in silence. She wasn't any calmer, so he tried for distraction. "So, you like barbecue."

She jerked and looked at him with horror. "What?"

"Last night. That was some good stuff. You guys get that often?" He flicked his eyes to her, then back to the road.

"You heard," she murmured, finally sitting back in her seat.

He shrugged. "Not really. I got the impression, at least. Then I saw your plate, and I put two and two together."

"I didn't think anyone noticed," she murmured, looking away. "I only meant to shut the girls up, not to make a demonstration for the entire group."

"Uh, I think everyone noticed," Hunter assured her with a laugh. "It wasn't very discreet."

Mal rolled her eyes and sank back completely in her seat. "Oh, good. I love being the center of attention."

"It was the best thing I've ever seen."

She looked at him with a doubtful brow raised.

He nodded once. "I mean it, Mal. That was perfect." Then he quirked a half grin. "The fact that you cleaned your plate just made it better."

Mal grinned back, to his eternal delight. "There's nothing else to do when it's Hal Barney's. How did you know I cleaned it? Were you watching?"

He looked back at the road. "I had money on you."

She burst out laughing. "How much?"

"Hundred bucks."

She hummed and sat back again. "Should have bet more. I snuck two helpings of cobbler from the kitchen after."

He had no response for that except to laugh again, and then they were at the shore, and she was all business again. She raced from the truck, gauged the sky, the mountains, and the approaching sun, and started snapping pictures. She bounced on her feet.

"Come here!" she called, waving him over. She took off her shoes and socks, yanked off her earmuffs, and splashed out into the water, not even bothering to roll up her leggings.

"What?" he laughed, heading toward her.

She giggled and hissed at the cold water, then took the second camera from around her neck. "Start snapping shots!" she said, tossing the camera at him.

He caught it easily. "Of what?"

"Anything!" she replied with another laugh, returning to the task at hand.

"I am not going out there," he informed her as he started to do as she said. "It's freezing."

Her laughter met his ears, and just then, the sun peeked over the ridge. It seemed that a beam settled itself specifically on her. She smiled and took pictures of the water, the sky, the mountains, anything and everything, the entire world seeming to delight her. She bent so close to the water he thought she was going to submerge herself, then she'd turn and tilt her camera up at a peak, at the dock, one particular tree that caught the sunlight... .

Hunter found it hard to swallow, transfixed by her, then he was taking pictures—of her. Just a few, because the moment could not go unnoticed. Then he took pictures randomly, not caring if he wasted her entire memory card on blurry nothings. He didn't even mind that suddenly he was getting his feet wet, or that he wasn't going to get a workout in this morning, or probably any other morning this week.

As far as he was concerned, they were all spoken for.

Mal was out of breath by the time she finished her shoot. She knew she'd been excitable and childish and way too giddy about a sunrise, and Hunter probably thought she was crazy, but he was being very nice about it.

Her initial impressions of him had been off, she could now admit. Yes, he was still the same impossibly gorgeous man from before, but like this, in a hoodie and sweats, he was also approachable. He wasn't as quiet as she'd pegged him, which was a fun surprise, and he was actually quite witty, which she never really expected from attractive people. Not fair, she knew, but snap judgments rarely were.

She was glad now that she'd gotten in his truck and gone with him today, despite her reservations at the time. It had been a much more productive morning than she'd thought. He hadn't made any smart comments about her walking barefoot in the sand now, her shoes in hand, the second camera once more around her neck with the first. He was chatting about the rowing teams that came to the resort on training trips and how his own team at UNC, which Tom had also been on, had done so. She wasn't really listening, but he had the kind of voice that was nice to hear no matter what he was saying.

"So how is it up at the house?" he said, changing the subject abruptly.

She looked at him. "What, the Hen House?"

He grinned, and she was still proud of herself for the name.

"It's... interesting," she said carefully.

"Very PC answer," he replied with a nod. "Care to expound?"

She considered, wondering just what she could say to him. "I'm not like these girls," she finally admitted. "I don't care about the calories in dinner or if my makeup is perfect or if my clothing looks like it's expensive even if it's not. I really couldn't care less about today being Designer Day. I'm actually hoping to avoid it. Jenna and Caroline are fine; they're closer to my level, but not much. I have nothing in common with these people."

"These people?" he prodded. "Your family and their friends?"

Mal snorted softly. "Friends. Show me real friends of anyone in this group, and I'll show you Santa's workshop."

"That sounds bitter."

"When you're called mediocre and too plump for your limited

height and 'only good enough for department stores' by people who've never actually spoken to you before, a little bitterness tends to show up." She scowled at the memories from last night, shaking her head.

Hunter nearly stopped, but didn't. "They said what?"

Mal turned to smile as blandly as she could. "Don't get excited. Let's just say I've gotten used to being treated like this by the upper class."

He didn't seem to like that any better, but that was all he was going to get from her. There was no way she was going to tell him about the last time she was with her cousins and what Jenna's preteen friends had said to her then. That was borderline therapy stuff, and it had taken too many pep talks and ice cream pints to get over that enough to be here.

Hunter folded his hands behind his back as he walked beside her, which was a very proper pose for a man wearing sweats. "So that's why you wanted to stay with your assistants."

"Which is why I expected to," she corrected. "As much as Jenna says I'm her favorite, she really doesn't know me. Not anymore. I thought I would be here more as the photographer and less as the cousin. But I guess I'm both."

"Is that a bad thing?" he asked softly.

She stopped for a moment, biting her lip. "I'm honestly not sure."

A squealing sound met her ears, and she looked toward the houses to see that they had arrived at the Hen House. Some of the girls were out on the second-floor terrace. Sophie was looking way too put-together for this time of morning, leaning on the railing in a silk robe, staring directly at the two of them. Her expression was disapproving.

Mal sighed and turned to Hunter. "Well, this is my stop, I guess."

He smiled. "So it is."

"Thanks for your help today. It really made a difference."

He shrugged easily. "Any time. Like I said, I love this place."

She returned his smile. "I can see that. And I can see why."

He stared at her for a moment, his eyes unreadable. Then he softly said, "Let me know when you need a dose of normal again. I'll help you out."

The uncomfortable feeling from the night before returned in an echo, but she was able to keep her smile. "Thanks," she said, though it came out as a whisper.

She pushed a strand of hair behind her ear and turned from him toward the house. She heard his footsteps in the sand after a second and exhaled a sigh of relief. She'd never last the week if she didn't find some control soon.

"What was that about?" Sophie demanded when Mal was close enough to her perch to do so without alerting the others.

A thousand snarky things came to mind as a response, but she plastered a polite look on her face. "I was getting some pictures of the resort this morning for Jenna, and Hunter ran into me. He volunteered to help me find some good places to shoot. He knows a lot about this place."

Sophie rolled her eyes and sneered. "Well, he should. He owns the place."

Chapter Five

Kids' Day was turning out to be a lot more fun than Mal had thought it would be. Too bad she was so cranky that it didn't matter. Taryn was having a blast on second camera, though, and even Dan was enjoying himself as he entertained kids and suggested angles and options for Taryn.

Mal was more content off by herself, doing her own thing, stewing in her thoughts.

Hunter owned the place. How did she not know that? That was a detail she should have been privy to, particularly when she was also doing shoots for the resort. And he'd said he was normal? The man was a walking mint!

Not only was he so far out of her league that it was ridiculous, but he was her employer! She had been checking out and getting ideas about a guy that she couldn't even sneeze in front of without getting a background check, and with only a week until all the craziness was done. A weeklong fling with a normal guy wasn't a crazy thing to imagine.

This was not crazy. This was certifiably insane. Her embarrassment knew no bounds.

She'd endured Designer Day this morning without complaint, even suffering two fittings for herself that Caroline had insisted on. The other girls had no idea why the photographer was being included in reaping the rewards of Jenna's generosity and connections with top designers, but as they'd all said they wouldn't be caught dead in those things, it wasn't a major concern.

Caroline assured her that they felt that way because they couldn't pull them off. Honestly, Mal couldn't have said what the outfits actually looked like. They might be in her closet, but she wouldn't have recognized them.

She'd gotten the pictures she needed there, assured Alexis that her nose looked fine, and agreed to only shoot Bethany from the left for the time being. Apparently, a blemish had sprouted, and she didn't want anyone to know.

Jenna and Caroline and Grace were playing with the kids now, but the other girls were holed up in the house getting facials and manicures or something, which made no sense, as they would all be getting their nails done the day before the wedding anyway. But Mal was glad to be away from them. Her cousins, she actually liked, and Grace had potential to be on the good list as well. She was the least snobbish of the group, and certainly the nicest to Jenna.

The men were golfing today, and she was grateful for that. She needed time to think, and any more time spent around Hunter would cloud her head. Or she might end up snapping at him. It wouldn't do more than get her fired and possibly blacklisted from high-end gigs, but she would at least feel better for it.

"Hey."

She froze, groaned in the back of her throat, and adjusted her camera to take more pictures. She would love to ignore him, but common sense told her she couldn't. "Hey," she replied stiffly.

Hunter came over and stood next to her, but she was more focused on the three kids dueling by the monkey bars. They waved at her, smiling broadly, and then continued their sword fighting. Maybe they'd come over here and sword fight around Hunter's kneecaps.

"The girl's the best one in that group," he said in an offhand way.

It was true, she was, but the fact that he identified that was grating to Mal. "Addie," she informed him.

"Excuse me?"

"Her name is Addie," she said more clearly. "She's the daughter of Tom's sister Karen, and her twin is Aimee, who currently owns the record for highest swing jump."

Hunter chuckled, which was also annoying. And lovely, drat him. "And who are the kids on the monkey bars?"

Mal gripped her camera so hard she was afraid she'd break the lens off, but she adjusted it and focused on the monkey bars in question. "Trevor and Harrison. They belong to Courtney. And the little one is Olive. She's a guest of the resort."

"Did her mom sign a waiver?"

"Of course her mom signed the waiver," she snapped. "So did the other five moms sitting at the picnic table." She exhaled slowly, trying to force her temper back. "Shouldn't you be golfing?"

"I hate golf. Boring game made for rich people. Actually, I'm just terrible and impatient. I'd rather be here."

The unspoken implication of his words was more irritating than his sweeping assessment of the game being for rich people—as if he wasn't one of them. She snapped one more picture of Olive, then lowered her camera to finally look at him. He looked impossibly attractive, somehow looking expensive in jeans and a white Henley shirt. Then there was the Rolex on his wrist, a class ring on one hand, and Ray-Bans hooked on the open collar. A rich man trying to seem normal.

"So, you own this place," she said without any fanfare.

He stiffened, and his brow furrowed. "Who told you that?"

She raised a brow. "Sophie. Why, is it some big secret?"

He sighed and put his hands in his pockets. "Yeah, I own the place, big deal. My dad inherited it, and we split ownership. I just recently bought out his shares, so he could go into retirement. What of it?"

His tone was defensive, and she matched his irritated expression. "Nothing," she said with a careless shrug. "That just seems like something you would tell people."

"Not me," he replied, shaking his head. "I didn't make this or have anything to do with it. I just make sure it stays this way—calming and beautiful and natural. It's supposed to be a haven, a refuge, a place to get away from everything. And you think I should take credit for it?"

She rolled her eyes and raised her camera again. "I think you should be honest about it."

"I was never dishonest."

Semantics? He was going to play it that way? Of all the… She snapped two pictures and walked a bit away, snapping a few more. Sure enough, he followed.

"You could have told me," she muttered.

"Would it have made a difference?" he asked, genuinely sounding interested.

Yeah, it made a huge difference. She swallowed and shrugged lightly. "Maybe."

"So why tell you?" She could hear him smiling, which only made her more irritated.

She sighed, snapped three shots, then lowered her camera and turned to him. "I deserve to know who I am dealing with."

The wind caught his hair and disheveled it just enough to make him seem almost human. "The same guy you were before," he insisted, his smile crooked now.

"I don't even know who that is," she snapped. "Here I thought you were normal. You even offered to give me more normal! You've got more money than Sri Lanka, and you think you can pretend to be one of the regular guys? You're filthy stinking rich, Hunter. You are one of the gang here."

He frowned and raised a finger. "Don't go middle class snob on me, Mal. I have money, and I can't apologize for it. I won't. Was I born to it? Yeah, but I've also worked hard for it. I earned my way to where I am. This place is all I keep of my family's inheritance. Everything else I've earned on my own, and people respect me for it. I'm not some rich boy who runs to Daddy when he wants nice things. Nobody handed me scholarships for my blue blood, and I bought my first car on my own with money I earned from jobs, not from handouts. You want something in life, you work for it, however you can, with whatever you've got, end of story. You know who taught me that? My filthy-stinking-rich parents."

She just stared at him for a long moment, mouth working. In a matter of moments, he had blasted her perceptions of him into smithereens. Her face was on fire, and she felt even smaller than she already was.

Okay, now her embarrassment knew no bounds.

She cleared her throat and called Dan over. He jogged to her, surprisingly all business for his usual backward hat and black V-neck. She handed him her camera and bag and told him to take over. He did so immediately, then she walked in the opposite direction.

"Where are you going?" Hunter asked, surprised.

"I've got to find a ladder," she said simply.

"What for?"

She picked at a leaf on her striped Gap T-shirt and sniffed. "I seem to have gotten myself into a majorly deep hole, and I'd like to get out of it now."

Hunter laughed once and grabbed her arm. "Hey, hey, come on, I'm sorry."

Mal turned to him, floored by his apology. "You're sorry? I called you a liar and held a grudge that you had more money than an entire country, and you're apologizing? Stop digging me a deeper hole. I'm the idiot here, not you."

He smiled, his teeth not quite touching and his eyes crinkling at the edges. "I never said I was an idiot, but thanks."

Mal folded her arms and sighed. "Look, why don't you just go back to the party guests, and I'll be the family photographer, and we can pretend this never happened?"

"What if I'm glad it happened?" he suddenly said, his smile fading, but his eyes still warm.

Mal stopped in the motion of scratching her ear. "Excuse me?"

If possible, his eyes turned bluer and warmer. "What if I enjoyed it?" he said in a low voice. "What if I've already started planning tomorrow's sunrise shoot, and I would rather listen to you ramble nonsense for hours than spend a minute listening to one of the hens try for legitimate conversation? I like you, Mallory. And I won't apologize for that, either."

Mal counted four heartbeats before her lungs decided to work. "Freaking A, you're intense," she eventually managed. "Give a girl a few seconds to breathe here."

One side of his mouth quirked back into a smile. "One Mississippi, two Mississippi..."

"Shut up."

He all-out grinned, which was quite a sight to behold. "So, where to?"

Mal shook her head. "No clue. I just gave away my camera, and knowing Dan, it'll be hours before he'll give it up."

"Back to the Hen House?" he suggested with a quirk of his

brows.

She snorted and shook her head. "Please. I thought I was going to die today."

He hissed with a wince. "That bad?"

Mal gave him a look. "Have you ever had to endure designer clothing with socialite snobs?"

He laughed, but his wince remained. "That sounds terrible."

"It's worse than you think," she assured him. "And there is nothing to eat. I had to have a salad for lunch—without toppings and without dressing. It was like eating leaves straight from the tree."

He took her arm again and steered her toward the lodge. "I can fix that."

"It's like three o'clock!" she protested, going along with it anyway. "Dinner is in a few hours."

He hummed an amused sound. "I think you'll be hungry by then."

"Come on, Hunter, it's not that bad, I was kidding." She laughed. "I was in a food coma so bad after last night that I could barely eat anything for breakfast. I felt like a whale."

He stopped and gave her a blatant and very thorough look over, his lips in a tight line. "Nope, can't see anything whale-like. Stop arguing. Let's go."

She grinned, wanting to burst out laughing. "That was the most perfect excuse to check me out I have ever seen. Bravo."

He shrugged. "I didn't need an excuse, but why waste a perfectly good opportunity? Okay, tell me: what food is in that house? We stocked it before everyone came based on requests, but if you're starving away, I can put in an order."

"Taryn already offered to sneak me Nutella and Froot Loops," Mal assured him as they entered the lodge. "I'll be fine, I promise."

Hunter gave her a hard look. "Woman cannot live on Nutella and Froot Loops alone."

"You underestimate my creativity," she quipped, taking the seat he pulled out.

He sat down across from her and leaned over the table, both hands in fists on the white tablecloth. "No. I don't. How hungry are you?"

She swallowed the urge to say "famished" and only said, "I could eat."

His perfect lips quirked into a perfect little smile. "Yeah, I got that. Why do I have the feeling you always 'could eat'?" He pushed away from the table. "Fine, Mallory Hudson, I'm forced to scrounge for you."

"Oh, come on," she protested, starting to get up. "I can scrounge for myself."

"Sit!" he ordered, pointing a finger at her chair. "I will not have the guests making a mess in the kitchens. Besides, I'm only getting ice cream."

She perked up even as she laughed. "Ice cream? That's supposed to tide me over?"

He gave her a look. "You object to ice cream?"

She sat back and grinned. "Not at all. Bring it on."

He matched her smile and nodded, then disappeared behind the kitchen doors.

Mal sat at the table, a grin fixed on her face, and wondered what in the world had come over this guy. This rich, powerful, gorgeous guy was going to sit in this lodge with her and eat ice cream just because… he liked her? She wasn't going to complain, but what was the endgame here?

"Oh, calm down, Mal," she muttered to herself, still smiling. "It's ice cream, not a proposal. Shut up and eat with the pretty man."

And that's what she did.

After dinner, she headed for the small cabin that Taryn and Dan, as well as the drivers, were staying in. She wanted to check out the pictures from today before they started editing, and she really wanted to avoid the Hen House as long as possible. She was supposed to go over to her aunt and uncle's house later to catch up, and waiting with her assistants would be better than waiting with the hens. Besides, she needed some pictures to show Hunter for his consideration and get a better idea of what he was looking for from her.

A smile lit her lips before she could stop it. Ice cream with

Hunter had been fun and surprisingly comfortable. They talked about her work, her adolescent years in Iowa, and, oddly enough, his Harley. He was very proud of it and absolutely appalled that she had never been on one. A scooter in Paris did not count, according to him, and he spelled out exactly why.

Mal had a history of guys that would have made people cry, not out of pity but out of hysterics, considering her age and fairish looks. But she was picky and she was busy—not that busy, but she claimed to be—and there wasn't exactly a line at her door. At best, she was friendly. At worst, the definition of awkward.

But something about Hunter made talking with him, and liking him, really easy. She refused to consider anything serious about it. He was a nice guy who said nice things, and if it made her time here more bearable, that would be great.

The fact that he set her insides on fire was completely beside the point.

Taryn and Dan took a minute to show her their cabin, which was rustic and way more Mal's style than the fancy, mansionesque Hen House. But then they went to the office designated for their work, and she saw that they had already been at work. The barbecue pictures were on one screen, and the Kids' Day on another, and so far, things looked good.

She pulled out her laptop and started loading the pictures from the morning shoot when she heard a throat clearing pointedly. She turned in her chair and looked at Taryn, who was turned to face her, pencil behind an ear, one brow quirked.

"Mallory," Taryn said in a sober voice that did not suit her. "Would you care to explain this?" She was pointing at a picture on her screen from Kids' Day, but it wasn't of any of the kids. It was adults.

Mal frowned. "I didn't take that."

Dan laughed loudly once, and Taryn shook her head as if Mal had missed a critical point. "Yes, I know that," Taryn said. "I did. Would you like to explain what is going on here?"

Mal looked closer and saw that it was a picture of her and Hunter on the beach. Taryn clicked a few more times, and Mal saw at least seven pictures, each one closer and more personal.

"What are you doing?" she asked, feeling a little panicked. "Are you stalking me, Taryn?"

Taryn snorted. "I was trying to get a picture of Hunter because— well, look at the man. He's like that cake that says 'Eat Me' in Alice in Wonderland." She broke off to glare at Dan, who was laughing hysterically, then she looked back at Mal. "So, I thought I'd snap a shot of him for my Drool Board at home, except I couldn't get a shot of him alone because he was too close to you and looking at you like you were Christmas. What's going on?"

Mal clamped her lips together and fought the urge to scream. It was one thing for Hunter to pay attention to her; it was quite another for people to notice. That was when things got out of hand.

"He helped me with the sunrise shoot this morning," she said slowly. "And didn't tell me he owns the place. That is us fighting about it and then him explaining. That's it."

"He owns the place?" Dan repeated loudly. "Oh, man, I didn't know I could hate someone so much."

"Bless whatever people created this man." Taryn sighed, clasping her hands in a prayer and looking up at the ceiling. "They should be sainted."

"He is not staring at me like any particular holiday," Mal corrected, her voice wavering with anger. "He's listening to my side. He's intense like that."

"I like intense," Taryn said, looking back at the picture.

Mal returned to her seat and sat heavily. "Have at him, then."

"Nah, he's in your bucket, babe," Taryn replied. "I'll take another fish."

"He's not–" Mal tried.

"Give it a rest, huh?" Dan interrupted gently, giving her a look. "Taryn's just giving you a hard time. Just fire her and be done with it."

And just like that, the topic was safer, as Taryn protested very vocally. They started joking about pictures and angles, and ideas volleyed back and forth.

Mal exhaled slowly and turned back to her computer, relieved that the familiar sound of their bickering was her soundtrack now. Anything to get away from that topic. She didn't want to be gossip fodder on this trip, and no pretty face with intense eyes and control over her lungs was going to change that.

As she clicked through the pictures Hunter had taken that morning, she found a few of her, laughing in the sunlight and taking pictures herself. They were actually quite good, but how had she missed him taking them? And why, exactly, was he taking pictures of her?

Her heart sank somewhere around her stomach, and she swallowed with difficulty. Part of her fluttered with flattery; the other part filled with dread. This was going to be trouble, she could feel it.

He was trouble.

Chapter Six

Hunter was waiting outside of the Hen House before dawn the next morning, deciding to forgo the beanie this time, but everything else was fairly the same. He'd prepared something special for the sunrise shoot for Mal, but he probably went too far. He was way too involved and invested and had too much riding on her expressions. He was probably freaking her out more than anything, and almost freaking himself out in the process. He'd never felt anything like this so fast. He rarely felt like this at all.

Actually, he might never have felt like this before.

All he knew was he needed to be around her, and he needed to be the normal that she wanted. He could be normal. He was fairly normal, compared to everybody else here, but what did that actually mean? What he needed was time, and unfortunately, there was not a lot of that to go around at this particular point and with their current restrictions. Every second counted.

The lower door of the house opened, and Mal appeared, wearing the same coat from yesterday, but this time in jeans and a warm hat, as well as gloves and boots. She still wore both cameras and had her satchel, but no thermos. She didn't look as if she'd slept well.

She saw him fairly quickly and did not have much of a reaction. She simply stared at him for a long moment, as if waiting for him to move.

"No cocoa today?" he asked softly, wondering why she was so far away. Maybe he was freaking her out. She'd called him intense yesterday, and yes, perhaps he had come off too strong, but he was feeling extremes with her, and he couldn't figure out how to manage that.

She blinked unsteadily. "I barely touched mine yesterday, so it seemed stupid to bring more." She lifted a leg to rub the boot against her other leg. "So, you really did plan out today's shoot, huh? I thought you were just saying that."

He shrugged. "I don't usually just say things."

She nodded once. "Good to know. Before I ask about that, is there any reason why I should be creeped out by you? And I'm not just saying this, Hunter. I'm being completely serious. I don't know anything about you except what Tom said the other night and what you said yesterday. I haven't asked about you because I'm not nosy, but you paying attention to me like this in a secluded place…" She looked at him helplessly. "I'm being honest here. Open. Cards on the table. Should I be creeped out by you?"

He reared back, stunned by that. She had been so carefree and full of banter yesterday, yet this morning, she was quiet and worried and nervous. "Mal, do I make you uncomfortable?"

"Yes," she said simply.

"In a good way or a bad way?" he asked, trying to lighten things a little.

She didn't take it. "Both."

He grunted softly. He liked that she was unsettled around him, but only so far as it could mean she might feel something for him if he didn't screw it up. He didn't want her to be scared or worried or anything but excited to be with him.

"I have a clean record," he told her, keeping his voice down. "No felonies or misdemeanors, nothing that is sealed or had to be expunged. I don't cheat, I play and fight fair, and I'm a very overprotective brother to a younger sister who taught me how to treat women. I'm spending time with you because I want to, and I want you to want to. I never want to do anything that will make you uncomfortable, so you just tell me, all right?"

She seemed to consider that for a moment, and he held his breath. Then she nodded. "All right."

He smiled as relief coursed through him. "I'm really glad you said that," he told her in a lighter tone. "It would really have messed things up if you hadn't."

Finally, she smiled, just a little. "What did you have in mind?"

He shoved his hands into his hoodie pockets. "What would you think about doing a shoot on the lake?"

She looked surprised. "What, like in a boat?"

He nodded slowly. "I could take you out to some good spots, show you the whole lake, maybe spark some ideas for future shoots?"

Her little smile grew, and his chest tightened. "That sounds awesome. Lead the way."

He wanted to smile again, but he held it back. He nudged with his head toward the road. "Come on. I docked the boat not far from here."

She fell into step beside him, looking around at the trees and the sky as if it were something new and fascinating. What did she see that he was missing?

"How was last night?" he asked, suddenly needing to hear her speak. "Any better?"

She groaned dramatically. "No! It was worse. Brittany and Bethany wanted to relive college dance team days with Jenna, and Alexis joined in, because she 'danced in high school,'" she mimicked with finger quotes and actually did a fair impression of Alexis, from what he knew.

He snickered and looked down at her. "What did they do?"

She returned his look with the most deadpan expression he had seen outside of an emoji. "They choreographed a dance to 'Call Me Maybe.' And incorporated singing into it. And they made Grace record it. It's going viral when the wedding is over."

Hunter laughed into a hand, fighting the urge to burst out laughing. "But was it good?" he asked when he could speak.

She shrugged, expression still carefully blank. "Sure. I mean, they're all very athletic and talented. But twenty-seven times through that song, not counting just parts, and with them trying to get Alexis up to par... Caroline and I were dying."

"What about Sophie?" he asked as the road opened up to the docking area.

"Sophie doesn't have facial expressions," she said with a sniff that reminded him of the girl in question. "We have no idea what she thought."

He chuckled at that. "Well, at least you have Caroline, right?"

She tilted her head in consideration. "Yeah, that's true. She played soccer at Tennessee while Jenna was on the dance team there. Honestly, my cousins aren't that bad, and Grace is okay. But the others…" She shuddered, then caught sight of the boat, and her brows shot up. "That's the boat?"

He bit back a grin. The speedboat was technically property of the resort, but he could use it whenever he wanted, and it was brand new. He had taken it out a few days ago for a test drive and loved it, so why not kill two birds with one stone?

"That's the boat," he said proudly, going out onto the dock.

Mal didn't follow. "I was picturing more of a rowboat."

He looked between her and the boat, then raised a brow. "Would you prefer a rowboat? I can drag one of those out if you want."

She was on the dock in half of a second. "Nope, this is just fine. Where'd you get it?"

He shrugged one shoulder. "I borrowed it."

She gave him a look, but said nothing.

He shook his head, smiling to himself, and got into the boat. "Stop judging me, Mal."

She smiled back and held her hands up. "Not judging. You poor, poor, very rich man."

He rolled his eyes and held out his hands for her. "Come on, smarty-pants."

She handed him her cameras and bag, which he promptly set on the driver's seat, then held his hands back out for her.

She surprised him by not taking his hands, but grabbing his upper arms instead. Before she could hop in on her own, he reached for her waist and lifted her. She snorted a laugh and gave him a funny look. He couldn't return it. He just looked at her, hands still on her waist.

"You're so tiny," he murmured, shaking his head.

She shrugged, her hands still on his arms. "Well, despite my uncle's stature, my dad was a jockey, so that started me out on the right foot."

"I like that you're small," he said softly, wanting to push a lock of her hair behind her ear, but unable to move his hands. "It makes me want to protect you."

She met his eyes defiantly, but there was something else in her eyes. "I don't need protection."

"I know," he replied at once, his hands jumping to her shoulders as if he could force down her rising energy. "And I like that, too. But it doesn't change the way I feel."

Her mouth opened, as if she were going to ask a question, but she stopped, exhaled, and just looked at him. The tilt of her head, her small frame, her wide eyes—all made her look more like a child. The question was still in her eyes, but he was afraid to know what it was.

He forced himself to step back and cleared his throat, then smiled. "All righty, Miss Photographer. Be prepared for quite the spectacle."

She laughed, all tension gone, and moved to sit on a bench nearby. "Don't hype it up if you can't deliver, Mr.... What is your last name, anyway?"

He turned to look at her. "McIntyre. C. Hunter McIntyre, at your service," he added, bowing slightly.

She raised a brow. "What's the C for?"

He made a face. "Carlow."

She clamped her lips together so hard he could nearly see her teeth through her lips.

"Go ahead," he dared. "Laugh. But it's for my grandfather, and he was really something."

She smiled, still biting on her lip. "I'm sure he was. He would have to be to pass that name down."

Hunter made a face and went to the other bench to pull out the blankets he'd brought. "Okay, Miss Hudson, what's your middle name?" he taunted, making a show of tucking a blanket around her.

She watched him with amusement. "Take a guess. Starts with an S."

He pretended to think, knowing he would most likely never get it. "Seraphina."

She rolled her eyes and pushed at him. He laughed and went to get his last surprise.

"Tell me," he said, going to the front of the boat. "I'm only going to guess ones that are out there."

"Shannon," she finally announced quietly. "It's my mom's

favorite cousin. She died in a tractor accident at sixteen."

He looked at her for a long moment. "It's pretty. Suits you."

She ducked her head for a minute, smiling, then looked up again with a teasing half smile. "Thanks, Carlow."

He snorted softly, shaking his head. "And to think, I'm being nice to you," he grumbled playfully, bringing a paper cup with a lid and a sleeve to her.

She took it with a surprised look. "What's this?"

"Cocoa."

Her mouth dropped open, and then one side slowly curved. "Seriously?"

He shrugged in what he hoped was a nonchalant way. "It's cold, and you like cocoa. It's the least I can do for creeping you out."

She flashed him a grin and held the cup with both hands, bringing it closer to her face. "Consider me totally and officially uncreeped out."

"Yes!" he whispered loudly, pumping a fist, which made her laugh. If only she knew that he was not actually playing his enthusiasm. He winked at her, then sat at the wheel and started the boat. "Okay, we gotta go or we'll miss the sun."

He drove her out to the middle of the lake and stayed far enough away from the houses to avoid disturbing anyone. A few of the guests and locals were out fishing, and he waved to them. He found himself talking to Mal a lot as she was taking pictures of this and that. He talked about his summers at the lake as a kid, fishing with his grandfather, when he first started taking part in the resort responsibilities… as a golf-cart driver. She gave him a hard time about that, but seemed to enjoy hearing his stories.

He showed her the house that had been his grandfather's, the one where all the best memories happened. It wasn't part of the resort, technically; it had been deeded over to a local family per his grandfather's will, but they were practically his own family.

They drove all around the lake, seeing the park and the hotel, the older homes that had been there for ages, as well as some of the newer, more modern places. She was particularly interested in the ruins and asked if there was a good story to go along with them.

"If there is, I don't know it," he said with a laugh, catching her disappointed look. "But it didn't stop us from pretending all sorts of things. My cousins, my sister, and I played for hours on those things. Never told the grown-ups. We can come back to that later, if you want. In the truck."

"I'd like that," she told him, smiling softly in a way that made him wish someone else was driving the boat. Then her attention was caught by something else, and she brightened. "Oh, the sun's coming up! Turn the boat just a bit."

He did as she asked and slowed the motor to still the water around them. There was hardly any wind today, so the surface of the lake was fairly still, but for the faint hint of a fog. The sky was perfectly clear, and if things stayed just as they were, she would get some amazing shots.

He'd looked up her work again last night, having forgotten what his publicity manager had shown him back when the contracts had been drawn up. And now that he knew her, he'd wanted to see her work, and he was beyond impressed. Tom, Jenna, and his team had assured him that Mal was a brilliant artist who could really help them out, and now he could see what all the fuss was about. Somehow, she took something simple and made it extraordinary.

What could she do with something already exquisite?

She pushed the blanket aside and started snapping, turning her body so she was more kneeling on the bench than anything else. She was completely silent, switching between cameras every now and then, and he could see they had different lenses, though what each was, he couldn't tell. She leaned over the edge of the boat, and he twitched with the urge to go and hold her heels.

There was no sound but the clicking of her camera and the water softly hitting the side of the boat. Occasionally, a bird chirped here or there, or a fish would flip the surface of the water, but other than that, it was complete silence. And he loved it. He could have sat like this for ages, just watching her work, seeing the concentration on her face, her thought process almost written across her features. He wanted to be able to translate that, to know what she was going to do before she did it.

Just then, the sun peeked over the ridge, and she snapped pictures rapidly, again leaning near the surface of the water. This time, he did get up and carefully went over to keep her from toppling overboard.

"Thanks," she said softly, not stopping anything.

He just squeezed her ankles in response.

After a moment, she turned. "Can we go over by that cove you showed me before?"

"Of course," he said simply, willing to drive the boat to France if she asked. Actually, he liked that idea a lot—not driving this boat to France, but taking her there. That idea certainly had merit. He shook the thought away and revved the engines to take them where she asked. After that, they only went to one more spot before she said she was ready to head back in.

"Get everything you wanted?" he asked.

She beamed at him as she settled back in and put the blanket over her. "Nope."

He raised a brow and turned to see her better. "No? Why not?"

She lay down on the bench and shrugged. "I never get everything I want. It's not possible, because I want to catch it all. Like I said yesterday, every sunrise is different. Someday, maybe I'll catch that magic moment I'm looking for, and maybe I did today. I won't know till I get in and look at them."

He watched her for a long moment, and she watched him. He bit the inside of his lip, then said, "But did you get enough?"

She smiled again. "Yeah. More than enough. Thanks, Hunter."

The softness of her voice did something to his legs and his chest, and he inhaled sharply, forcing a smile in place. "Don't thank me, Mal. I just really wanted to drive this boat."

She smirked. "Uh-huh. Boys and their toys."

He chuckled, then glanced back again. "Why are you nicer in the mornings?" he asked, genuinely curious.

"Am I?" she asked, coming up on an elbow.

He gave her a nod. "Yesterday, you were sweet as pie in the morning, then bit my head off in the afternoon."

"Yesterday, you lied to me," she pointed out with a quirked brow.

He opened his mouth to argue the point yet again when she overrode, "Okay, fine, you withheld certain information."

He would give her that one.

"My point is," he said with a satisfied smile, "you are nice again this morning. I'm just wondering if you are going to be mean to me later."

She pursed her lips, and her eyes narrowed. "Are you withholding more information?"

Was he ever. But he didn't think she wanted to know about his feelings yet. He shrugged. "What do you want to know?"

That made her smile. "When can we do the full resort tour and shoot?"

"Today."

"Really?" she asked, sitting up and folding her hands in front of her.

He nodded thoughtfully. "Yeah. Today works. You've got fittings today, right?"

She rolled her eyes. "Ugh, yes. You do too, I think."

He winced. "Touché. But it's not tuxes, just suits. So that's nice."

"You don't like tuxes?"

He mock-shuddered. "Hate them. It's why I hate black-tie affairs and only go if I have to."

She grinned and rubbed the back of her neck. "Well, hurrah for no tuxes, then. I hate taking pictures of crabby people."

He gave her a look. "I would not be crabby on Tom's wedding day."

She raised a daring brow. "If you were in a tux and partnered with Sophie?"

That made him wince again, with great dramatics, and she giggled. "Thankfully, we will never have to know," he replied, shaking his head. "I'm in a suit and paired with Caroline. I think, except for Tom, I win."

Mal nodded, grinning. "I think you do." She wrinkled up her nose and looked at the approaching shore. "Do I have to go back to the Hen House? It's not only dress fittings; its makeup tests too. Why do they need pictures of that?"

Hunter laughed and slowed the boat as he neared the dock. "Why do they need any of this? You could always pretend to take pictures…"

"Now there's an idea," she mused, pulling at her lip thoughtfully.

He shook his head and docked the boat carefully. "Well, you just text me if you need saving. I'll come up with something." He hopped out and tied the boat.

Mal stood up and gave him a calculating look. "I don't have your number," she said carefully.

He took his time to look at her, a smile playing at the corners of his mouth. "No worries. I have yours."

An open smile formed, and she looked like she wanted to laugh. "How'd you do that?"

"Your contract, remember?" He shrugged. "I have connections."

"That's for business," she reminded him, grinning.

"Exactly," he said simply, holding her gaze.

Her smile faded. "What are you doing, Hunter?" she asked in a soft voice.

He took her hands and helped her out of the boat, then still held them as they stood there on the docks, keeping her eyes on his. "I don't know why," he responded quietly, "but I can't seem to leave you alone."

"Oh," she murmured, swallowing once. "I'm sorry."

"Don't be," he told her. "I'm actually enjoying it."

Mal tried for a smile as she peered up at him. "Being my babysitter?"

Hunter wasn't going to let her play this off. He shook his head slowly and reached up to push a strand of hair behind her ear. "Being with you. It's an adventure. It's entertaining. And I really don't feel like doing anything else."

Her green eyes widened, and her lips parted. "Oh…" she finally whispered.

He pretended to adjust another strand and let his thumb graze her jaw just briefly, then dropped his hand. "Come on," he said as he stepped away. "I'll walk you back."

She cleared her throat and started walking. "I can do it myself," she quipped almost steadily.

"I know," he told her as he came beside her, walking close enough to occasionally brush arms. "But I really want to see if any of the girls wear those green facial masks to bed. That way, I can picture them like that all the time."

Mal snorted and nudged him. "Jerk. I think you just want some of my secret Nutella stash."

He considered that and looked up at the sky as if weighing the options. "Green masks… Nutella… I think it balances out. Let's do both."

Mal laughed again, and the sound echoed faintly in the morning air, and somewhere in the vicinity of his heart.

Chapter Seven

Mal was going to shoot somebody, as soon as she found a gun. This was, without a doubt, the longest morning of her entire life. For all its pleasant start, the subsequent hours were doing their utmost to obliterate any and all good feelings that might have remained from it. It was a sad thing to state that the dress fittings had been the best part of the bridesmaids' adventures thus far, probably because all the girls had known what they looked like and only got to complain about the fit, which was quickly adjusted to each girl's tastes. The boysenberry one-shoulder gowns flattered everyone's silhouette and had just enough sparkly things to calm the girly girls without offending the rest of them.

The hair and makeup tests, however…

"Retract the claws, kitten," a soft Southern accent calmly broke through her thoughts before she could properly process her frustrations into an appealing picture.

Mal glanced at Caroline, who finished her hair, makeup, and fittings ages ago and was sitting on a nearby sofa, looking as though she had been posed for a magazine shoot. Except she looked just as bored as Mal. If it weren't for the fact that she was looking up at Mal through her now heavily lined and falsied eyelids with a half curve to her mouth, she might have been just as miserable too.

"Don't tell me you're enjoying this," Mal muttered as she pretended to take more pictures of Bethany and Sophie, still in their chairs with the hairdressers fussing at them.

Caroline snorted softly and switched her crossed legs. "Nope. I have no idea how a girl with a pixie cut can take three hours on hair, but what do I know?" She shrugged and looked over at the window seat where Jenna was sitting, anxiously watching her friends. "Call me crazy, but I thought this was all supposed to revolve around the bride, not her bridesmaids."

Mal followed her gaze and sighed. "Yeah... Are they always this mean to her?"

Caroline didn't have to ask what she was talking about. Subtle insults, and not-so-subtle insults, had been flying back and forth ever since they arrived, from all the girls except Grace. Mal wanted to snap back but held her tongue, feeling it was not her place. But Jenna just smiled and laughed as if it had all been jokes, and her friends laughed too.

It wasn't funny, and it had to hurt.

"Yep," Caroline said tightly. "Drives me nuts, and I've told Jenna they aren't really her friends, but she won't listen to me. She knows they're being mean, but she doesn't rise to it. I don't know if that makes her sweet or stupid, but God love her, I can't do anything about it."

Mal hummed a noise of discontent, then looked at her cousin again. "You look great," she said, changing the subject.

Caroline gave her an amused look. "Thanks. It's a bit much for my taste, but it will do for Jenna. The hair, I like." She turned her head, and, really, the sweeping updo was very flattering on her. Mal was convinced no one else could pull it off that well.

"The hair is awesome," Mal assured her.

A fake, trilling laugh came from one of the other girls, and Mal groaned and gave Taryn a look, which was returned with similar sentiments.

"What about your hair and makeup, Mal?" Caroline asked. "What are we doing for you?"

Mal gave her a dirty look, and Caroline laughed and took her hand. "Come on, chica. Just because you're low maintenance, and do it very well, doesn't mean we can't gussy you up a bit."

Mal eased her hand away, smiling at her cousin's earnestness. "No. I just work here. I'm just the help, Caroline."

Now it was Caroline who gave her the look. "Call yourself that again, and I'll fix your face up real nice."

Knowing Caroline, she would too.

Mal swallowed nervously. "You're scary, you know that?"

The blinding smile was back. "Yeah, I've heard. And if I didn't love my twin so much, the rest of the girls would think so, too. Besides, come wedding day, you're part of the family in more than name only. You have to dress up then."

"I'll figure it out when that time comes."

"As long as you let me do it, I'm good with that."

Normally, Mal would have shied away from that, but Caroline had good taste and sense, and it might not be so awful to let her have her way. It would have been hard to fight her at any rate.

Sophie was finally satisfied with her look and turned to Jenna for approval, which was immediately given, not that Sophie actually cared. And Bethany… Well, she just whined, but once Brittany, Alexis, and Jenna convinced her she was perfect, she suddenly loved it.

"Blessed day," Mal groaned, capping her camera.

"Did you actually take any pictures?" Caroline muttered as she got up and came beside her.

Mal lifted a brow. "That is for me alone to know."

Caroline smiled and scrunched Mal's loose bun. "I'm glad you're here. You're like the only real person in this bunch."

"Tom's sisters seem nice," Mal pointed out.

Caroline shrugged. "Yeah, but they don't hang with us, so it's not the same."

Just then, Grace appeared with a tray of sandwiches and brought them over to where Caroline and Mal were.

"I know the others are on some bizarre fruit-and-nuts diet or something," she whispered, looking around conspicuously, "but I couldn't stand it. I asked Rosa in the kitchen to whip up something. Y'all mind turkey and cheddar?"

Did Mal mind? She'd been dying for real food, anything with more calories than she could count on her fingers and toes. Despite her Nutella and Froot Loops stash, she felt on the verge of starving all the time. She was tempted to hug Grace, but she resisted the urge and just smiled and took one.

"Bless your heart, Grace," Caroline said heavily as she took one as well. "You always were my favorite of Jenna's friends."

Grace smiled and scratched self-consciously at her own updo. "I'm all about figure, don't get me wrong, but I'm not gonna starve for it."

"Why is the photographer eating?" Sophie said with a sniff. "We are over here. Come on, do your job."

Mal slowly turned to face her and raised a brow, which was mirrored rather superiorly. "I am doing my job," she said quietly. "And one part of that involves not passing out from hunger when I'm taking pictures of you. Don't worry, Sophie. I have plenty of shots of you already."

Sophie blinked in uncertainty, and Mal felt satisfied about that. No doubt Sophie didn't expect Mal to respond, only to obey or perhaps to fight, but Mal had dealt with tough customers in the past, and she was professional about it. Plus, there was the fact that Sophie didn't know what shots Mal had of her, and Mal's complete control over them just had to be unsettling for a perfectionist like her.

"What about me?" Brittany asked from behind her. "You didn't get me without any makeup, did you?"

"I've got the ones of you," Taryn said in her best I'm-trying-not-to-kill-you voice. "No worries. You look great."

"Not in that dress, I won't," Brittany pouted, looking in the mirror and frowning at her hair again. "I look like a pageant runner-up. Are we gonna look this tacky and cheap on Saturday?"

Grace gasped from somewhere behind Mal. Taryn made a subtle choking motion with her hands behind the girls, and Mal only blinked. Jenna looked embarrassed beyond belief, and her mouth worked as if she didn't know what to say. Mal wasn't surprised. Jenna was a nice girl. Caroline, on the other hand, cracked her knuckles, which caused Sophie to look at her in a sort of disgusted surprise.

"Jenna," Mal said with what was hopefully a kind expression, "if you don't mind, I have an appointment with the resort."

Jenna looked like she wanted to cry, but she nodded. "Of course, sweetie. Go ahead. See you at dinner?"

Mal smiled tightly and nodded. "At the lodge. I'll be there."

"Are you going with Hunter?" Sophie asked with another look.

Every girl in the room froze and looked at Mal, mixtures of interest and horror written on most faces. Jenna and Caroline looked surprised, and Taryn was wide-eyed and terrified.

Mal shrugged and picked up her bag. "Not sure, Sophie. All I know is I'm supposed to be at the office in twenty minutes, and someone is supposed to take me to some locations they think would work. If it is Hunter, I'll tell him you said hi." She turned and left the room without looking at anyone else, her face absolutely flaming.

Three minutes later, she got a text from Taryn: *You are my idol.*

Follow-up texts soon came from her cousins. Caroline sent three thumbs-up emojis, and Jenna's was a longer, very detailed apology that Mal did not have time or patience to actually read.

That house was going to kill her, and if she had to do any more abrupt subject changes to avoid living in a remake of Mean Girls, she would consider vaulting off the third-story terrace.

She was relieved to be going out to the resort and taking pictures, but why did Hunter have to be the one taking her? If people suspected how much time they had been spending together the last two days, and how much she was starting to like it, things would only get uglier. Despite how much she hated girls like Sophie, that sort of high-end clientele was very influential. She needed them to like her in order to achieve her goals—not have them spreading rumors about her and feeling resentful.

There wasn't anything she could do to keep Hunter from taking her today, but she could determine the direction of the day. All business, no flirty fun like the morning shoot. She needed to work, not be distracted, and no matter how gorgeous he was or how he made her feel, she would shut down all awareness of him. He would be just another client.

She could do that, right?

Something was seriously up with Mal, but for some reason, she wasn't talking about it, and it was beginning to drive Hunter crazy. They'd been driving around in a golf cart for almost two hours now, and all he'd managed to get out of her was business. Any attempt of his to tease or flirt resulted in a quick shift of topic and a drop in temperature.

At this point, it was practically thirty below.

She wasn't rude, not by any stretch, but she was formal—professional, pleasant, and yet carefully distant. He didn't enjoy it at all, and it was going to make what was coming up more awkward.

He wanted the Mal from this morning, the one that was comfortable and charming and made his heart skitter around like a pinball machine. This Mal made him nervous and doubtful, and he would have to admit, a little insecure. He had been making plans, for heaven's sake, and all of them involved her. Right now, he wasn't sure any of them were going to work out.

This tiny, moody photographer with snarky responses and warm smiles was taking over his life at a rather alarming rate. He was more than happy to let her do so, but he'd rather hoped the course of said life would run smoother with her at the helm. Daily convincing her of his sincerity and the value in trusting him was going to get very, very old.

He watched her as she snapped more pictures of their newest renovated house, unable to help smiling as she muttered things to herself. He caught a few more of her made-up swear words, as Dan had called them, and made a mental note to someday ask her about them. Assuming they were ever on friendly terms again, of course.

"All right," Mal finally said, turning back to face him. "I think that's enough here. What next?"

He carefully turned his smile into the polite, borderline insincere one he used on all his clients, most of his employees, and some of his associates and friends.

"There's a classic, small cottage not too far from here," he told her, gesturing for her to lead the way back to the cart. "Ralph thinks it might appeal to the clientele that have a more rustic taste."

Mal made a face of consideration, then nodded. "Makes sense to me. Some people want a real getaway." She situated herself in the seat and met his eyes squarely, just a hint of her smile in them.

It was the friendliest she'd been all afternoon, and he let himself warm up a little. "Exactly," he said, taking his own seat. "Some people actually like 'all this wood,' and there are cabins we can photograph later for them."

She smiled in earnest then, but it faded just as quickly, and with it, his hope for the day. "Whatever you need," she murmured, tucking a strand of hair back into her bun. "Ralph said there was a lot on the resort I could use. It just depends on what you want from me and where you want it to go."

Hunter sighed as he drove to the cottage. "I think it would be best for you to use your own judgment on the scenic stuff, Mal. I can give you an idea of houses and property, resort details and the like, but you're the artist."

She looked away from him, not that she had even been looking at him, and nodded. "Sounds good."

He groaned inwardly. This was going to be a disaster, and it was supposed to be dramatic and maybe romantic. Maybe he would just forget the whole thing. She didn't need to know, right?

His more rational side kicked him. Of course she needed to know, and he needed to do it. She would be impossible for the rest of the week if he didn't. She would be happier this way, ultimately, even if it was presumptuous on his part.

And it was nothing but presumption on his part.

He was nosy, interfering, overbearing, and self-serving, no matter what good intentions started it all. But hopefully, that wouldn't work against him here. After all, it's not as if she knew where to find him if this all went south.

He glanced at her as they approached the house, and her demeanor changed. She lit up, and the first genuine smile of the afternoon appeared. He bit back a grin and let the elation of victory wash over him.

"This is perfect," she breathed when they stopped, not moving from her seat. "This right here is exactly what I picture in a place like this."

Hunter stared at it for a long moment. It really was one of his favorites on the resort, and not just because Mal liked it. Or because it made him think of her. Or because he could picture her here.

He'd liked it before today.

But he liked it more now.

"Do you want to go inside?" he asked softly, keeping his voice conversational.

She looked at him wide-eyed. "We can do that?"

He had to smile at that. "I'm the owner," he reminded her, tilting his head. "I can get whatever keys I want. You can see inside any house you want."

Her grin was wild and breathless as she nearly leaped from the cart, leaving him rather wild and breathless as well.

It didn't take Mal long to take pictures of everything. The first floor was simply a large living room and spacious, rustic kitchen. Almost the entire back wall, however, had been turned into windows, and the view was truly spectacular. While not one of the more prominent views, it was sheltered in a beautiful section of trees near a stream, and glimpses of the lake could be caught through the woods if she looked closely enough.

"This is incredible," Mal said to herself, but loud enough that Hunter caught it. She went to the back door to go out onto the deck, pausing to catch something the windows were doing.

"It's yours," Hunter blurted out.

Mal froze, took one picture, then lowered her camera. Slowly, almost horrified, she turned to face him. "Say what now?" she asked, her voice barely controlled.

Hunter scratched the back of his neck anxiously. "Well, not yours, not like that. I'm not giving you a house, that's… That would be ridiculous. But I could, if I wanted to. If you wanted…"

"Hunter."

He sighed and put his hands into his pockets. "I reserved it for you. You're staying here now." He shrugged lightly, his eyes never leaving hers. "I thought you'd like it."

She blinked once, then again, and put her hands on her hips, looking down at the floor. "My stuff is already here, isn't it?"

He winced. "Yeah. It's in the master bedroom downstairs."

"And what about Jenna?"

"I told her you needed more privacy and personal space for work and easier access to various resort locations, but you didn't want to say anything to upset her." He quirked a brow and gave her a knowing look. "All of which is the truth, I might remind you."

She looked up at him, and the green glint in her eyes was enhanced by her emerald top and only made her more captivating. "And who said you got to make those decisions? Seriously, Hunter?

People are already talking, and your interference is going to make more of a spectacle of us than there already is."

"So what?" he argued, coming over to her. "Mal, you were miserable over there! I just wanted you to be happy, and I know you will be more comfortable on your own."

"Yeah, and it's very sweet, and the house is perfect, but the fact that you knew that, that you even thought that…" She exhaled sharply and rubbed at her head. "It's too much. With everything else, it's all too much." She looked up at him again, her expression unreadable. "I need this to be private too. I need to not be the topic of conversation. It's crazy enough as it is. Can you do that, or do I need to file a restraining order?"

He wanted to laugh, but she looked completely serious.

"I'm sorry that I've made you uncomfortable," he said softly. "I never meant to do that. Well, maybe a little, but only in a good way." He gave her a hint of a smile and was relieved when she returned it. He looked at her for a long moment, then admitted, "I just can't seem to let you out of my sight. I told you yesterday that I like you, Mallory. And today, I like you even more. And you're going to have to get used to it, because I have no intention of stopping anytime soon."

Her eyes widened, and she chewed on her lip for a moment. "Oh…" she finally whispered.

He took two steps closer to her. "Still want a restraining order?"

She cleared her throat briefly. "I-I plead the fifth."

He wasn't quite sure he heard her correctly, but he caught the tone of her voice. "That's not a yes," he pointed out, keeping his voice steady and slow.

She nodded once, her eyes on his. "Correct."

His heart lurched against his ribs. "So… no?"

"I didn't say that." She tilted her head, as if considering her options.

Hunter let a slow, sly grin cross his face. "Sweetheart, that's a wide-open invitation to a guy like me."

Mal smirked up at him. "A guy like you? What are you?"

He reached out a hand to touch hers. "Determined," he murmured, daring her to pull away.

She blinked slowly, once, twice, then swallowed and interlaced their fingers.

He smiled, unable to do anything else, and nodded. "Okay. Let me show you the rest of the house."

It didn't take long, as the house was small, but Mal was so delighted with everything that it took twice as long as it should have. She raved about the kitchen and refused to let him bring in an employee to cook for her. He'd seen to it that the basics had been supplied for her, along with her precious Nutella and Froot Loops and a massive selection of cocoa. According to her, that was all she would need.

He paused in the kitchen, still holding her hand, the tour of the place finished. He needed to get back to Tom and the guys, and dinner was at the lodge in an hour and change. But something else needed to be said before he left, before she was apart from him and back in her own head.

"Mal," he said quietly, stroking her hand, "I need you to stop fighting me. I need to know that the version of you I leave is the one I get back. Decide now if you are in or out, sweetheart. Because I'm not going anywhere. And with how you're holding my hand right now, I get the feeling you're okay with that. Am I right?"

She looked at him for a long moment, chewing on her lip again. But he never felt anxious, never doubted for a second. Her hold on his hand was secure and sweet; he knew where her heart was.

The question was if her head was willing to follow.

"Yeah," she finally admitted, allowing a smile to curve shyly across her perfect lips. "You're right."

He grinned. "I know." He brought her hand up and kissed the back of it. "See you at dinner." He slowly released her hand and headed for the door.

"What, you aren't sending a car for me?" she teased, following curiously.

He half turned and gave her a look. "You said private, Mal. I can do private. In fact, I am very good at private. I may be better at private than I am at public. But you'll have to forgive my eyes. They've never been very good at keeping things private."

He winked and left the cottage, smiling at her choked laughter as he did so.

Chapter Eight

Feeling better about how she was dressed for this dinner and more chipper than usual, Mal sat in a corner of the room, observing the others as they entered.

Hunter was a genius, really. One hour in her new place, and already, she felt rejuvenated. She would have to talk with Jenna tonight, just to make sure she was really okay with it. It had been so important to her to have Mal there, and this hardly seemed like an appropriate thanks.

Mal waved at her aunt and uncle as they entered and earned waves and a wink in return.

"Can I sit here?"

Mal turned in surprise to see Tom indicating the chair next to her. "Where did you come from?" she asked bluntly.

He grinned. "I was out on the terrace just there. Came in to greet Cady and Drake, but I saw you and wanted to come here first. We haven't had a chance to get to know each other."

Mal couldn't help but smile back. Tom was just that guy. "Of course, please sit."

"Thank you," he said as he did so, leaning back casually in his seat. "So, Mal… I'm sorry. Can I call you Mal?"

She laughed and waved her hand. "Please do."

He chuckled. "Jenna never calls you anything else, so I got used to it. It means a lot to her that you could come."

Mal sighed and twisted her fingers. "I was stunned when she asked me. It's… it's been years. And there are other photographers, better qualified ones."

"She wanted you, Mal. And after I saw your work, I was almost as excited. The fact that you were family was just a bonus." He gave her a half smile that probably melted kneecaps. "You really are very gifted. I trust you know that."

There really wasn't a way to answer that, so Mal just murmured, "Thank you." Then she asked the question that had been eating at her for months now: "How in the world does a UNC boy get a Tennessee girl? How does that even work?"

Tom laughed out loud and rubbed his ear as he glanced over at his soon-to-be in-laws. "Well, it hasn't been without its difficulties. Drake and I don't talk about sports ever, and Caroline lords over me whenever she can. Lucas doesn't care; he's just happy I'm not from Florida or Georgia."

Mal had to laugh at how perfectly her family fit into the stereotypes she'd pegged them for.

"Cady's just happy there's a wedding," Tom added, smiling fondly. "And Jenna doesn't say anything about it unless our schools play each other, so it's fairly safe most of the time."

"How did you meet?" she asked, feeling more comfortable with him by the minute.

He turned back to her with a raised brow. "You don't know the story?"

She shook her head. "All I know is the public version, of which there are at least seven, and I know Jenna better than to believe you guys met at a Tough Mudder."

Tom threw his head back for one barking laugh. "Yeah, that one is the most ridiculous of them all. Truth is, we met at a hotel in Lexington. I was in town for business meetings; she was getting ready for the Kentucky Derby. One morning, we were both in the workout room at the same time—she was wearing a UT tank top, and I was wearing a UNC shirt, and somehow it didn't matter. I couldn't take my eyes off her, and she 'accidentally' broke the treadmill, so I offered my assistance." He grinned, and his eyes twinkled at the memory.

"Of course you did," Mal snorted, shaking her head. "Did you fix it?"

He smirked and made an amused noise. "No, turns out she actually broke it in her enthusiasm. So, we ran away and agreed to meet up for lunch to see if we got caught. The rest is history."

Mal burst out laughing and put a hand over her eyes. She could just see Jenna trying to be smooth and pretend to break something, but actually break it in the process. She was just that sort of cute and uncoordinated person when she got excited, though she was all grace and poise at every other time.

"I've been addicted to her ever since," Tom said with a smile. "She could ask me for anything in the world, and I would get it for her."

"Does she?" Mal asked, turning in her chair to face him more. "Ask you for things?"

Tom gave her a look, his eyes seeming bluer for the pinstripe in his shirt. "What do you think?"

Mal considered that. "Honestly, I can't see Jenna asking for much. She's pretty much the most perfect person I know."

"Exactly. Try getting perfection to fall for you." He shook his head and took a drink of the water on the table.

"Try being related to it," Mal muttered.

Tom smirked and turned thoughtful. "I get the impression you don't ask for much either, Mal."

She shrugged and sipped her own water. "I've learned not to. For all my ambition to be someone in the world, I try to live as quietly as possible. Which reminds me," she added, sitting up, "why didn't Hunter know I was Jenna's cousin?"

Tom exhaled and craned his neck. "Yeah, he asked me that one too. Jenna would have told everyone in the entire world that her cousin was taking the pictures, and that would have been enough for some people. Not her bridesmaids, of course," he admitted with a snort, "but everyone else. I'm afraid the decision to keep that a secret was mine." He gave her an apologetic sort of look.

She frowned, her brow furrowed. "Why, though?"

"Business," he said simply. He put his glass back on the table and sat forward. "You see, Mal, I know what it's like to be tossed into the Hudson world when you're not ready for it. I come from a wealthy and high-end family in North Carolina, it's true, but I didn't have Jenna's star appeal until I was dating her. I'm used to it now, so I don't mind. But when she wanted to bring you in, I was hesitant. No reservations about you, but this is a big thing, and for someone who doesn't have any connections to this sort of world, it would be a hard sell. I didn't want your connections to be an issue. And I figured if we could get you something that might appeal to your artistic and professional side…"

"The resort contract," Mal said, nodding in realization.

"Uh-huh." Tom smiled. "I knew this place well enough to know that someone with vision could have a lot of success. I mean, the place works for the hobby photographer to have once-in-a-lifetime shots; what could a professional do? But again, I didn't think you'd want someone to bring you on just because of Jenna. So, we kept that under wraps. Sold it to them just on your skills and portfolio alone. Hunter looked at them himself and was convinced, and the lawyers did the rest."

Mal shook her head and sat back in her seat, crossing an ankle over her knee. "So, I really did get it on my own."

Tom's smile grew. "You really did, kiddo." He winced. "Sorry, you're not that much younger than me. I shouldn't call you that."

She chuckled and took her glass of water again. "You can call me whatever you want, Tom," she assured him. "We're family now. Anything goes."

He inclined his head in thanks.

They sat there in a companionable silence, watching the rest of the group trickle in for dinner. Jenna saw them together and grinned, waving at Mal, looking much more at ease than she had earlier.

Tom whistled low under his breath.

Mal glanced at him in surprise, but he just grinned.

"Just when I think she can't get any prettier," he murmured, shaking his head.

Mal laughed. "You are completely head over heels, aren't you?"

"So far gone," he groaned as he pinched at the bridge of his nose. "Three years with her, and I still can't breathe."

Mal shoved at his knee with an exasperated noise. "You sound like a Hallmark movie."

He laughed and shrugged his broad shoulders with ease. "I know, and I fully admit it."

Mal looked over at her cousin, mingling and smiling nonstop. "That's good," she said quietly. "Jenna's that sort of person."

"Hunter really likes you, you know."

She jerked and gave Tom a strange look. "Say what?"

Tom glanced to the doorway where Hunter and two of the guys had just come in, talking to each other. Mal also followed his gaze. Hunter was engaged in conversation with the others, but his eyes were on Mal. For a full set of heartbeats, she couldn't move, couldn't look anywhere else.

This guy was single? And looking at her like that? In public?

She swallowed and dropped her gaze to the table. "I'll kill him," she muttered.

Tom chuckled quietly. "Somehow, I doubt that, Mal. Hunter likes you, and he doesn't like anyone."

"He told you?" she asked, meeting his eyes.

"Didn't have to. He's my best friend, Mal. I know him. He's private about just about everything in his life, perfectly composed, professional, reserved almost to a fault. But he is also driven and ambitious, generous, and makes things happen." Tom shifted and nudged Mal with his foot. "In college, they didn't have a rowing team at UNC. Hunter wanted to row—something to get him on the water and keep him in shape for rugby. The school wouldn't sanction it, so Hunter started a club. Raised the money from frats and other organizations at school, and before you know it, there was a club rowing team. He was a freshman at the time."

Mal choked on her water. "Good heavens," she gasped, coughing. That was a fairly good picture of the sort of person he was, and apparently always had been.

"What Hunter wants, he gets," Tom said simply. "No matter how much work he has to do for it."

Mal twisted her lips and considered the man in question for a moment. "You're saying I should just give in."

"No way."

She turned back to Tom in surprise. "No?"

He shook his head with a mischievous grin. "No. A little fight never hurt anyone. Make him work for you. Trust me, it'll be worth it."

She gave him a look, and he laughed. "I know," he said. "You've known me for like a minute, and I said 'trust me'."

She grinned, as that had been her thought, more or less. "I'm willing to give you some good faith," she told him. "Any advice?"

He mused on that for a moment and eyed Hunter in thought. Hunter caught the both of them staring at him and looked between them in confusion, then concern, then outright wariness.

Mal smiled at Tom. "Well?" she prodded softly, seeing the rest of the girls come in and knowing Tom would have to go make nice soon.

"Don't let him take control," Tom said slowly. "Not all the time, anyway. He's used to being in charge. Throw him off a bit. Could be fun."

She raised a brow as he got up. "Fun for me or fun for you?"

He smiled. "Hopefully, both." He looked at her for a long moment, then added, "I'm glad you're here, Mal, and I'm really glad Hunter likes you. Like I said, he doesn't like anyone."

"He likes you," she pointed out.

"Well, I didn't give him much of a choice there," he scoffed, his smile going crooked. "And apparently, neither did you." He winked and pushed off the chair, going to the rest of the group and slipping his arm around Jenna's waist as if it had been designed to be there.

Taryn and Dan were suddenly on one side of her, chatting about something or other.

"What were you doing?" Taryn asked absently as she set her purse down.

"Getting to know my new cousin," Mal said, nodding her head at Tom as he pointed at her from across the room.

"Oh yeah?" Dan asked, fidgeting with his collar.

"I'd like to—" Taryn started in a low voice but was cut off by Dan's elbow in her side.

"And?" Dan continued, as if nothing had happened.

"Quite possibly my new favorite person ever," Mal said without hesitation. Then she turned to face them. "How did the rest of the day go?"

Hunter didn't think they would ever get away. He'd done his part by getting to the furthest corner of the room, the one closest to the door, but that was as far as it got. If it wasn't because of Mal snapping random pictures, it was the notice of just about every person in the room. He could hardly just toss Mal over his shoulder and say, "Well, we're leaving now!" without causing some serious problems. He wouldn't make it three steps before some evil eye, from someone else or from Mal herself, would make going anywhere impossible.

He wanted to know what she and Tom had been talking about. He wanted to know what she thought of the house. He wanted to know if anything had changed in the last hour.

He wanted to be alone with her. Because that was the only way he could have her. In public, he was the best man, and she was the photographer, and apparently, that was some insurmountable obstacle. Only in private could they work.

"Hey, Mal!" Jenna called, breaking through the various conversations. "Didn't you want to get a sunset shoot before the week is out?"

Mal looked confused for just a moment, wrinkling up her nose. "Yeah…" she said slowly, not quite comprehending.

She was really cute when she did that.

Jenna suddenly had a very knowing look on her face. "Well, tonight is probably your best bet. Y'all better take off now before you miss it."

Mal still looked confused, but she and her assistants got up and gathered their things.

Jenna was Hunter's favorite person ever, possibly even more than her fiancé, and he was indebted to her. He slipped out the door, having not been addressed by anyone in at least five minutes. Hopefully, it would be ten more before his absence was remarked on. Maybe someone else would leave, and then it wouldn't even be a thing.

He waited for them out by the carts, crossing and uncrossing his arms like an anxious teenager, looking at his watch, and wondering what in the world was taking so long for them to get down here. Finally, they appeared, and Mal wasn't looking ahead, just talking to her assistants.

"Honestly, you guys just go back to the house. I'll take some quick shots and be done in a jiffy. Then we can edit together tonight, and it'll be great."

Dan opened his mouth to respond when he saw Hunter, and his mouth curved into a smile. He nudged Taryn, and she, too, caught sight of Hunter. Her eyes lit up, and she fought to keep from laughing.

"Know what, Mal? That's a great idea," Taryn said, clearing her throat. "We'll head to the house while you go shoot. But we don't need to edit tonight. There's plenty of time. Just take your time. Relax. Enjoy."

"What?" Mal said, looking at her. "What are you…?" She followed her gaze and saw Hunter, then stopped dead in her tracks. "Ah-ha."

Hunter sighed and looked at the others. "She says that like it's a bad thing."

Mal rolled her eyes. "I take it you're going on the sunset shoot with me?" she asked him pointedly.

He shrugged one shoulder. "Am I invited?"

"Yes," the assistants said together.

He nodded. "Thought so."

"Isn't that up to me?" Mal asked, looking around.

"No," all three answered at the same time.

She threw her hands up in the air, but smiled. "Fine. Care to drop them off at their place?"

"Sure thing." He started toward the parking lot. "We'll take the truck. You guys mind riding in back?"

"Nope!" they replied in chorus.

Hunter put his arm around Mal's shoulders. "I like these two," he murmured. "Very smart kids."

"Shut up," she muttered as she pushed at him.

Soon enough, they were alone, and the moment they were, he took her hand again, faintly sighing at the relief of being able to touch her again. He was getting more pathetic by the minute. But, despite Mal's cynical expression, she was holding his hand just as tightly.

If that wasn't enough to make him rightfully pathetic, he didn't know what was.

She gave him no direction, letting him drive them around however he wanted. He took her to one of his favorite spots, the place they had gone just yesterday morning on their first sunrise shoot. It would be that much better in the evening, and he couldn't wait for her to see it. Hand in hand, they walked from the road up to the spot, and he heard Mal's soft "oh" of appreciation.

"We've been here," she said, glancing at him.

He nodded. "It's better in the evenings, so I didn't think you'd mind."

She turned and looked over the expanse before them, sighing. "I don't."

"Do your thing," he encouraged, letting go of her hand and sitting down to watch.

She surprised him by only taking a few pictures and then coming to sit by him. His look made her duck her chin bashfully and shrug. "I'll get what I need."

They sat without speaking for several minutes, and Hunter spent most of that time looking at Mal, who purposefully stared ahead at the view. She was stunning just like this. The golden glow of the fading sun on her skin, the warm evening breeze sending stray tendrils of hair dancing, the green in her eyes dancing with flecks of gold… He was transfixed by her, heart and soul.

"What are you looking at?" she finally asked, her face still forward, though the hitch in her voice told him she knew exactly where he was looking.

He smiled at her defensive tone and the very telling catch. "You," he said simply. "In the evening light. It's beautiful."

She swallowed hard. "Stop it."

"Stop what?" he asked as he reached out to replace a strand of hair the breeze had dislodged, keeping his fingers on her jaw.

"I can't think," she whispered.

"Then don't."

He turned her face toward him, steadied her eyes with his own, and felt his breathing match her own uneven pace. His hand moved, and he gently parted her full lower lip from her upper with his thumb. He leaned forward and pressed his lips against hers for a sweet, soft kiss.

Surprisingly, he was shaken by such a simple connection, and instantly wanted more, but he didn't want to overwhelm her. He broke off gently, touching his forehead to hers, and felt satisfied at the small sigh she released. He started to pull away when her hands came to his face on either side of his stubbled jaw, and she pulled him back to her.

"You're going to miss it," he whispered, teasing her by staying just far enough away that their lips didn't touch.

"Miss what?" she replied, her eyes still closed.

He smiled against her lips and then kissed her again, taking all the time in the world to do so properly.

Chapter Nine

Hunter was exhausted, and the early and ungodly hour of this sunrise shoot was just brutal. Dreaming of Mal, reliving her kiss over and over, had made sleeping fairly impossible, and as much as he wanted to enjoy this quiet time with her, he also really wanted to sleep.

But he wasn't going to. He would just deal with it and catch up when he had to drop her back off at her place. The group resort tour wasn't until after lunch, so that was plenty of time.

Mal wasn't chatty this morning, and he was grateful for that. She'd smiled shyly when he'd picked her up, but after that, nothing had been said. It was uncomfortable between them this morning, more than it had been last night, but it was the sort of ticklish uncomfortable that made him smile—or would have made him smile if he had energy to. Thankfully, the site for the sunrise shoot wasn't far. All he had to do was get her there without crashing and then sit for a while until she was done.

They almost matched this morning with their hoodies and jeans, and she'd gone further by wearing a hat as well. For someone who had apparently just rolled out of bed, she looked far too attractive like this. Something about Mal always looked good, whether she was in sweats or flannel or dressed up. But she wasn't stop-dead-in-your-tracks attractive. No one would ask to take pictures of her, she wouldn't draw comment, and people probably forgot her face if they weren't paying attention. Maybe that was why Hunter loved looking at her so much.

He could see her.

"Come on, sleepyhead," Mal teased softly from beside him. "I'll be quick, and then you can go back to bed."

It took him a minute to realize they were stopped, and he'd been staring out of the windshield for a while. "Sorry," he mumbled, clambering out of the truck and heading toward the site, holding his hand out for her.

Mal chuckled as she took his hand, squeezing it. "Go sit down. I'll be right there."

He gave her a tired smile and did so, leaning against a rock, his arms and head resting on his knees.

Either he fell asleep, or it was a matter of moments and not very many camera clicks before there was a hand on his knee. He looked up and saw Mal shaking her head at him, smiling. He started to scoot over for her, but she gently moved his knee aside instead.

"Let me in," she murmured, avoiding his eyes.

His eyebrows shot up as he realized what she meant, but his legs moved of their own accord as Mal situated herself between them, leaning back against his chest.

"This is a pleasant surprise," he whispered as he nudged her head, resting his chin on her shoulder.

She laughed low in her throat. "You think after yesterday I'm supposed to be shy, Mr. You're Going to Miss It?"

He smiled and nuzzled her ear, just enough to make her squirm. "You didn't seem to mind."

"Mind?" She laughed again. "My brain was working backward with how you were staring at me, and then that kiss? You were right; you have got skills."

He hummed and ducked his head against her. "Skill's got nothing to do with it, sweetheart. You drive me crazy, and I'm not responsible for my behavior, skills or no skills."

She tensed, then pulled his arms around her, and he was more than happy to comply.

"Either way," she said in a carefully indifferent tone that didn't fool him, "your pickup lines need work."

"I beg your pardon?"

"Oh, come on. You had to know that was cheesy."

He shrugged against her and held her tightly, burying his head more securely between her neck and shoulder. "Yeah. But, in my experience, women like cheese."

"This time," she replied smugly as she leaned more fully into him. "Now, shut up. The sun is about to come up."

Hunter didn't move from his position and felt his breathing slow and deepen. His body relaxed fully against and with hers, more comfortable than he had been in years.

"You're missing it," Mal whispered, and he could hear the smile in her voice.

"No," he mumbled sleepily against her. "I'm not."

She let him doze for a while. Then, as the morning began to warm, stirred and got to her feet. "Come on, let's get back. Lots to do today."

He grumbled and reached for her, but she only laughed and kept carefully away. She grabbed his hand and hauled him to his feet.

"Cruel woman," he muttered, rubbing at his eyes and shoving his hands into his pockets.

She smiled and nudged him with a shoulder. "Not gonna hold my hand?"

He glared at her. "No. You're being mean."

She laughed out loud and slung her camera over her shoulder as they headed back to the truck. "What are you, seven?"

He sighed and allowed himself to smile back. "If I touch you, Mal, you might not go anywhere all day. I'm feeling very possessive today."

Her eyes widened, and she pursed her lips, then took a measured step away from him.

He nodded once, looking at the truck even as his hands fisted in his pockets. "Good idea."

"We have got to work on your intensity," Mal muttered, shaking her head.

Hunter opened the truck door for her, then got in on his own side. Nothing was said as they drove back down to Mal's cottage, and Mal was surprisingly fidgety. When he was more coherent and alert, he would have to talk to her about that. If she was really put off by his intensity, he could back off.… At least, he could try. He hadn't been lying; she really did drive him crazy, and he almost didn't recognize himself.

Almost.

They pulled up to the cottage, and he threw the truck in park, glancing over at her, looking so small on her side of the truck.

"This is your stop," he said, leaning to poke her with a finger in her thigh.

Her lips quirked, and she looked up at him with an unreadable expression that stopped his heart. Before he could think, she reached over, slid a hand around the back of his neck, and tugged his lips to hers for a soft, thorough dismantling of every single brain cell he had. She broke off and took advantage of his stunned silence by giving him a crooked smile and a suggestive lift of her brows, then she scrambled out of the truck and went into the house.

Once sanity, sense, and sensation returned to him, he managed to put the truck into drive and get back on the road.

That little minx…

So much for sleeping.

It was two o'clock in the afternoon at a remote resort in a roomful of people, and Mal was ready to come out of her skin. She should have been seven levels of controlled here, in her zone, assistants at her side, and a multitude of amazing photo-ops at her fingertips. But her fingers were twitchy, her palms were sweating, and pretty much every word being said sounded like a buzzing in her ears. She had just enough focus to take quality shots, but conversation and smiles were completely beyond her.

It was all the fault of the ridiculously good-looking man in a blazer and T-shirt with those just-tight-enough stonewashed jeans. He had been staring at her all flipping day, the same smoldering, patella-pulverizing look that made her wish she was wearing a muumuu. She was grateful he was the one giving the tour and thus had to be up front and speaking most of the time. His tone was perfectly professional and controlled.

His eyes, however…

He was an attractive man before she'd started to like him, before he'd started spending sunrises with her, and certainly before they'd kissed and he'd set her world aflame. Now he was like the entire dessert menu at the Cheesecake Factory, and she had a gift card.

"Sweet mother of Abraham Lincoln," she hissed as her eyes clashed with his again and her face and neck flushed at once.

Taryn and Dan snickered, and she elbowed whoever was closest.

"Honey, if I were getting looked at like that," Taryn said out of the corner of her mouth as she checked her camera screen, "I would not be standing here taking pictures."

Mal glared at her and fumbled in her satchel for another lens as the group moved out of the house to the back patio to admire the view. This was one of the premier houses on the resort, apparently, and had some great and rich history, and the family who owned it had done a lot of work to make it both rustic and modern… and some other stuff that Mal had completely forgotten. But it was located above many of the others, so the view was spectacular.

If only someone would let her appreciate it.

Was this what it was going to be like all the time? She was going to die. A slow and painful and rather embarrassing death.

The girls headed off in one direction, the guys in another, all chatting aimlessly. Hunter had stopped his tour guide act and was talking with Caroline at the moment, thank goodness. Mal focused on the amazing view she had, wondering if the homeowners would mind if she came back. She could only imagine how fantastic this view was at sunrise and sunset, with morning fog, with rain coming in… She wanted to see this view in every season and in every condition.

"Taryn, can you get a focal point shot of that tree on the ledge?" she asked, clicking away madly. "I think you could get a spectacular aspect."

"She's already doing that," a distinctly non-Taryn voice murmured from behind her.

Hot and cold shocks exploded up and down her back, and she gasped at the contact on her arm. Hunter gripped her tightly, pulling her away from the patio and the view.

"What are you——?" she tried, resisting initially.

"Stop talking," Hunter ground out.

Mal looked back toward the others, but no one paid any attention to her except Taryn and Dan, who waved. Then Caroline saw her and raised a brow.

No one tried to stop them.

"Hunter," Mal said carefully, trying to avoid stumbling on the walkway.

He shook his head and opened the side door to the house, moved to the glorious and state-of-the-art kitchen, then tossed Mal into a pantry just to one side and followed. He closed the door quickly, her arm still in his grasp.

She didn't have time to say anything before he had her up against the wall. He took her camera off her neck, slid the satchel down her arm, and in the same motion, managed to get a hand behind her ear while his thumb grazed her jaw.

And then he waited.

Mal looked up into his face, trying her level best to be mad at him. "You are ridiculous," she scolded, her voice sounding harsh and rasping to her ears. "I thought you were going to be reserved. You said you could do that. Well, nothing about you is reserved, pal. You're making a scene, which I specifically asked you not to do. I am going to get so much crap for this! What in the world has gotten into you?"

Hunter apparently didn't hear a single word. He stared at her, eyes flicking between her lips and her eyes. She held her breath, waiting, and then he kissed her. Softly at first, just once. Then his other hand came up to match the first, and his kiss became hard, insistent, and possessive. She was unable to move, to think, to breathe... Everything was suddenly and completely attuned to him.

His lips were magical and wicked, and she had no idea how to match them, how to keep up, and she felt herself growl in impatience. He angled her face up, their difference in height more enhanced by the cramped pantry, but their forced proximity only made things hotter, more exciting, more... something.

He kissed her deeply, parting her lips with ease and skill, draining her of thought and any resistance she'd ever had. His hands cupped her face, fingers stroking and gripping against her cheeks. He wrung every ounce of sense and pleasure from her, kiss after drugging kiss, and soon, the wall was the only thing holding her up.

When he finally saw fit to give her a break, her hands were

gripping his lapels, and his chest was moving just as fast and unsteadily as hers. There was some comfort in that, at least. If she was going to be completely senseless, at least he was there too, to keep her company.

"What was that for?" she eventually gasped.

He stroked her cheek, one hand leaning against the wall above her. "After your little stunt in the truck, I haven't thought of anything else all day. I needed to see if I imagined it." He waited a beat. "I didn't."

Mal swallowed hard and slid her hands on his blazer. "Wow."

One side of his mouth curved up. "Is that a compliment?"

"Sure," she managed, clearing her throat. "I just…" She had no idea what had come over her this morning; she'd only known that she had to kiss him on her own, just once, in case it never happened again. "I thought it was a one-time thing," she admitted lamely.

His eyes flashed dangerously, and he kissed her again, slowly and maddeningly raw. She broke off with a whimpering gasp, the only sort of noise she could make. Hunter layered her jaw with grazing kisses, then brushed his lips across her earlobe. She shivered, his hand moving from her face to her waist, pulling her tight into him. Mal kept her eyes closed, though her eyelids twitched and fluttered with the rest of her.

"Nothing about this is a one-time thing," he growled into her ear, breathless and panting a little. "Nothing."

"Even the pantry bit?" she managed to quip, finding her voice at last.

His low laugh sent a ripple through her. "Especially the pantry bit."

She slid her hands around his waist under his blazer and cleared her throat again. "Better make it worth my while, then. We've only got a few minutes, and I need something to tell the others when they find out."

Hunter made a noise of amusement and appreciation. "Tell them to use their imaginations."

And then, still smiling, he kissed her again.

Feeling much better about life in general, Hunter walked into the entertainment room at the lodge. It was already mostly filled, and the first group was ready to go on. He hadn't thought that Jenna and Tom would have included the events at the resort into their extravaganza schedule, but when he'd shown them the calendar, they had both insisted that the live music and karaoke night be part of their package. He didn't mind, not at all, and it would give the tourists and locals something to talk about, when they were permitted to. He really enjoyed spending time with his guests and neighbors.

Mal was on one side of the room with Taryn and Dan, giving direction. He wouldn't distract her. Not again. She looked over at him and seemed to lose her train of thought. He smiled and inclined his head, but made no move to go toward her. He saw the flash of relief and pleasure, and she returned his smile, then went back to work as if nothing had happened. He wasn't entirely sure what was going on between them, but he was enjoying it.

He headed to the table where the rest of the group was, ordered a drink from one of three waiters floating around, and settled in to enjoy what was destined to be an entertaining, if not at times downright hilarious, evening.

The first group turned out to be a folksy bluegrass ensemble that was really quite good, and the crowd enjoyed it. They were followed by a number of fair but fun karaoke numbers from various audience members, and then a truly stirring young man with an acoustic guitar.

Hunter saw Sophie furiously texting away on her phone during and after that one, which was a clear indication of his talent. Her father was one of the biggest names in the music industry and, while Sophie didn't inherit his taste or his ears, she knew what he liked and looked for.

During the intermission, the wedding group mingled again and warmed up to the idea of participating. Hunter glanced at Mal, who was at the end of the table, camera in her lap for the moment. She rolled her eyes once and folded her open cardigan closer around her, as if settling in. Taryn, meanwhile, was poring over the karaoke list, and Dan was shaking his head at her.

There was an interesting family dynamic between those three, and Hunter liked what he saw. Mal was not what he would call a people person, and she was struggling to reconnect with her family while maintaining her self-image and allowing for their wealthier eccentricities. She'd never talked to him about it, and he wasn't sure she would, but he could see it.

He pulled out his phone and texted her quickly.

What are you singing?

She glanced at her phone briefly, then looked up directly at him, her expression incredulous. He shrugged, and she snorted softly, shaking her head before texting him back.

You first.

He smirked but didn't look back at her. Instead, he looked over at the stage, where three of Jenna's bridesmaids were about to sing. It was horrible. But then, they knew it was going to be, and it was all about fun, wasn't it?

He'd never do something this impulsive and exposing; it just wasn't in his nature. But he could appreciate the bravery of doing so if you were serious, and the lack of inhibition if you were not.

Two more acts followed—one, a sweet duet from an older couple he'd seen at the resort every year for at least five years, and the other, a group of guys doing a fantastic a cappella rendition of "I Will Wait." Hunter made a note of that one, signaling to his MC to get the necessary information from them. Talented and popular acts were always worth bringing back.

"Now what?" Jenna asked quietly of the table. "Who's next?"

"Not it," Tom answered, putting a finger on his nose, which most of the group followed.

Lucas sat forward. "I think everyone in the group should do at least one number. Call it a dare."

That was received well with hushed voices and significant looks.

Hunter looked at Tom with a raised brow, and Tom shook his head. "Hunter has a forfeit. He runs the place."

Lucas rolled his eyes but smiled. "Fine, fine, boss man doesn't have to. But that means we get some wings off tab."

Hunter grunted and shook his head with a smile. "Sure, whatever you want. So long as I'm not going up there." He flagged down the waiter and put in an order for them.

"I think Mal should go next," Sophie said with a sneer in her voice.

Hunter's smile faded, and he turned to look at her in disbelief. He wasn't alone.

Sophie pretended to look surprised. "Didn't you say the entire group? She's part of it, right?"

Mal was wide-eyed and small at her end of the table. "I don't think—"

"And I know what she can sing," Sophie interrupted, looking at the music list, though her eyes didn't move across the page. "'Alone' by Heart."

The entire table went silent, no one stupid enough to mistake her real meaning, not even Bethany. Hunter fought the urge to look at Mal and the following urge to punch the table.

Caroline, sitting two seats down from him, snatched the paper back from Sophie. "Here's an idea, Sophie. How about you go next and sing 'Don't Speak' by No Doubt?"

Uneasy laughter broke out, and Mal quietly excused herself from the table, camera in hand, and moved to one side of the room, taking pictures of the Journey cover band currently on stage.

Hunter watched Mal like a hawk, looking for the barest hint of hurt or distress from her. He never saw it. She was as calm and cool as a cucumber, and he was proud of that.

You okay? he texted quickly.

She glanced down at her phone, then looked over at him in surprise. She smiled, rolled her eyes, and made a small gesture with her arms and shoulders as if to say, "Of course."

He gave her a warning look. He didn't want her to pretend, not with him.

She huffed and looked down at her phone.

I don't care about Sophie. And I could totally rock 'Alone' if I wanted to.

He smiled and looked up at her again, sending her a wink, which she returned.

Someone at the microphone cleared his throat, and Hunter looked to the stage to find Lucas there. "I would like to dedicate this song to my cousin Mallory," he said with a hand on his chest, looking at Mal. "I love you, and you're hot. If we weren't related, this would be my song for you."

That earned him three whistles from their table, and Hunter sat back with a smile. Mal was going to kill Lucas no matter what song he sang after this. What followed was a dramatic, heartfelt, and surprisingly decent rendition of Survivor's "The Search Is Over," and Hunter suspected, looking around the room, that Lucas would have quite a fan club before the night was out.

Mal was taking pictures of the whole thing and smiling, shaking her head. According to multiple sources, there was just no explaining Lucas.

When the applause died down, Lucas spoke again. "And now, ladies and gentlemen, for an encore, I present to you a Hudson cousin special. So, if my lovely sisters and cousin would join me up here…"

There were gasps and squeals and mutterings of murder as Jenna and Caroline went up. Mal stayed rooted in her place.

Lucas was staring at her with a lifted brow. "Mallory, if you don't get your butt up here, I will tell this entire room about that family trip to Charleston when you were seven."

Mal's eyes went wide. She swallowed, and her brow snapped down. She handed her camera off to Dan, who was grinning gleefully, and he and Taryn stood together in the back, plotting their angles.

Mal made her way up and stood by Caroline, smiling in spite of her glower at Lucas. Then Mal met Hunter's eyes, and her shoulders dropped in a sigh of defeat that made him smile.

"This is a real treat, ladies and gents," Lucas was saying now. "This is something that has not been done in fifteen years. All our lives, we worked tirelessly on one song together, and one song only."

All three of the girls went wide-eyed and looked at each other.

"The Hudson cousins present… 'Dancing on the Ceiling.'"

The room broke into applause, and it looked like Lucas wasn't going to live very long after this, but something he said to the girls made them smile. The music started, and they were off.

And they were good.

More than that, they were having fun, and soon everyone in the room was—except Sophie, who was not impressed. But nobody cared. They were up on their feet, dancing and singing along, clapping to the beat.

The cousins danced, harmonized, and seemed to know exactly

what the others would do. Clearly, there had been much rehearsal of this song in their younger years, and they remembered every bit of it.

Mal was alive on stage, and he could see the years of distance melting away between her and her cousins. She moved to the beat in her place, though she was clearly not a dancer. She didn't care, and neither did anyone else. This was a side of her he'd never seen before, and layers of Mal's inhibitions were falling away one by one before his eyes.

He liked what he saw. He liked it a lot.

The song ramped up, and Lucas turned his focus to the audience, playing to their excitement and enjoyment, while Mal and the girls turned into a trio, playing off each other and having a blast while they did it.

Hunter couldn't pay attention to the others, not even with the charm and beauty of Jenna and Caroline to contend with. They might have been the ones everyone else watched, but not him. There was no one but Mal, for him—Mal on the stage, Mal behind the camera, Mal drinking cocoa in the mornings… Mal as she was at any given time.

She was a constant surprise, and for the first time, he really liked surprises.

Thunderous applause met the end of the song, and all the cousins were laughing hysterically.

Sophie, not to be outdone, forced Alexis on stage with her, and they butchered "Hips Don't Lie," raising several concerns from patrons about their blood alcohol content level. Pity they did not have any such excuse.

Lucas saved the evening again with Reed and the rest of the guys by leading the room into "Friends in Low Places," but Hunter only pretended to sing along. He kept looking over at Mal, now back with her assistants and taking pictures, invisible to everyone else again.

In his opinion, Mal had never looked more gorgeous than laughing with her cousins on stage. And all he wanted to do was pull her onto his lap and tell her how proud he was of her and how beautiful she was. And ask her to sing for him again. But he couldn't.

He texted her instead.

And her blush and smile was worth it.

Chapter Ten

Sunrise was becoming a favorite time for Hunter. It didn't matter where they went or how much they talked or didn't talk. Being with Mal was enough. The opportunity to hold her and steal several kisses was enough. Even without that, watching her work was enough.

She was truly brilliant, visionary, and artistic. The most inconsequential things were fascinating and of great interest to her. Mal could make something beautiful out of things that Hunter couldn't even see. She tried teaching him, showing him what she saw through her lens, and the two just did not seem to be comparable. She tried and tried to get him to understand what she did and how she could do it, but his brain just did not work that way.

That didn't mean he couldn't appreciate her genius and find her work absolutely brilliant. He told her that so much she was beginning to hate him for it. He knew that for certain because she kept telling him.

"If you don't stop that," she said with a very pointed glare, "I really will hate you, and you will not get any kisses from me."

He grinned at her from where he was leaning on a rock near the old ruins. "Stop what?" he asked, folding his arms. "I'm only staring."

Mal rolled her eyes. "Exactly. But your stare is one thousand megawatts stronger than a regular person's. I refuse to be stared at like a piece of hamburger." She gave him another look and went back to taking pictures.

Hunter gave her a second, looking her over. She was in her jeans and hiking boots, the white jacket from the first shoot, and one of his beanies. She was gorgeous and natural and everything he had ever wanted.

"You're not hamburger," he said slowly.

"Thank you."

"You're a perfectly cut, seasoned, and tender piece of prime rib-eye steak."

Mal stumbled as she whirled, cheeks flaming and eyes wide. "Stop that!" she screeched.

He shrugged one shoulder, curving his mouth into a smile. "What? What did I say?"

"You say things like that, and then I get all fluttery and nervous. And stop staring at me with those intense eyes!" She waved a hand in the air and turned away from him, facing the lake.

Hunter pushed off the rock and slowly sauntered toward her. He didn't say a word, and she didn't move when he got close. He simply slid his arms around her waist, pulled her against him, and waited. Soon enough, she relaxed in his hold and leaned back with an irritated sigh.

"Am I ever going to be really mad at you?" she asked with a hint of a smile in her voice.

He chuckled and pressed a kiss against her ear. "Probably not," he whispered. "You like me too much."

"Maybe." She leaned her head back to rest on his shoulder. "How long is this going to last, Hunter?"

That gave him pause. "What are you talking about?"

"This," she said, tugging briefly at his arms, but not dislodging them. "How long is this going to last? Because it's moving really fast, and we're in our own lovely little world here. How long until you realize that I'm just some solidly middle-class girl with impossible aspirations who's dipping her toes in water she doesn't belong in?"

Hunter dropped his arms from her and turned her to face him, his emotions suddenly going haywire, his vision turning an interesting shade of red. "What are you talking about, Mal?"

She wouldn't look at him, and he didn't want to force her, so he just squeezed her arms.

"What?" he asked again.

She swallowed once. "You're too good for me," she mumbled. "Way too good. And I don't want to be played."

It was as if some cosmic vacuum had sucked all the air from his lungs. He couldn't breathe, couldn't think, and his equilibrium was suddenly and entirely focused on her as its center. She thought this was some off-the-cuff fling? That he was some rich guy with nothing better to do?

"Do you really think," he began slowly, fighting for control, "that I am playing with you? That this is a fling?"

She shrugged, still not looking at him.

He exhaled carefully, drawing it out. "Then I have been doing a miserable job of courting you."

Her head finally came up, and her curious, red-rimmed eyes met his. "What?"

He took one hand and cupped the side of her face. "Mal, I don't fool around. I don't play or fling, and I most certainly don't care where you think we are on the class and fortune spectrum. None of that matters to me. How many times do I have to tell you that I like you, that you're beautiful, that I want to be with you, for you to believe me?"

"I just… I didn't think things like this happened," she whispered. "They don't happen. Not to girls like me."

He stroked her cheek softly. "Well, it's happening, baby. To you. Despite what you think, there are no girls like you. There's just you. You need to stop putting distance between us that isn't there."

She reached a hand up to pull his head down and touched her forehead to his, swallowing hard. "I'm sorry," she whispered, her voice choking.

He shifted to kiss her forehead gently, then went back to touching foreheads and let his nose graze hers. "Don't be sorry," he told her. "Just see what I see. I'm getting tired of fighting you for you."

She leaned her head to kiss him softly, then buried her face into his shoulder, and he held her for a long while, the sunrise unnoticed by either of them.

She eventually stirred and smiled at him. "Have I ever told you how ridiculously good you smell?"

He grinned and raised a brow. "Really? What do I smell like?"

Her smile turned impish. "A man."

A hiccup hit his chest, and he laughed to cover it. "Well, good. I would hate to smell like something else." He looked up at the sky. "I should get you back and let you get ready. We get to spend all day together."

"Do we?" she asked, taking his hand and letting him lead her back to the truck.

"Lake Day," he reminded her. "We rented the tour boat and reserved it for the party only. Fun in the sun, on the water, and a fully stocked bar and concessions." He stopped and turned to look at her with a suggestive quirk of his brows. "What kind of swimsuit do you wear, Mallory?"

She laughed and shoved at his chest. "I will be fully clothed at all times, dude. Best thing I can say is I might wear shorts, and maybe, just maybe, you'll get a glimpse of my shoulder."

Hunter gasped dramatically and clamped a hand on his chest. "I don't know if I can take it…"

Mal rolled her eyes and got into the truck before he could get the door for her. He chuckled and got in himself. He opened his mouth to say something when Mal suddenly turned to face him.

"Did you call me baby out there?" she demanded, looking a touch irritated.

He clamped his lips together on a laugh, then returned her look with one of his own. "You would prefer muffin? Or maybe pumpkin? Snookums? How about my little kumquat?"

Mal winced and rubbed at her forehead where the beanie sat. "Fine, fine, call me whatever you want, but nothing stupid or cheesy. And absolutely nothing in front of the others, you got that?"

"Yes, ma'am," he said obediently as he started the truck.

"And keep your gorgeous megawatt eyes to yourself," she muttered. "I need to have brain capacity in public."

Hunter smirked and backed the truck up. "Yes, dear."

Hunter behaved himself rather well on the boat. It was Mal, actually, who was having trouble. She couldn't stop staring at him. Whether that was his fault or hers would be up for serious contention later. He knew the effect he had on her. His near-constant smirk today told her everything.

He was more dressed up than the other men, but still far more casual than Mal had seen him. A pair of well-loved blue jeans, Sperry's, and a white button-up that hung open and rolled at the sleeves, with a white tank top underneath. His hair was disheveled by the wind, his scruff was tempting, and he wore his Ray-Bans the entire time, which honestly did nothing about the intensity of his eyes.

She knew when he looked at her. Her entire body lit up when those eyes hit her. And she got very, very warm—warm enough to take off her oversized peach T-shirt and just go with the double-layered tank tops underneath.

Hunter smirked broadly at that one, but thankfully stayed on his side of the boat. She stayed as far away from him as she could bear, hanging near Taryn and Dan whenever she could. Obviously, they had to separate at times to get pictures of different things and at different angles, but they stuck together as the outsiders of the group.

Taryn found great enjoyment in Mal's behavior and took it upon herself to point out various things to her. "You're drooling," she said with a snicker as she made her way behind Mal.

"So would you, if you had him," Mal bit back, her mouth curving.

Dan choked a little on his drink and marked an invisible tally in the sky while Taryn grumbled under her breath. Mal glanced around and saw, to her surprise, Reed was away from the rest of the group, sitting in a lounge chair, with a pencil and notebook in hand.

The Hollywood Heartthrob wasn't trying to get with any of the bridesmaids? That was odd. She wandered in that direction, covering with the camera and new angles, knowing Hunter's eyes were following her. She glanced at him occasionally, and his attention was riveted on her.

Yikes.

Reed didn't seem to notice her coming, his notebook propped up against his bent knee, tanned skin contrasting brightly with the white pages. He was shirtless, like most of the guys, and she was woman enough to appreciate the fine show of muscle on display. His dark hair tousled in the breeze, flapping against the sunglasses on his face, and she restrained the impulse to take a picture. Nobody needed more shirtless pictures of Reed Summerfield in the world. Except maybe Taryn, and she would already have taken twelve.

"Hey, picture lady," Reed said quietly when she was close enough, still focused on his paper. "Come to get the money shot?"

Mal snorted and pointedly turned her camera toward the back of the boat. "Yeah, the houses on this side are amazing."

"Ouch." Reed paused to rub his chest just over his heart but didn't sound wounded at all. "She bites too."

"Reflex," she replied, snapping a few more photos.

Then she turned back and saw, to her surprise, that he was sketching. She moved closer and peered over his shoulder, looking from the group of people toward the front of the boat, then back to his paper. He was sketching all of them, and he was good.

Really good.

"You sketch?" she asked, lowering her camera and leaning on his chair.

He shrugged. "When I'm bored. Or stuck. Habit from hours on set as a kid with nothing better to do."

His voice was flat, but she had the sense that the Summerfield family had been less of a family and more of a corporation. That couldn't have been easy for a kid to grow up in.

"Well, it's good," she told him, straightening. "Like, really good."

For the first time, he looked up at her. "Yeah? Not just saying that?"

She gave him a look. "You need me to tell you it's good?"

"You don't seem the type to try to flatter me, so yeah."

She smiled at that. He was right; she wouldn't. "It's good, Reed."

He flashed a smile of too-perfect teeth that probably would have made other girls light-headed. "Thanks." He looked back down at it and flipped a few pages, showing her more. "People are easy, once you get the hang of it. I tried landscapes for a while, but I couldn't get it right."

"It's a struggle," Mal agreed with a nod. "I've got it easy with the camera, but I still miss tons."

Reed shook his head at once. "Not easy, Mal. You've got it harder. You've gotta catch what we're already seeing but make it different, make it more. You have to change what we think we see."

He shrugged. "I just can't draw trees and rocks. Much better at pretty girls."

She chuckled in spite of herself. "Do you draw dirty pictures, Reed?"

He looked up at her with a jaunty smile and a raised brow. "You offering?"

That made her laugh, and she shook her head at him. "No, sir."

"I know," he said, still smiling. "Just joking."

He went back to work, and Mal watched him for a moment, intrigued by the detail he put into Sophie's hair, and what a difference the detail made to the sketch. He knew what he was doing, despite his nonchalance, and that intrigued her, too. There was a deeper side to this guy? Did anybody know that? Somehow, she doubted it.

"You're not as bad as I thought you'd be," Mal murmured, fidgeting with her camera strap.

Reed glanced up in surprise. "I'm usually considered much worse."

"Yeah, well, I'm willing to bet you don't let your guard down much."

His lips quirked, and he pushed his sunglasses up on top of his head. "Same to you, picture lady."

They shared a small smile, and Mal wondered if her perception of rich people ought to be tossed overboard for fish chum.

"Wanna get a drink?" Reed offered, tilting his head toward the bar. "Totally platonic, I promise."

Maybe not.

The words were sincere, his tone even, but there was a very rich, very intense man with skin-scorching looks that would take exception to that drink, platonic or not.

"I'm, uh… sort of, uh…" Her cheeks were starting to heat, and she prayed he would think it was a sunburn.

"Spoken for," growled a low voice from behind.

Mal stiffened and glanced back to see Hunter watching them both, about three feet behind her.

Reed slowly raised a brow at Hunter, then looked back at Mal. "Right," he drawled, not sounding disappointed or surprised. "Three's a crowd." He tapped his sunglasses back onto his face and shrugged. "I'll just keep sketching bridesmaids I wouldn't touch with a ten-foot pole."

A guy with his reputation saying that? She had a hard time believing it. "Grace is okay," she told him. "Nice girl."

He snorted and waved her off. "Yeah, all the more reason not to touch her. It's me."

Mal frowned, moving back toward the others, inhaling sharply when Hunter subtly stroked her back as she passed him.

"Please don't play with fire, baby," he murmured, moving back toward his former spot. "I'm the jealous type."

Gah. She swallowed and lowered her head, pretending to look at the screen on her camera.

Too much. Much too much.

"Honey, Sophie is about to shoot lasers at you," Taryn muttered when Mal got back. "I think she thinks it's a tennis match between you two, her head keeps whipping back and forth, and she's gonna need Botox for the wrinkles she's forming."

Mal glanced over at Sophie, who looked like she could have spat at her. She sighed and adjusted the camera straps. "Well, I can't help it that he likes me and not her, even when she does her best to show off her crazy trim legs."

"Might be crazy trim, but your calves are much hotter."

Mal turned to look over her shoulder at Lucas, who was now by the bar getting a drink.

He shrugged helplessly. "I'm your cousin, but I have eyes. Denim cutoffs are a nice look for you, kiddo."

"Don't call me kiddo. I'm older than you!" she protested, ignoring his compliment entirely.

Lucas grinned and stood to his full height, looking down at her pointedly. "Yeah, but you're tiny. I win."

Mal rolled her eyes and took in the group without her lens for the first time in hours. Caroline and Jenna had followed her style, wearing their swimsuits under their clothes, but they had not seen it necessary to take off their shirts as she had. Grace and Sophie opted for sundresses, though Sophie's was a crocheted number with a skimpy bikini beneath. The other three were either in partial or entire swimsuits and more interested in tanning than socializing. Most of them wore oversize hats as well.

The guys were all shirtless except for Lucas, Hunter, and Tom. Taryn was having a field day with the sideline reporting there. Dan and Lucas sat at a table nearby, both wearing backward baseball caps, more interested in the baseball game on TV than anything else onboard. Dan was mouthy enough as it was, but if he started hanging out with Lucas? That would be trouble.

Jenna suddenly met her eyes and smiled her brilliant, beautiful, perfect smile. There wasn't anything to do but smile back, and Mal lifted her camera in a silent question.

Jenna nodded and pulled Tom closer, and their interaction was so intimate that Mal started snapping shots before they were ready. These were the moments she lived for as a photographer—the unplanned, spontaneous, natural moments that captured the essence of a person or a place. The artistry of her subjects was always revealed in these unexpected glimpses into life as they knew it.

She managed to get a few shots of the world's most perfect couple, earned herself a familial wink from Tom, and then took a few random shots of everyone else before setting the camera down and finding herself a drink

"Taryn?" Sophie suddenly called in her fake-sweet voice. "The sun is hitting me perfectly right now. Can you get a shot of it?"

Taryn gave Mal a look that made her clamp down on her lips hard. "Sure, Soph," Taryn called back casually, tossing her braid over one shoulder. "Lemme change lenses real quick."

She turned and pretended to shuffle things around in her bag.

"What lens are you looking for?" Mal asked out of the corner of her mouth, knowing she had the right one on at the moment.

"Something that highlights and emphasizes all-natural ugly," Taryn replied. "Got one of those?"

Lucas and Dan snorted behind them.

"Sadly, no," Mal told her with a click of her tongue. "But play nice. She bites."

Taryn snarled. "So do I." She quirked her brows as she picked up the camera again and left.

Mal watched for a long moment, chewing her lip absently. Sophie stared back, expression disapproving and superior. How did someone get that way?

"I can throw water on her and see if she melts," Lucas offered.

Mal laughed and squeezed the back of her neck. "Not sure what would happen there. She might explode into a burst of steam."

"There's an image," Dan muttered. "Might end up killing you, man."

"Eh," Lucas said with a shrug. "Least I can do after she tried hitting on me the other day."

"Did she really?" Mal asked, turning to look at him.

He shuddered. "Yep. I've had nightmares ever since."

Mal gave him a look. "Why would she hit on you?"

He returned it with a cocky half smile. "I'm really very pretty, Mal-Mal. But I don't like gold-digging snobs with an inflated sense of self-importance." He winced. "She didn't like my refusal."

"She doesn't like much, it seems." Mal sighed. "Except Taryn."

Dan laughed once in disbelief. "She doesn't like Taryn," he told her. "She just hates you."

"I know, but why?"

Lucas coughed and gestured surreptitiously. "One guess, darlin'."

Mal followed his finger and saw Hunter staring blatantly at her, looking like a GQ model that belonged on a poster in her bedroom. He leaned on the boat railing, arms folded, which happened to highlight his perfect physique, and a breeze tousled his hair as if spreading fingers through it with the same loving motion she suddenly wanted to. She swallowed hastily, and her cousin laughed.

"Go for the win, Mal," Lucas urged softly. "If for no other reason than to be able to shove it in Sophie's face."

Mal smiled softly, but not at Lucas.

At Hunter.

And he smiled back.

Maybe neither of them were very good at public after all.

Chapter Eleven

Mal's phone buzzed on the nightstand next to her, and she pried her eyes open blearily to get it. It couldn't be the alarm for her sunrise shoot; it was way too dark in the room for it to be that time. One look at the clock told her it was indeed that time, which meant that—

A loud roll of thunder interrupted her thoughts, and she flopped back down on her pillow. No sunrise shoot today, then.

She fumbled for her phone, disconnected it from the charger, and squinted at the blinding light of her screen. There was already a message from Hunter.

No shoot today, babe. Get some extra sleep.

She smiled and replied back, *Yeah, I need it after last night.*

You cowgirls have a late night? he wrote back, and she could just see his crooked half smile filled with insinuation.

She smirked. *I hate bachelorette parties on principle, but last night was the worst. I spent most of the time trying to find Jenna and Caroline outside.*

She waited for his response, which took longer than she expected, but then, she knew he wasn't the sharpest knife in the drawer in the early morning.

They left? he finally responded.

She thought back to the night before and shook her head again even now. It was the stupidest thing she'd ever seen or heard of, all the girls trying to be stereotypical cowgirls but looking more like Daisy Duke working at Hooters. And then there was the guy…

The girls surprised Jenna with a stripper, she wrote, hoping that would be enough for him to understand.

Oh… he texted in return, which made her sigh in relief.

She tilted her head in thought, then smiled and said, *On the plus side, he looked like Matthew McConaughey. But Jenna never wanted a stripper. She and Caroline left the moment he appeared, and she was really upset.*

His response was immediate. *I can see that. Did the others stay?*

Again, Mal shook her head, silently laughing now. *Oh, I left Taryn for all that stuff. I got out of there to find my cousins. She said they had a great time. Lots of dramatics and drinking. Bethany slapped Alexis for making out with the stripper. Sophie came dressed in a flannel that was identical to mine from BBQ night, but decided leather shorts were a better touch. Maybe she thought you would be there.*

She bit her lip as she waited for his response, wondering if he would take the bait.

On that note, I'm getting off and finding forks for my eyeballs. Go to sleep, beautiful.

She set the phone aside and hunkered down into the warmth of her bed. A lazy morning might be just what she needed after all the excitement this week. And a morning free of Hunter might just clear her head a little.

After getting more shuteye, she puttered around the cottage for a while, texted with Taryn, who was thankfully not as hungover as expected, but it didn't take long for her to be completely stir-crazy with nothing to do. The day's scheduled events were canceled, which would only really upset the kids, as it was supposed to be a kids' water day.

Hunter had apparently done some scrambling with Tom and Jenna, and they found a house above the resort that had an entire movie theater screen in their basement. The family was not using the house, so they were able to shuttle the kids there instead.

Jenna and the girls were off doing a fitness Bridal Bootcamp thing spontaneously, and Mal had been invited, but hot yoga with the Barbie gang was not her idea of fun. She'd sent Taryn a message about it, knowing how she loved being among the group, but apparently last night had been enough. And while Mal might be out of her comfort zone on this whole extravaganza thing, there was no way she was going to spend her time taking pictures of the girls under these circumstances.

The problem was that she had nothing left to do. Taryn and Dan were editing everything, and she'd only be in the way, looking over their shoulders.

A faint rumbling of thunder gave her pause. The storm would make for an excellent addition to her resort repertoire. She imagined some of the vistas and views she had seen so far over the course of the week, and the idea of catching them again with the clouds and the rain… It could be brilliant.

In a strange twist of fate, just at that moment her phone buzzed, and Hunter had texted her.

Don't go out today, okay? Really slick and more rain on the way. I'm dealing with resort stuff, but I'll come by later and pick you up.

Mal didn't think that required a response from her. Despite what Hunter thought, she had a job to do, and she'd been out in far worse weather than this for a shoot. She texted Taryn her plan and gave her an estimated time she should be back so they could edit these together. Then she tossed her phone onto the couch and hurried to get her boots and coat. This was a perfect opportunity for her, and no overprotective resort owner was going to ruin that.

Hunter finished the rounds at the few houses that tended to have trouble when it rained, checked in with the grounds crew to see if there was any trouble with landslides or trees down, and fielded four phone calls with Tom about Jenna's worries for the wedding on Saturday. He repeatedly assured his friend that everything would be fine in two days. The forecast showed things clearing up this evening, and nothing else coming until next week.

He prayed the forecast was accurate.

Hunter drove down to Mal's cottage, wanting to see her, hoping they could grab lunch, and generally just wanting to be with her. The next few days were going to be crazy, with the wedding on Saturday and rehearsals and everything tomorrow… It might be the only day they would actually get to spend time together.

And then what?

He didn't really want to think about what came next. How could he explain to her what she made him feel and how deeply he felt it? After less than a week? It was certifiably crazy, and he knew it.

It didn't change the fact that it was the truth.

He'd never really made plans with regards to his personal life; he was too busy with his professional and business life. Everything else came and went along with that. But now… he had plans—or the dream of them. There were so many things he wanted to do and see with Mal, so many ideas constantly swirling about his head, and nothing seemed impossible.

It would have absolutely terrified him if he weren't so delighted about it.

There were no lights on at the house, which was unusual. It was still raining and rather dark, for it being almost one o'clock. He knocked several times and saw no movement from inside. He pulled out his phone and texted her quickly, waited a few minutes, and frowned again.

She was usually fairly quick with her responses. She was practically married to that phone; it enabled her to communicate with her assistants, mark the locations she had photographed recently, and keep her calendar of tasks and contracts on hand.

If she wasn't here, she was probably with Taryn and Dan.

He rushed back to the truck, brushing the water from his sleeves and rubbing at his hair. He would be soaked through if he spent too much time out there; his jacket might be waterproof, but it was not deluge-proof. Rainy days at Lake Lure were one of his least favorite things.

He pulled out his phone again and called Taryn.

"Taryn Chase, artistic goddess and creative genius extraordinaire, how might I serve you?"

Hunter looked at his phone for a second, shaking his head. He would never understand that one. "Taryn, it's Hunter. Is Mal there?"

"Hunter?" she squawked. "How did you get my number? Shut up, Dan, and watch the red eye. You just made that kid look like a demon."

Hunter sighed and looked up at the ceiling of his car. "Taryn. Mal."

"Right, yeah. Sorry, boss man. Um… Mal. Not here."

He frowned. "Not there? Where is she?"

"Not with you, I take it?"

He didn't answer.

"Right. You wouldn't be calling if she was. Well, she must still be out on the shoot, then."

Hunter's ears perked up at that. "On the what now?"

She must have caught the sharpness in his tone, because she slipped on whatever she was saying and stopped. "Um… Mal said she was going out for a shoot? You can catch really amazing things in a rainstorm, particularly with the views you've got here."

He growled and gripped his phone more tightly. "I specifically told her not to go out today!"

There was complete silence on the other end. Then, very weakly, Taryn squeaked, "I suppose now would not be the time to tell you that Mal doesn't like being told what to do?"

Hunter hissed and brought his phone down, tempted to throw it out of the window, but somehow managed to find a bit of control. He replaced the phone at his ear. "Do you know where she went?" he asked, his teeth grinding together so hard his ears hurt.

"No," Taryn said apologetically. "But I'm willing to bet it's a place she's already been. Days like today, you don't take chances. You go where you know you'll win."

Hunter hung up the phone, tossed it onto the seat next to him, and sped off up the road he had just come down.

If Mal wanted to play with fire, she had picked the right starter. This was going to get ugly, and while he was absolutely crazy about her, this particular brand of crazy had limits. Ignoring his text about safety up here was right up there.

Knowing Mal, she was not properly dressed for this weather, wandering where there weren't paths, and only concerned about getting the perfect shot. He had a fairly good idea of where she might have gone.

He drove toward the first area he had taken her to for a sunrise shoot. It had an incomparable view, and there were several places along the way she could have stopped for quality shots to distract her.

When he got to the point where he'd almost run her over that first morning, he watched more carefully. Sure enough, two curves later, there she was, drenched and trudging through the trees, smiling and looking for all the world as if she were in her element.

He screeched to a stop, threw the truck into park, and clambered out, slamming the door behind him. Mal turned to face him, her hair in two braids, though several strands clung to her cheeks. She wore a black track jacket over a V-necked shirt, jeans, and boots, so she wasn't a complete idiot, which was comforting. Or, at least, it would be when he could feel comforted about anything.

"What do you think you're doing?" he barked as he marched toward her, stopping at the edge of the road and looking up at her on the hill.

Her brows rose at his tone but then snapped down again. "I am doing my job."

The flatness and defiance in her voice irked him. "I told you not to go out today," he said, trying to moderate his tone. "It's too dangerous, and–"

"Yeah, you told me," Mal interrupted, raising her voice. "Did I respond? Fun fact, Hunter: I do not like being told what to do."

Hunter felt a growl well up in his chest. "I don't care what you like or don't like, Mallory. You don't know the area, and it's dangerous in this weather. When I told you not to go out, I wasn't doing it because you might get your hair wet. You could seriously get hurt."

"I don't need you to look out for me!" she cried, flinging her arm, causing her feet to slide.

Hunter jerked anxiously. "Are you kidding me?" he yelled. "Mal, it is torrential out here, and you've been slipping and sliding all day! Your boots are covered in mud! Do you have any idea how easy it would be for you to go tumbling down a ravine and no one ever know?"

"Oh, come on, the chances of that are–"

"Is your phone on you?" he interrupted, hands on his hips.

She opened her mouth, then scowled. "No, it's at the cottage. Probably on the couch."

"You never go anywhere on this resort without your phone, you hear me?" he ordered, his voice rising perceptibly. "What if you had gotten lost or hurt or something went wrong?"

Mal groaned up at the sky. "You are such a freaking worrier, you know that? Why do you even care?"

"Stop arguing!" he bellowed, growing irrational in his anger. "Get in the truck!"

She raised a brow. "No."

"What?"

"I am a photographer, Hunter." She hefted her camera for emphasis. "This is what I do and who I am. And no overprotective, bossy, nosy resort owner is going to stop me from doing that."

Hunter felt his lip curl in a snarl and pointed one finger at the truck. "Stop being stubborn and stupid and get in the truck, Mallory!"

"You are ridiculous!" she screeched. "I can't believe you have a problem with this. You know what this means to me!"

She was growing more and more rooted in, he could tell, but he was not going to bend on this one. "Get in the truck!" he bellowed. "If you won't get in on your own, I will pick you up and force you in myself."

Mal snorted and folded her arms, looking at him. "Right."

"Try me."

She stared at him for a long moment, then exhaled with all the dramatics of a moody teenager and marched over to the truck. Hunter went to his side and got in, waited for her to do the same, and then started driving again.

It was utter silence in the truck for quite a while, him gripping the wheel so tightly it would probably be permanently dented, and Mal looking out of the window, arms and legs crossed, as far away from him as humanly possible. He would have sworn steam was coming off both of them, curling with their mutual fury.

Mal shivered, and he glanced over to see her shaking, tucking her arms and legs more tightly against her. Silently, he reached forward and turned the heat up and turned the vent toward her.

She looked toward him barely and muttered, "You're going the wrong way."

"I'm not taking you back," he told her simply, keeping his eyes focused on the road, trying not to wince every time the wheels slid on the road. He was going to have to talk to someone about the road conditions.

"What?" she cried, her legs coming uncrossed.

He shrugged one shoulder. "My place is closer, and I can keep an eye on you there."

"I don't need a babysitter," she spat defiantly.

"Tough."

She sat back heavily against the seat. "I'm drenched," she said. "I need clothes to change into."

"Got it at the house," he clipped.

"From all the other women you've dragged up there?" she snapped, trying to level him with a glare.

He spared her one brief, disbelieving look. "Really, Mallory?"

She pushed a dripping lock of dark hair behind her ear. "Sorry," she said, managing not to sound petulant or sarcastic.

And just like that, his fury was banked down, and he could breathe again. He was still stinging, and fear prickled at his heart, but at least he was rational once more. "We're almost there," he murmured softly.

She nodded once.

Hunter exhaled slowly and prayed there would be something to salvage after this.

They pulled up to the house, and Hunter found himself holding his breath as Mal saw it for the first time. She stared wide-eyed for a long moment, then looked at him with a raised brow. "Really?" she said with a hint of irony.

He tried not to smile. "What?"

She scoffed and propped her feet up on his dashboard, somehow having removed the muddied boots without him knowing. "It's… little."

He smirked. "Just the entrance. It's built into the mountainside. You can't really see the whole thing from this side. You need to see the back or the side. In fact, you probably already have."

She looked at him, curious. "How's that?"

He leaned his head back and listened to the rain hitting the truck for a moment. "Down on the shore, where the lodge is? Have you seen the house up high with the back wall of windows?"

"Yeah," she replied slowly, almost sighing. "I've never lusted after a house before, but that one…" She trailed off, and her hand trembled as she put it on the armrest and turned to him. "Are you saying this is that house?"

He laughed and groaned, rubbing his hands over his face. "You lusted after my house? Oh, that's just great…"

"Hunter," Mal said in a strained voice, her body tense and practically coiled in her seat. "Can we go in?"

He rolled his head on the headrest to look at her. "You think I brought you up here to sit in my truck?"

She suddenly looked very small. "It would be the perfect punishment."

He watched her for a moment, blinking slowly. "Well, I'm not the torture kind of guy, sweetie. So yeah, we'll go in. And I'll make you lunch, and then you can fall asleep on my couch in front of the fire. But there's something I think you'll want to do first."

She looked wary but interested. "Oh yeah?"

He nodded slowly. "You'll need your boots."

She tucked her feet back in them, then looked at him again.

He hid a smile, the tension in his chest easing. They would be all right. "I don't want to deprive you of your photographic opportunities, but you have to be safe. The outdoor fireplace is just down those stairs, and there is a perfect vantage point of the lake. Take what you need, and we'll go in after that."

Her mouth popped open with an audible sound. "Are you serious?" she squeaked.

"I am."

She stared at him in awe. "Really?"

He laughed once. "We're not going to get wetter than we already are. Yeah, go take your pictures, and if the weather clears while we're up here, I'll take you wherever you need to go for more of them. But only if it clears. Understood?"

She nodded so fast he thought he missed it, and then she was out of the truck, racing toward the stairs he had indicated.

He sighed and shook his head, then followed. The things he would do for this woman constantly amazed him—like driving around the resort in the middle of a torrential downpour, screaming at her like a deranged father, and hauling her up here as if she was grounded for life. For someone who was known for being cool and calm and controlled, he was having quite the emotional awakening. If he didn't go completely insane because of her, it would be a miracle.

She tossed one hesitant smile back at him as he watched her, and his entire being lurched toward her helplessly. As he suspected he always would.

Chapter Twelve

"Don't get drool on my floor. The cleaning service doesn't come until next week."

Mal heard Hunter's jab, but she couldn't manage to close her mouth as she took in the grand spectacle and sheer awesomeness of his house. He held her arm steady as she struggled to take off her muddy boots, mostly because she was too busy gawking and craning her neck to see up as high as she could. He was right; the house wasn't little at all. It was huge.

He sighed, still holding onto her arm. "I'm not going to get you to change first before I show you around, am I?"

Mal grinned wildly at him. "No way, pal."

His smile turned quizzical, and her stomach fluttered. He shook his head and released her arm. "All right, come on."

He led her around the stairs, which were a gorgeous hardwood. She craned her neck up to see where they led but couldn't get a glimpse. He took her down a hallway toward the far side of the house, the floor beneath her feet perfectly smooth and polished wood that was a dark, almost cherry stain, and her damp socks slid none-too-gracefully along them. She traced the walls aimlessly with her fingers for a sort of balance, her pulse still racing with the excitement of being here—in Hunter's house. She swallowed a large, almost burning lump in her throat and turned her gaze ahead, only to gasp once more.

He'd brought her to the dining room, which was large, open, and had glass windows from floor to ceiling on two sides.

"Dining room," he said unnecessarily, gesturing with one hand. "Doors lead out to the outdoor grill and firepit you saw before."

She went to the windows, tempted to put her hands and face on them like a kid at a candy store. The view was spectacular. She had known that from the pictures he'd allowed her before they'd come in. But to live here and see it all the time? Over a bowl of Froot Loops? That was unreal.

He stepped back and pushed a door open behind him. "Kitchen; a bit much, but we like food, so we went all out."

Mal turned and poked her head in. He wasn't kidding. It was a restaurant quality, stainless steel kitchen with state-of-the-art appliances. Eight chefs could fit in there, no problem.

"Who cooks?" she asked him, tilting her head.

He raised a brow. "Me. And Mom and Dad and Uncle Sam... We all do, but when we're all here, we hire someone to come in."

"Uh-huh," she murmured in disbelief, turning to go back down the hallway. Really, she was putting on a show for him. She was ridiculously impressed with this place. It was just the right mix of rustic and modern, well-furnished and well-maintained without reeking of excess, and the place even smelled like Hunter. Warm. Rustic. Clean. And just that barest hint of all-natural earthiness that somehow soothed her and scorched her all at once.

Hunter stepped around her and opened another door they had passed before. "Office," he said simply, waving his hand dismissively.

She peeked in and smiled. One half of the room was certainly an office, the other half had a couch that probably folded out, and those killer tall windows with the perfect view. And a balcony.

She nudged her head toward it. "For when you're lost in thought?" she asked.

He shrugged with a small smile. "Fresh air is good for thought, don't you think?"

"And a couch for naps?"

"A good nap does wonders for me."

She snickered and let him pull her back out.

"One more," he told her, "then we go upstairs, and you get dry."

She rolled her eyes with a snort.

He laced his fingers through hers, and she could feel him holding his breath. Then suddenly, they were in the massive great room, which was open to the second story, and had those grand windows covering most of the two external walls. The same wood floor throughout the house was most prominently displayed here, and the third wall was entirely made of stone with an expanded natural fireplace at the base.

Several couches and chairs and rugs were spread about the room. A few end tables and desks were here and there, and massive bookshelves filled to their limits took up the only wall space not occupied with windows or stone. It was, without a doubt, the best room she had ever seen.

Hunter chuckled and tapped her chin, now gaping once more. "Grotesquely extravagant?" he suggested softly.

She shook her head slowly. "It's perfect," she breathed.

He squeezed her hand tightly. "Come on," he said after a moment. "We're dripping on the floor."

She looked down and saw, much to her dismay, that he was right. "Oh, good night," she muttered, mopping it up with her socks. "I am so sorry. This floor is real too, and I'm ruining it."

Hunter laughed once and tugged her behind him as he led her from the room. "Honey, it's my house, not a hotel. Trust me, these floors can take it. They've seen worse."

"You're just saying that," she grumbled, adjusting a strand behind her ear.

"Yep. 'Cause I'm the kind of guy who 'just says things,'" he drawled, giving her a look over his shoulder.

She returned his look and followed him up the stairs, peering over into that great room once again. She really hoped that was where Hunter had imagined her taking a nap, because that's where she was headed.

Hunter took her into the first door on the second floor and pulled her in ahead of him. "This should do it," he murmured, sounding a little bit awkward.

The room was fairly simply decorated, but in a tasteful, distinctly feminine way. There was a spectacular view of the lake, a queen bed with a pastel flower embroidered coverlet, and an oversize chair with matching ottoman. The walls were hung with pictures, and she moved over to the nearest one.

A gorgeous blonde woman dressed in the most perfect fall ensemble ever created was throwing leaves at Hunter, both of them grinning perfectly. It could have been a haute fashion photo shoot. Mal swallowed down a bit of bile. What was this?

"This is Audrey's room," Hunter said softly from behind her. "She's my little sister."

Mal turned and saw him leaning against the doorframe, watching her. She tried not to let her relief show as she swallowed.

"She's pretty," she complimented, glancing back at the photo. "Like movie-star pretty."

"I tell her that, but she seems to think I'm biased," he mused.

Mal smiled at him, seeing a whole new adorable side of him. She slowly meandered to the next picture, this one of a much younger Hunter and Audrey on a dock in early morning with an older man with fishing gear.

"Grandpa Carlow?" Mal asked, without looking back at him.

"The man himself," Hunter answered, coming up behind her. "Through and through Irishman, loved family, fishing, and Guinness, usually in that order. Sometimes those last two got reversed."

Mal laughed and touched the picture gently. "You two adored him."

"Couldn't help it. Irish charm. He had it. Dad, Uncle Pat, and Uncle Sam have it. It must dilute with Americanization or something, because Deacon and I don't have any of that."

Mal looked up at him incredulously. "You don't have any Irish charm?"

He quirked a half smile. "No… but I can do a perfect Irish accent, if that counts for anything at all," he said, displaying the accent in question.

Mal had to steady herself with one slow blink. "Don't do that," she said faintly, laughing. "Not without warning." She cleared her throat. "Who's Deacon?"

"My one male cousin," Hunter replied, sounding amused. "The rest are girls."

"How many?"

"Twelve."

"Good heavens!" she cried, looking back at him.

He shrugged. "Irish."

She moved on to another picture, this one of Audrey in sweats and a T-shirt, clinging to a walker, but with a brilliant smile on her face, tears in her eyes, and sweat on her brow. "What's this?" Mal asked quietly.

Hunter exhaled softly, but she heard a lot of emotion behind it. "Nine years ago," he started, his voice rougher than she anticipated, "Audrey went for a run while we were here. Not unusual, she's a fitness nut. It started raining while she was out, but we weren't too concerned. She was a big girl, knew the area, so Deke and I didn't think anything of it. But when three hours went by, we knew something was up. We split up and drove around the resort, tracing her usual running paths, fighting the wind and the rain. It was getting dark…"

Mal stared at him openmouthed. "What happened?" she whispered.

He swallowed hard and folded his arms uncomfortably. "I found her. I don't know what drew my attention to that patch of road, but I got out of the truck and went over to look down the ravine. There was Audrey…" He cleared his throat and shook his head. "She was unconscious, gash on her head, and her leg was twisted in a way that no leg should twist. Blood all over it. I got down to her, called 911, called Deke… I rode with her in the ambulance to the hospital. Deke called my parents, and we just waited. Her leg had been badly cut and broken in three places, lots of surgery to fix it, and the doctor said it might not work. They asked us about cutting it off, if it came to that. But it didn't. She made it." He shook his head again and pointed at the picture. "This is the day in rehab that she finally managed to stand up on her own. She called it her personal V-Day."

Mal looked back at it, unable to help smiling at it. "Best day ever."

"Actually," he said with a catch in his voice, "that one is." He pointed at a picture on the adjacent wall.

Mal wandered over and grinned broadly. It was of Audrey crossing a marathon finish line, arms raised in victory over her head, laughing at the camera.

"I don't think I've ever been prouder of her than I was that day."

Mal could hear that big-brother pride in his voice, and her smile softened. She turned to look at Hunter for a moment, then walked over and wrapped her arms around his waist.

He smiled in surprise, but returned the gesture, cocking his head at her. "What's this for?" he asked.

She shrugged. "You're cute."

His smile turned warmer, and her toes curled in her socks. "I thought I was overprotective and a worrier and way too nosy."

She tugged him closer, feeling her cheeks heat. "You are. But you're also cute, and I like you."

His eyes darkened, his smile faded, and something about his soaking wet hair and skin and clothes made him smell even better than normal, the scent filling her lungs and seeping through her skin. He put one hand under her chin and slowly tipped her face up. "I like you, too," he murmured, his voice almost a growl.

Mal inhaled slowly, her lips parting all on their own, and Hunter took advantage of it, grazing his lips along hers. Once, twice, three times, he passed over, barely touching, but enough to drive her crazy. She moved her head to brush their noses, letting her lips fall against his, catching his bottom lip between hers for a moment.

Hunter's hand shifted, and he cupped her jaw, sealing his lips more firmly over hers, somehow wringing a more exquisite response from her than their little closet venture had, though the two could not have been more different. That had been frantic and passionate and heady.

This was slow and gentle and filled with tension, emotion, restraint…

This… this was a maddening, grazing, hardly-able-to-breathe, toe-tingling, stomach-curling onslaught that was heating her from the inside out and draining her of thought and sense and everything in the world but him.

This, she could get used to.

Assuming she lived through it.

After another gentle, teasing brush of his lips, Hunter broke off with a hint of a despairing groan. "Okay," he rumbled, sounding punch-drunk as he stepped away from her. "I gotta get out of here. Shower and get changed; Audrey has clothes that should fit you."

"Okay," Mal replied, sighing more than speaking, dazedly looking him over and wondering how in the world she had this man at her fingertips.

Hunter stepped back farther, reading her thoughts with far too much insight. "Stop looking at me like that," he warned, his voice strained. "I gotta get out of here."

Mal smiled knowingly. "You said that already."

"It bears repeating. Just… stop." He held out a hand as if he could actually stop her, then he turned and headed out the door, glancing over his shoulder at her again. She caught the flash of heat and hunger there, and she shivered. Yeah, it was probably best that he left.

Things were getting a bit toasty.

She finally looked down at herself and threw her hands in the air. She was a drowned rat. He should have forced her up here instead of indulging her desire to see the house. She hurried over to the bathroom, quickly stripped down, and jumped into the pristine marble shower, trying to ignore the perfect water pressure and thoughts of how much it cost to have such a room.

She'd always been fast in the shower, and this time was no exception. While the water was soothing and just the right temperature, she'd never seen the point in taking forever and found little relaxation in hygiene. Her grandfather used to joke that she never actually washed anything, just got wet and got back out. Somehow, he always managed to sound impressed when he said that.

Wrapping herself in a perfectly thick towel, Mal got out of the shower and padded over to the moderately sized closet, instantly liking Audrey for her taste in clothing alone. It was simple, fashionable, and good quality, without any of the ostentation Mal would have expected from a girl of her fortune. She probably looked like a model in these things. But then, she was related to Hunter. He knew how to dress and never looked anything less than perfect.

Audrey in real life would probably terrify her, and then quickly become a girl she could laugh over coffee with.

Mal grabbed the most inexpensive clothing she could find, settling on a pair of dark-wash jeans, a long T-shirt, and an oversized sweater. She glanced in a basket just inside the closet door and grinned at the collection of fuzzy socks.

Yep, Audrey was on her good list.

She heard some noises coming from the floor below and tiptoed out of the room to the landing, rubbing her hair in the towel. Hunter was still in his wet clothes, but he'd taken his jacket off. The fire was now built up and roaring in the fireplace, and he was rearranging furniture of all things. The massive and comfortable-looking couch was now pulled in front of the fire, and he was moving the chairs that had been there somewhere else.

Mal bit her lip and smiled as she watched him, taking pointed pleasure in watching that man work in clothing that clung to him. She wasn't usually so fascinated by a guy's physique, but none of her past relationships had involved someone so spectacularly formed. There was something graceful in the way he moved, his muscles coiling and uncoiling with just the right amount of artistry and magnetism. He was a masterpiece in and of himself, just as he was, and she suddenly wanted to send his mother a fruit basket or flowers or a convertible.

He stood, put his hands on his hips, and nodded once, then started for the stairs, never once looking up. Mal scurried back into Audrey's room, hung the towel up, and waited until she heard him walk by. Then she poked her head out and watched him walk into the room at the end, pulling his T-shirt over his head with both arms.

She nearly swallowed her tongue as she caught sight of his back, even more perfectly sculpted than she'd thought it would be. She would have to remember that she was a back kind of girl. She hadn't known that before this.

Hunter tossed his shirt somewhere and ran his hands through his hair, half turning and giving her a spectacular view of his front side.

Chest and abs would also have to go on the list.

He scratched at his scruff and twisted, unknowingly baring more to her view. Mal choked back a whimper of appreciation. Maybe just his chest and abs.

Real men didn't look like that. And yet, there he stood. A real man, who really liked her and who really drove her insane and really knew how to kiss her.

He finally moved out of sight, and Mal found herself staggering backward against the doorframe. She blinked hard and realized she was literally biting her knuckle. Shouldn't she have noticed that before? She straightened up and fumbled her way back into the room, reaching for walls and the bed and anything else that would keep her from falling over.

Another shower suddenly seemed like a really good idea. A very, very cold shower.

Several face washes and fanning episodes later, Mal made her way down the stairs. She wandered around the main floor and heard some noise from the kitchen, which made her smile. She wasn't the only one quick in the shower, then.

She poked her head into the kitchen and saw Hunter pulling things out of the fridge and a pot from under the counter. A set of speakers in the corner was playing slow jazz, and Hunter moved to the beat. He was freshly changed into a perfectly fitted dark gray T-shirt and jeans, and oddly enough, he was barefoot.

Mal grinned and came into the room fully. "What's on the menu, chef?"

He looked up, gave her a slow appraisal, and his mouth curved. "Hello, gorgeous."

She blushed and tucked an invisible strand of hair behind her ear. "Hey, hot stuff."

He choked a laugh and winked at her as he moved to the sink to fill the pot with water. "Don't tease me, baby. And don't get excited either; it's nothing fancy. Mac and cheese. From a box."

Mal smiled and came over to his side of the counter. "Sounds great."

He smiled down at her. "Audrey's clothes look good on you."

"She has great taste," Mal informed him, pushing the sleeves back. "I like her already."

Hunter's smile grew, and his eyes crinkled. "I thought you might."

Mal considered him for a moment. "That story you told me. About her leg? That was why you got so crazy about me in the rain, wasn't it?"

He set the pot down and turned on the burner, taking his time to answer. He turned, facing her. "Yeah, it was. I'm sorry, sweetheart. I just get fired up about that."

"I get it," Mal said as she came over to him. "You have good reason to be worried about that. I'm sorry I made it so hard for you. I should have listened."

He straightened up and kissed her forehead softly. "I get angry when I get scared. Forgive me."

Mal laughed softly through her nose. "I guess I have to, since you're showing me the house and feeding me and all that."

He laughed and stepped aside, going for the things he pulled out of the fridge. "Yeah, the house you wanted so badly."

Mal shrugged, folding her arms. "It has its perks," she drawled.

Hunter gave her a look that made her grin. "Topic change," he instructed.

She hummed and leaned against the counter. "If you had to sing at karaoke night, what would you sing?"

"Easy," he said simply. "I wouldn't."

Mal rolled her eyes. "Yeah, I know, but if you had to."

He looked at her again. "I wouldn't."

She tossed her hands up. "Really? It's a hypothetical!"

He raised a brow as if she were missing the point and not him. "Yeah. And hypothetically, I wouldn't."

Mal pinched the bridge of her nose and shook her head. "You are impossible."

"But you like me," he said pointedly, using a spoon for emphasis.

"Debatable," she replied with a shrug.

His frown made her grin again.

"Fine, rephrasing the question. Favorite kind of music? And don't tell me you don't like music, I saw you dancing around in here."

Again came the quirked brow. "I know how to dance, Miss Hudson, and what you may have witnessed in here does not constitute dancing."

She held up her hands in surrender. "Sorry, excuse me."

He snorted. "Honestly? I probably like this stuff best." He gestured at the speakers. "I'm an old soul, I guess. Jazz has always been a favorite. In fact, there's a jazz night for the resort guests and locals tomorrow night down at the pavilion. I was thinking about going." He gave her a questioning look. "You like jazz?"

Mal chewed on her lip for a moment, watching him with a smile on her lips and somewhere in the middle of her chest. "Yeah," she said softly. "I like jazz. I'll go with you."

He fought a grin and pretended to be casual. "I don't remember asking."

"Tough," she said simply.

He stared at her for a moment, then shook his head. "You are something else, you know that?"

She smiled. "So are you."

The moment, whatever it was, hung between them for a time, suspended in the air and coursing through them and swirling around them. Something unspeakable and fantastic and perfect and completely overwhelming. How was it possible that this crazy good-looking, intense, funny, charming man was available for her picking?

Or for anyone's at all?

She was suddenly breathless with the giddiness of how lucky she was.

A hissing sound behind her made Mal turn in surprise. Hunter was at the stove in three strides, picking up the pot and letting the boiling water and noodles settle before returning it to the burner.

He gave her a scolding look. "You are ruining lunch. Stop distracting me and go over there."

Mal laughed and scooted away from him. "I'll just go into the great room and sit by the fire. Okay if we eat out there?"

"Baby, I'd let you eat anything anywhere in this house, so long as I was with you," he told her without any hint of irony or fawning.

Mal's eyes widened, and she cleared her throat. "Right. I thought we talked about toning that down."

"How many Mississippis will that take to settle?" he asked with a crooked grin.

Again, she cleared her throat. "About seven."

He nodded. "Awesome. Getting better."

She rolled her eyes and pushed the kitchen door open. "Only you would see that as a challenge."

"Blankets are in the ottoman," he called. "And save me a seat. Next to you."

She turned back and poked her head in. "I thought I was supposed to be warming up and taking a nap."

His slow, smoldering grin made her legs ache. "You are. I'm

helping."

"Shasta!" Mal exclaimed as she straightened and put a hand over her eyes.

Hunter chuckled. "Come on, Mal, I'm playing. I'll tuck you in and hold you tight, and you can ask me anything you want. I'll tell you my whole life story, if you want—beginning to end. Funny stories, twenty questions, truth or dare, whatever strikes your fancy."

She gave him a curious look. "Really? Mr. Filthy Stinking Rich with his very private life is going to let me in?"

His lips quirked at that, and his smile softened. "Just for you, baby. Whatever you want."

Mal returned his smile and headed toward the great room, feeling unsteady again. Because she was fairly certain that what she really wanted wasn't his life story or his hopes and dreams for the future. She would even pass on this house, as perfect and jealousy-inciting as it was.

What she really wanted was him.

And that was a particularly terrifying thought.

Chapter Thirteen

"I can't believe you made Aunt Cady snort at dinner. You're supposed to be Mr. Doesn't Like Anyone, and suddenly, you're the life of the party?"

Hunter gave her a look as he stirred their mugs of hot chocolate in her kitchen. "Are you upset or surprised, Mal?"

She drummed her fingers on the counter. "Surprised, I guess…" she mused slowly. "You've made a point to not be particularly social so far."

He made a small sound of amusement and picked up the mugs, nodding his head for her to exit the kitchen before him. "True, but that's just because most of the people here annoy me. Your family is great, Tom's family I know already, and if you haven't noticed, I make Mrs. Yardley laugh all the time."

Mal frowned as she flopped down on the couch and reached for her cocoa. "I hadn't noticed. She laughs?"

Hunter frowned and sat down next to her, flinging his arm on the back of the couch around her. "Yeah, she does. She's a great lady, Mal. You'd like her."

Mal made a face. "If you say so. I like Tom well enough. His sisters are distant, but okay. His brothers…" She made an indecisive hand gesture.

Hunter chuckled and sipped his drink. "I would love to take you to one of my family reunions. You could analyze the lot of us and have a field day."

"Stop that," she muttered, leaning into him. "I'm just not a people person. Particularly rich people."

"Snob."

Mal shifted uneasily against him and could feel his quiet laughter.

"Sorry, sweetheart, you're just going to have to get used to it," he said with a sigh, pulling her closer. "With your talent, you're going to be spending a lot of time around people, maybe even rich people. Be as antisocial as you want in your private life, but you'll have to at least pretend to be a people person sometimes."

"Selectively social," she corrected with a sip of her cocoa.

Hunter snorted and took a drink from his own. "Right. Sorry, I forgot."

Mal looked up at him for a moment. "There is one question I forgot to ask you earlier."

He looked back at her in surprise. "Really? I remember feeling rather interrogated before you finally nodded off."

She elbowed him hard, and he grunted a laugh. "Seriously, though," she said, sitting up. "Where do you actually live? I know you probably have condos or houses in a lot of different places, but where is home?"

He made a face in thought. "Right now, Atlanta."

"Really?" she said, unable to hold back her own surprise.

"And what is wrong with Atlanta?" he asked defensively with a raised brow.

"Nothing," she assured him quickly, pushing a strand of hair out of her face. "I just figured you'd be somewhere a little more... I don't know, famous?"

Hunter laughed, leaning his head back against the couch. "I'm not famous, babe. Atlanta is a great city, and we've done very well there. Headquarters can stay there as far as I am concerned, but they really don't need me. I'm considering moving over to a smaller branch to try to build up more."

"Where would you go?" she asked, truly curious.

He shrugged. "Chicago, Dallas, Columbia... My mom wants me to come to Baltimore sometime in the near future, so that's always an option. Audrey suggests Seattle all the time, since that's where she is. Or I could visit the overseas branches. London is always a good idea, right?"

Mal stared at him in wonder. "Uh-huh," she murmured, settling back. The man could quite literally go anywhere and be successful.

Nothing was out of the question, and with his drive and skill set, he would revolutionize any place he went. He held all the power in the world in his hands, and he knew how to use it.

"Did I lose you there?" he asked, nudging her.

She shook her head and leaned against him. "You take a pretty active role in work, don't you?"

He nodded, resting his chin on her head. "I try to. I can't get away from the boardroom entirely, but I think hands-on is a good way to go—assuming I don't get in the way. I don't want anyone feeling like I'm looking over their shoulder, but if there are improvements that need to be made, I'll step in. I think I'd get bored if I just sat in my crummy office all day, ruling the empire by mobile device."

Mal snorted and patted his knee. "Yeah, I'm sure you have a really crummy office there, dude."

He laughed and kissed the top of her head. "It has a shocking lack of artwork. Know anyone that could help me out there?"

She slowly sipped the last of her cocoa. "I think Dan might have some pieces that could work for you."

Hunter growled and moved his mouth to the side of her neck just below her ear. "I don't want Dan's help…"

She arched her neck with a shiver. "No? Well, Taryn is pretty good, too. I can put in a good word for you."

He snatched her mug away and set it on the table behind the couch with his and turned, forcing her to lean back against the armrest while he loomed over her, his arms bracketing either side of her.

"Not Taryn," he murmured with a slow shake of his head, leaning down to kiss her chin, then down the column of her throat.

"No?" she gasped, trying to find some sense of wit and thought before he disintegrated the last of it.

"No," he said simply, coming back to place a slow, leisurely kiss on her lips.

She wrapped her arms around his neck with a sigh when a knock on the door interrupted what was destined to be a fantastic make-out session.

"Seriously?" Mal said to the ceiling, frowning in her

disgruntlement.

Hunter laughed and pulled her up to a sitting position. "You expecting anyone?"

She gave him a look as she rose to her feet. The knocking came again, more insistent, and Mal folded her cardigan around her. Whatever this was, it had better be good or she would be seriously ticked off. She opened the door to find Caroline standing there in sweats, an oversize T-shirt, and her hair loosely braided over her shoulder, large Coach tote on her arm.

"Caroline?" Mal asked in surprise.

Her cousin wrinkled her nose. "Can I claim sanctuary here tonight? I'm about to kill people."

Mal laughed and stepped back, scratching at her hair. So much for her evening plans… "Sure," she said with a shrug.

Caroline grinned and stepped in, dropping her bag. "Thanks," she said heavily. "Seriously, when it's my turn, remind me how nuts this is, okay? I'm just gonna elope."

Mal nodded knowingly. "Noted."

Caroline turned to look around the place and saw Hunter sitting on the couch. "Hunter?"

He smiled and waved. "Hey."

Caroline whirled to face Mal, eyes wide. "Am I interrupting something?" she whispered loudly.

Mal glanced nervously at Hunter, who only lifted a brow and smiled. "Uh, not really?" she answered in a completely awkward way.

Her cousin's eyes narrowed. "Uh-huh. You've got maybe three minutes before Jenna gets here, so…"

"That would be my cue to leave," Hunter announced as he got up from the couch.

Mal turned to him with a wince. "I'm sorry," she said, coming over to him.

"What for? Girls' night with your cousins seems like a good idea to me."

She made a face. "Yeah, but…" She looked up at him and sighed impatiently.

His smile told her he understood what she wasn't saying. "Yeah," he said quietly, stroking her cheek, "but there's always tomorrow. I'll pick you up at the usual time."

Mal pouted. "Okay."

He pressed a soft kiss to her forehead. "Call me later?" he whispered.

She nodded, unable to keep from playing with his shirt, taking note of the taut skin and muscle she could feel beneath.

He gave her a wink and headed for the door, grabbing his leather jacket from the bench. "Caroline," he said politely as he passed her, "have a good night."

"You too, Hunter," she replied, never once looking away from Mal, arms folded over her chest. The minute the door closed, Caroline came over to her. "You have thirty seconds to tell me what that was," she said quickly, eyes dancing.

Mal's throat and mouth worked opposite of each other as she scrambled. "Um, would you believe me if I said nothing?"

Caroline snorted once. "Nope. I saw the two of you just now, sister, and that ain't nothing."

Mal rubbed her hands over her face. "I have no idea what it is," she admitted. "It just sort of happened, and it hasn't stopped, and… I like it?"

Caroline grinned slowly. "Oh, girl," she said, heavily accenting her Southern drawl. "That boy has worked you over like nobody's business."

Mal made another face. "Am I pathetic?"

"Heck no," Caroline laughed, shaking Mal's arm. "If I didn't have Ryan, I'd be all over that myself. You guys got plans?"

Mal smiled, unable to resist the contagious excitement Caroline was giving off. "We do sunrise photo shoots every morning, and tomorrow, he's taking me to jazz night down at the pavilion."

Caroline suddenly seized both arms. "Mal. You have got to let me do your hair and makeup for that. And I have a dress for you."

"No," Mal said at once, shaking her head. "I'm going as me, and nothing you have will fit me."

Caroline glowered at her so darkly that Mal was actually a little nervous. "Who said I was going to make you anyone else? You have to sleep at the Hen House anyway tomorrow night, and I do so happen to have a dress that will fit you. I pulled some aside for you on Designer Day, since you wouldn't touch a thing. I promise, it is totally you, and it will drive Hunter absolutely crazy—in a good way."

Now that sounded like an idea Mal could get behind. She chewed her lip in indecision.

"Come on," Caroline begged. "Don't you trust me?"

Mal met her eyes for a long moment, then sighed. "Yeah, I trust you. Okay, you're hired."

Caroline squealed and hugged her quickly. "This week just got that much better!"

Mal hesitated a long moment, then winced. "Caroline, do you know anything about… Hunter's past?"

Caroline pulled back with a sharp look. "His past? What, like, his record?"

Mal shook her head quickly. "No, no, I mean…"

"Ohh," her cousin said knowingly, nodding now. "Girls. Gotcha. Not much at all, only that it's been a bit for him. Someone said he got his heart broken, but I don't know how much I believe that. He doesn't seem broken to me. But then, I'm not that close with him, so who the heck knows?" She frowned at Mal. "Why?"

"I just… I don't know." Mal wrinkled up her nose and knitted her fingers. "I don't know why he's… with me. I don't match, you know? I'm not his type."

Caroline gave her a look. "I saw him looking at you, sweetie. He thinks you're his type, and I'm pretty sure he would know."

A knock at the door effectively ended the conversation.

"That will be Jenna," Caroline said with a sad smile. "The girls were on a roll today, and she's had enough. I'm gonna go make popcorn."

Mal went to the door and opened it, stepping back automatically to wave Jenna in. She was wearing absolutely no makeup, looked downcast, but still was gorgeous.

"Really?" she asked in a small voice.

"Please," Mal said with a laugh, waving her in again. "I think we could use a Disney night. What do you think?"

Jenna smiled and instantly pulled Mal in for a tight hug. "Oh, thank you for being you."

"You're welcome?" Mal replied, returning the hug as best as she could for not being a hugging person.

Jenna stepped back and pulled her hair back into a low ponytail. "I just can't take those girls tonight. I hated that I had to have so many bridesmaids, and I know they're mostly tacky girls with no taste and less morals, but friends are hard to come by in my world, you know?"

Mal had no idea, but she nodded sympathetically all the same.

"And they're not all bad," Jenna said as she sat down on the couch. "Not all the time, anyway. Maybe this is just too long. But it's my week and my wedding, so they can just shove it."

"Hear, hear!" Caroline bellowed from the kitchen.

Mal laughed and shook her head. "Caroline, I think there's Fresca in the fridge. We'll need that too!"

"Heck yeah, we will!"

Jenna grinned up at Mal. "You are the best, you know that?"

Mal had to smile in return. It was impossible not to. "So are you, sweetie. So, what are we watching tonight?"

"You have to ask?" Caroline called out.

"*Little Mermaid*," they all said in unison, the sisters with glee, Mal with a smile.

Of course.

"No singing this time," Jenna scolded loudly, turning her head to yell at her sister.

"You are the one who has to sing the daughters of Triton song," Caroline shot back as she appeared. "Just because you can remember all the names."

Mal laughed and took a bowl of popcorn from her. "You can't?"

Caroline sniffed and sat down as Mal rummaged for the DVD amid the house's massive collection. "Of course I can, now. Aquata, Andrina, Arista…"

Mal rubbed her eyes and glanced over at the couch, the light from the TV casting warped, blue shadows over everything. Jenna was sprawled across the couch, while Caroline was on the floor below her. Both had several pillows and blankets around and under them, and both were fast asleep.

Mal had dozed off in the middle of their second movie, and it appeared they had, as well. She reached for the remotes and turned everything off, grabbed her phone, and stumbled into the bedroom, crawling into her bed. She looked down at the phone screen, checking the time, and then decided that she could call Hunter, like he asked. If he didn't pick up, that was his own fault.

Besides, she wanted to hear his voice again.

He picked up after two rings. "Hi," he murmured sleepily, his voice rough but she could hear the smile.

She smiled back. "Hi."

There was silence for a few seconds, and then she heard rustling from Hunter's side. "So…" he drawled suggestively, "what are you wearing?"

Mal burst out laughing and pulled her covers up under her chin. "Flannel pants and a high school T-shirt," she answered, trying to match his tone.

His low laugh rumbled in her ears. "That is so sexy."

She snickered and then sighed. "I'm sorry. I really wanted to spend tonight with you."

"Oh, yeah?" Hunter replied, his tone pointed and amused.

"Not like that!" she protested, drawing another low laugh from him. "You know what I mean."

He exhaled audibly. "I do. And I'm sorry, too. But I am glad you spent time with your cousins."

"Me too, actually. They aren't like the other girls."

He made an amused sound. "No, they aren't. Did you think they were?"

Mal sighed and made a face. "I don't know. No, I guess not."

"Did you have fun?" he asked quietly.

"Yeah."

"You sound surprised."

She smiled as she thought about it. "I am. It's been years. Literally, at least ten. But tonight, we watched our same favorite Disney movies, *Little Mermaid* and *Sleeping Beauty*, and we laughed at all the same parts we used to, and… I don't know, I just… I forgot how much I like them."

That seemed to satisfy him. Then he asked, "So why'd you come if you didn't know you liked them?"

"Money," she said bluntly, feeling a hint of shame. "Opportunity. And I remembered being kids together, and we had a ball back then. I couldn't say no to that. To her."

"I'm really glad for that, Mal," he told her softly, and again, she could hear him smiling. "I can't tell you how much. Whatever it was that convinced you to come, I'm… I'm glad."

Mal bit her lip on a silent squeal and closed her eyes. "Me too," she finally answered, trying to keep her voice as calm and casual as possible.

Neither of them said anything for a few moments.

"I miss you," Hunter groaned petulantly at last.

Mal snickered softly. "You saw me three hours ago," she reminded him.

"Too long," he grunted. "I miss you."

Mal didn't know what to say. Did she tell him the truth? Did she play it off and back away from the tension she was feeling?

"Mal?"

She swallowed hard. "I miss you, too," she finally whispered, something in her chest bursting and stealing her breath.

Somehow, Hunter knew. She could hear it in the way he exhaled, could imagine him smiling in the dark, just as she was.

"Good night, baby," he said, his voice a soft, velvety caress. "Sleep tight."

She looked up at the ceiling, shaking her head. "Good night."

She hung up, set the phone on her nightstand, and curled into a ball on her side. A small squeal escaped her, and she grinned into her fisted hand, burying her face.

Where in the world was Mallory Hudson, and what had happened to her?

Chapter Fourteen

A wedding rehearsal always seemed like a weird idea in Hunter's mind. How many times could you mess up walking down an aisle?

Apparently, several.

He was on his fourth time going down with Caroline, who had long since stopped grinning and now muttered things that kept him relaxed.

"You guys are naturals!" Jenna called from behind.

"I've never felt less natural in my entire life," Caroline muttered, blowing hair out of her face.

Hunter snorted. "At least they let you take your shoes off."

She tilted her head in consideration. "True. But we're still walking like it's a funeral. Can't we just quickstep it?"

"I dare you to try."

She glared up at him. "Don't do that. Then we'd have to do this again when we're obviously the best ones in this whole party, and then I won't get to help a certain someone get ready for a certain something."

Hunter looked down at her in surprise, caught the warning brow raise, and swallowed. "Right. Fourth time's the charm, right?"

"Exactly."

"Do you want them to go slower?" Grace called from her place at the front.

"No!" Hunter and Caroline, and a few others, said at once.

They were out on the lakeside gazebo, where rows of white chairs adorned with fabric and ribbon had been set up, a long roll of white linen spread along the stone aisle, and the gazebo itself decorated with matching ribbons, fabric, and flowers. It would all be adjusted in the morning for the wedding, but for this afternoon, it was good enough. His crew had outdone themselves, and Jenna was beyond pleased with the results, which meant Tom was pleased, which made everyone else happy, too.

Caroline and Hunter parted at the right spot and went to their respective places at the front and turned to watch Jenna and her dad one more time.

The flower girls had already lost their patience and had been given permission to go off and play, so their part was skipped, which Hunter was grateful for. They'd squabbled two of the three times they'd come down, and it drew things out more painfully for all of them.

Drake looked about as happy to do this again as the rest of them and was saying things under his breath that made Jenna giggle.

Hunter heard Tom catch his breath after one laugh and was about to tease him when he heard another laugh nearby. Mal had been standing near her uncle and cousin, heard the last comment, and was now laughing behind her camera. The camera came down, and she looked at the display screen, laughter still on her face.

His breath caught, and he had nothing to tease Tom about.

Mal looked up at him, raised a brow, and turned back to plan angles with Taryn and Dan, who would be doing the pictures during the ceremony. Mal had been informed she was sitting with the family during that time, which made her smile, but also left her flustered. As much as she liked her assistants, she was a control freak with her projects, which was pretty endearing, Hunter thought.

She'd been her usual sweet and mischievous self at the sunrise shoot this morning and more cuddly than normal, which didn't bother him one bit. They talked about their childhoods, which was a revelation. Mal was very open with him about the death of her parents and moving to Iowa, living and working on her grandfather's farm, living in a small town. She'd overcome a lot of obstacles and skeptics to become what she was today: a world-class photographer with high prospects. No farm girl from Iowa, in their minds, could do that.

But one did.

Hunter didn't have as many stories to share with her, having grown up all along the east coast without any difficulty or objections to his future, but he and his cousins had managed to get into their fair share of scrapes over the years. He and Deke alone had caused a dozen hospital trips for themselves and the girls, but his older cousins were just as vicious, only sneakier about it. The McIntyre family was not exactly shy and retreating, particularly not from each other.

Mal had been surprised, though, at some of their adventures. She claimed Hunter was so reserved and careful. How could he have been reckless or come from a family like that?

How, indeed.

He'd thought about that, wondering how he had become the man he was now. Was it something he had to prove to himself? That he was to be taken seriously and not just because of his family name and fortune? It had worked, whatever it was. He was still the same person with his family, but he rarely opened up for anyone else.

Until Mal.

"Aunt Cady, you can't cry now!" he heard Mal say with a laugh, slipping an arm around her aunt in the front row. "It's the rehearsal!"

Her aunt dabbed a tissue at her heavily lined eyes and sniffed. "I'll cry if I want to cry, Mallory Jo. I'll be crying all day tomorrow; just think of this as a practice test."

Mal grinned and shook her head, and so did Lucas, standing at the end of the line. "Mama, you're a goddess, and you know it," he called.

Cady smiled broadly at him. "Baby boy, you got something brown on your nose."

Caroline and Jenna chortled loudly, and the minister shook his head with a grin.

"Right, back to work," he said over the general conversation. "Mr. Hudson, you give your daughter away…"

"She's away," he said, releasing her and holding his hands up in surrender.

Jenna rolled her eyes. "Nice, Daddy."

"…and go join your wife," the minister continued as if nothing had happened.

Drake did so, giving a quick peck on the head to Mal as she slid past to take more pictures.

Hunter did not come from a particularly demonstrative family, and he knew Mal was not a hugger generally, but the warm affection from her aunt, uncle, and cousins fascinated him. They were loud, but loving, and though they had not seen Mal in ten years, they treated her as if she'd never left, and from her accounts, never made her feel guilty about it. And now, seeing Mal interact with them, he wondered if this wasn't some part of her nature too, just something she'd forgotten. Mal grinned at her uncle and then went back to business behind her camera.

"Jenna and Tom, you say your vows," the minister said, peering over his spectacles as he held the order of events.

"Blah, blah, blah, I love you, etc.," Tom said, making Jenna grin.

"Exactly," praised the minister. "I say my spiel, and yadda yadda yadda, you are man and wife, kiss the bride."

Tom made a show of dipping Jenna and kissing her, which earned some whoops and hollers from the rest.

The minister chuckled and waited for them to be set to rights. "And I present you as the mister and missus. Wait for applause, and down the aisle with you."

Tom and Jenna marched their way down. Hunter offered his arm to Caroline, and they followed. Mal snapped a picture of them, and Hunter cast a wink at her that earned him a scolding look. The rest of the group followed perfectly, and they all held their breath and waited to be dismissed.

"All right, y'all," Jenna finally said over them all with the help of a whistle from Tom. "Thanks for your patience. Dinner's on your own or at the lodge. Boys, you got Stag Night later, I guess a text will be going out with details. Anyone brings a stripper near my man, I will beat you with a tire iron."

That was met with some chuckles, and Hunter noticed some of the girls looked ashamed.

"Tomorrow morning, we've got breakfast at nine with the rest of the family members that are coming in for the wedding," Jenna continued, holding Tom closer. "We turn in phones after that. You can pick them up when you leave the reception for the night."

Some of the group grumbled, but Hunter actually didn't mind that. Tom and Jenna had thought of everything for the security of their wedding, and it should work. Wedding guests would turn in their phones when they arrived at the resort before they were shown to the venue, and it should not prove to be an obstacle, as everyone that had been invited knew about their wish for privacy. His only concern would be keeping track of Mal throughout the day with all the running around they would both be doing, but so long as he stayed close, it shouldn't be a problem.

But when the wedding was over, when Jenna and Tom left for their mystery honeymoon, when everyone started going back to their lives…

What was the plan then?

"Okay, dismissed!" Tom called out, cupping his hands over his mouth.

People began dispersing, and Hunter looked for Mal but couldn't find her. Caroline saw him and took pity on him.

"She's headed over to her cottage," she told him. "I'm bringing things over to help her get ready, and then I'll take her stuff back to the Hen House for tonight. You pick her up at six thirty, all right?"

Hunter gave her an assessing look, then sighed. "Take care of her, okay?"

Caroline reared back. "Tonight? Oh, buddy, you better take care of yourself. She is going to knock you off your feet."

He smiled, then said, "No, I mean after. Tonight, at the house."

Caroline's expression softened, and she patted Hunter's arm. "I gotcha. Rest easy, Hunter. I'll take care of our girl."

He swallowed a lump that had formed and nodded, turning to go back to his truck.

Tonight was going to be special for them; he could feel it. It might be the last night they had together before the real world took them back. He wasn't letting her go, he knew that much, but where did she stand?

Where did they stand?

"Mallory Hudson, if that man does not want to eat you with hot fudge and a spoon, I am checking him for a pulse."

Mal snorted and teetered on the heels that had been forced upon her. They weren't especially tall or crazy; in fact, they were quite perfectly Mal's style, if a bit more strappy. Mal was just ungainly and uncoordinated and the tiniest bit nervous.

"Seriously, girl, come look at yourself," Caroline insisted, waving her toward the mirror on the back of the closet door. Mal shook her head and fumbled with the jewelry Caroline had brought, looking for something that might match.

Caroline heaved a sigh, then grabbed Mal's arm and yanked her toward the mirror. "I said come look, and I meant come look!" she ordered.

Mal glanced up, and her eyes went wide at the sight of herself.

While she had been self-conscious when the little black dress had come out, now that it was on, it looked fantastic. It fit her absolutely perfectly without being tight and flattered what little figure she had. The material was light and flowed while still clinging to her, and the halter-top left her feeling secure even with the plunging V-neck. She'd never been grateful for not being particularly well-endowed before, but it was ideal for this look, and her waist looked even smaller than normal, thanks to the ruches and silver ribbons there.

Her legs looked long and fit, which was a bizarre experience for her, and thankfully, Caroline had given her a dress with a skirt that hit just above her knees. Anything shorter, and Mal would have vetoed it. It swished and twirled in a subtle, yet fun way, and for a night of dancing with Hunter, she was all for that.

"Oh my…" Mal managed, unable to find just the right words to describe this.

Caroline squealed. "I knew the dress was perfect. You look like a jazz goddess. What do you think about the hair and makeup?"

Mal hadn't even noticed. But when she looked, it was impossible to not notice. Her hair was perfectly curled à la style of the forties, gathered and pulled and pinned to the side—the most perfect loose ponytail ever. Caroline had done a beautiful job on her makeup, giving her a smoky eye that made the green of her irises really pop, foundation and blush for a cleaner complexion, and sealed it all with a dusty rose lip color.

As arrogant as it sounded in her head, Mal would have to agree with Caroline on this one: she looked like a million bucks. There were no words for this. She met Caroline's eyes in the mirror and just gaped, which made her cousin grin and nod.

"And I know just what to do for your jewelry," Caroline announced, going over to the box and bringing some things over. She handed Mal some small, silver earrings that were a simple line of five black and silver rhinestones and dangled just below her earlobe. Subtle, but with a statement.

"Nice," Mal said, smiling for the first time.

Caroline chuckled low in her throat. "No, this is nice."

She draped a necklace around Mal's throat and fastened it in the back. Mal swallowed in surprise. The necklace matched the earrings except for one detail: the chain on which the matching pendant hung formed a Y so long the pendant sat quite squarely in the center of her deep neckline, just above the skin of her exposed chest. Mal squeaked out some noise of protest, but it only made Caroline grin more.

"Just enough to draw the eye," Caroline said quietly. "And with enough flair to kick a man in the stomach."

She patted Mal's hip affectionately. "My work here is done! I've got your overnight bag, and I claim privilege of being your stylist tomorrow, too." She hefted the bag over her shoulder and gave Mal a serious look in the mirror.

Mal laughed and ran her hands over her front. "With skills like this? You're hired."

Caroline winked at her. "Go get 'em, tiger." She clicked her tongue and left.

Five minutes later, there was a knock on the front door. Mal's heart leaped into her throat, and her palms started to sweat. Somehow, she made her way to the door without tripping and hesitated just long enough to inhale and exhale, then opened the door.

Hunter looked as perfect as ever. His scruff, which would come off for the wedding, was impeccably tempting, his hair was less perfect than normal, which was somehow more perfect, and he was dressed to kill. A simple pair of black trousers and a white button-up shirt, no tie, sleeves rolled back, and open at the throat.

He was every woman's fantasy. And he was staring at her with wide eyes and parted lips.

"I feel shockingly underdressed," he finally said as he studied her up and down, his voice rough.

Mal blushed and looked down at herself. "I should change," she murmured awkwardly.

"No, you should not," he insisted, forcing her to look up at him. He smiled softly. "You look beautiful. You always look beautiful."

Her cheeks flamed again. "Hunter…"

He exhaled a laugh, shaking his head. "Mallory, I'm having trouble catching my breath here, so give me a second."

Mal felt a smile tick at the corner of her lips. "One Mississippi…" she drawled slowly.

Hunter met her eyes with a grin and shook his head again. "There's my girl." He reached for her hand and gave her another thorough look over. With a heavy exhale, he said, "I'm way out of my league tonight, but I enjoy swinging for the fence."

"Out of your league." Mal snorted, her fingers curling instinctively over his. "Please. Caroline insisted I wear this tonight, and I feel ridiculous."

"Caroline is my new favorite person after you," Hunter said plainly. "She knows what she's doing."

"What's she doing?" Mal asked, feeling impish and curious.

He raised a brow. "You tell me."

Mal fought the urge to bite her lip as the tables were suddenly turned on her. Yet again, she felt her face and neck heat. "She… she wanted me to drive you crazy. In a good way."

Something in Hunter's eyes caught fire, and his smile turned smoldering. "Mission accomplished. In the best way."

She grinned and tilted her head. "Thanks. Shall we go?"

"I think I'm the one who needs to say thanks," Hunter muttered as she took her handbag and exited the house. "But yeah, let's go."

They drove down to the pavilion, and Mal was enchanted by the changes they'd made for the evening. The entire pavilion was now hung with basic light bulbs that gave the perfect aura to the place and fit in so well with the music coming from the band on risers, who had multicolored lights around their backdrop. And they were good—not in an amateurish way, but a real could-be-recording-artists way. She said as much to Hunter as they approached, and he shrugged with a smile.

"We attract all sorts here," he said in an offhand way. "Just wait till you hear their vocalists."

He squeezed her hand and smiled. Mal felt his excitement and matched it with her own.

Most of the people there were old, but not all of them, and they all seemed to know each other. When Hunter and Mal entered the pavilion, everyone called out to Hunter in excitement, and he grinned openly and waved to a few of them.

Mal watched with fascination as he greeted every single one of them by name, asked after kids or other acquaintances, and held light, joking conversations with back slaps and high fives.

He was an entirely new person.

But somehow, it was still him.

This was the version of him that Mal had come to know in their private moments—this easy, warm man with no airs or distance. His quick smile and quicker laugh was a hit, and he was truly adored by his guests.

And he wasn't leaving her out of it.

He introduced her to everyone he talked to, holding her hand or wrapping an arm around her waist, keeping her close and leaving no doubt in anyone's mind, least of all hers, as to where his head was. She earned herself some gentle ribbing from some of the older men, and they were ecstatic when she played along.

Hunter disappeared for a moment when someone needed to discuss a problem at their rented house, and Mal found herself leaning on the railing of the pavilion, looking out at the lake under the light of the moon. It was one of the most surreal moments of this trip, with the band playing smooth, emotional jazz behind her.

Could anything on earth be more perfect than this?

"Darlin', gimme five minutes to get my car, and I'll take you away from here," rasped an older voice near her.

She turned with a raised brow to the old man now leaning beside her, his smoking jacket, no doubt once well fitted, hanging on him like a sack. But his eyes twinkled and the hint of cigar on his breath reminded her of her grandfather.

"Where'll we go?" she asked, leaning closer.

He wheezed a laugh and gave her a wink. "Saucy girl. I like you."

"Arlo, leave the girl alone, will ya?" cawed another male voice. "Honestly, your wife is right over there; show some respect."

Arlo gave the newcomer a look. "Don't get involved, Richie. You haven't had a broad since the seventies. You wouldn't know what to do."

"You can't call them broads anymore," Richie scolded as he came to Mal's other side. "It's disrespectful." He shook his head and looked at Mal. "I apologize for my friend's rudeness, miss. His wife doesn't let him out much."

Mal grinned, looking between the two of them. "How long have you two known each other?"

Arlo chuckled and looked at the taller man for a moment. "Fifty years?"

"Near enough," Richie said with a nod, folding his long arms over his sweater vest. "My Ann and his wife were girlfriends from school, and we all met here by accident one year. After that, the girls did just about everything together, so Arlo and I had to get along—or else." He made a slashing motion across his throat.

"It wasn't that bad," Arlo assured her with a smile. "Ann was too soft-hearted to threaten anything in the world."

Richie smiled and sighed. "Yeah, she was one of a kind, my girl. And she could dance like an angel." He looked at Mal with a quirk of one furry brow. "Can you dance?"

"Only with me," Hunter said as he appeared as if by magic. He clamped a hand on Richie's shoulder, smiling. "You should know better, Richie. You want to dance with a pretty girl? I think Mrs. Howard could use a dance."

"Judith?" Richie said with interest, looking across the dance floor. He suddenly straightened his bow tie. "Excuse me."

That drew chuckles from the rest of them, and as a new song started up, Arlo patted Hunter on the back. "Enjoy your dance, Hunter. Hang onto this one, eh?"

Hunter smiled and met Mal's eyes. "I intend to."

She had to swallow hard as Hunter slowly pulled her onto the dance floor and into his arms. The soft strains of "As Time Goes By" floated on the breeze, the piano and saxophone playing off of each other in flirtation.

"Are you having fun?" he asked as they slowly moved to the music.

She nodded, smiling at him. "The music is amazing. Honestly, this is the best I've felt all week."

Her answer pleased him, she could tell, and he pulled her closer. "I'm glad."

"You know everyone here," she commented softly, smiling as Arlo led his cute wife onto the dance floor.

Hunter nodded, humming in agreement. "I make it a point to. Grandpa did that, Dad did that, and it's become the trademark. But I like doing it. People trust a place with owners and managers they can put a face to." He turned his head so his mouth was close to her ear. "But then you get guys like Arlo and Richie thinking they can make moves on my girl, and I have to remind them who's boss."

Mal half giggled while goosebumps raced across her skin. "Yeah," she murmured low. "I was this close to running off with them."

Hunter chuckled. "I knew it." His hand on her back tightened, and he touched his head to hers, slowly dancing with her in this perfect place, with this perfect feeling between them.

And then, very softly, so low she wasn't sure she heard it at first, she heard him sing, "Moonlight and love song, never out of date… Hearts full of passion, jealousy and hate…"

"You don't sing," she whispered, her words as shaky as her breath.

"I never said that," he replied and continued to sing along in her ear.

Mal swallowed hard and slid her hand to the back of his neck, resting her face against his shoulder. He serenaded her softly, just for her ears, and his voice was velvety smooth and sensual, not to mention perfect. He could sing, however unexpected and impossible it seemed, and she might be the only person who knew it.

There were no words for that, either.

But here, dancing in his arms, his lips at her ear, words weren't important.

Hunter couldn't take his eyes off of Mal, and it was obvious. He'd been getting teased about it all night, residents and visitors alike seeing just how taken in he was. He didn't mind. He could shrug it off and laugh about it, because he knew very well it was true.

She was an absolute vision tonight, and he would always remember the way she looked here, the way she felt in his arms, and how right it felt. He was going to have to tell her at some point. Tonight. There was no possible way he could hide it anymore, especially not when it should have been fairly obvious.

They took a breather after "As Time Goes By," and he drifted to collect his bearings again, speaking with the bartender and the manager, making sure things would be cleaned up and ready for the wedding reception tomorrow—anything to take his mind off the breathtaking woman who had stolen his heart.

It was productive, but it didn't exactly work. Mostly because he never stopped looking at her, and she looked at him just as much.

A peppy number ended to applause, and the lead vocalist took the microphone again. "Ladies and gents, we're going to slow it down again. This is one of our last numbers of the night and one of our favorites: 'It Never Entered My Mind.'"

The piano started in slowly, and then the cymbals, and when the trumpet began its soulful notes, Hunter found himself moving in Mal's direction, unable to do anything else.

She saw him coming, and he saw her throat work, then she came to him on her own. Without a word, she put her hand in his, wrapped the other around him, and laid her head on his shoulder. Slowly, they began to sway, and Hunter would have sworn they were the only people in the world, let alone on this dance floor.

All he could feel was Mal's hand in his, her arm around his neck, her body brushing against his. It was enough to drive a man insane, but despite that, somehow, he was comfortable. It felt natural to hold her like this, to move like this with her in his arms. He leaned his head on hers, eyes closed, and moved with the music, unaware of anyone or anything else.

Their bodies moved together as one. He was leading, he supposed, but only in the loosest sense of the word. He could dance, had learned years ago, but this was something else—something entirely beyond comprehension or skill. Dancing with Mal wasn't like dancing had ever been. It went beyond anything physical and wasn't something he could even describe.

His heart pounded frantically in his chest as sensations flooded him. With the music drawing on his emotions and his heart in his arms, it was all too much.

But it was all so right.

Suddenly, he wanted to be away from here. He wanted Mal to himself, without any distractions. Just the two of them together.

"Let's get out of here," he whispered.

Almost sleepily, Mal nodded against him, and she let him lead her out of the pavilion, fingers entwined. They walked down the stone steps to the beach, pausing only for Mal to remove her shoes, which she held in her other hand. They didn't speak for a while, just walking and letting what was passing between them flow on by some unspoken agreement. He didn't care; he just wanted to be with her.

"I want to put my feet in the water," Mal suddenly said, her tone playful.

Hunter reluctantly let her fingers slide from his, but he grinned as she waded out ankle-deep. "That's what you did the morning of the first sunrise shoot," he reflected softly.

She laughed and tossed him a grin. "Yep! What can I say? I love walking in the water."

"I fell in love with you that morning."

Mal jerked, the water splashing loudly against her calves, and stared at him wide-eyed. "What?" she half cried, half whispered.

He cleared his throat. He probably shouldn't have said it so bluntly, but it just came out that way. "I fell in love with you," he repeated. He offered a small, unapologetic shrug, smiling warmly and watching her.

She was frozen as she stood in the water, watching him. Waiting.

"I'm in love with you," he said simply. "I've been in love with you this whole time. I haven't said anything because I know how crazy it is, and I was afraid it was all one-sided and I couldn't risk you running off when I feel this way and–"

"It's not one-sided."

He stopped—his heart and his words and his breath all at once.

He stared at her, something intense and burning growing within him.

Mal shook her head, swallowing. "It's not one-sided," she said again, much quieter.

Before he knew what he was doing, he marched into the water, reaching for her face, and kissed her hard. Her arms twined tightly around his neck, her lips parting instantly, returning his kiss with a fire of her own. She clung to him, desperate and frantic as he was, her feet no longer touching the ground as he held her.

He couldn't feel enough, couldn't breathe enough. Everything was solely and completely drawn up in Mal, in loving her, in the heady rush of delight in knowing that the insanity of his feelings was matched in her. They kissed deeply, tasting each other as if for the first and last time, again and again, as if it would never be enough.

It would never be enough.

Then their kisses became softer, more tender, searching and comforting and soothing. Grazing passes of lips, settling and unsettling all at once. Hunter shifted his mouth to capture her lips fiercely, drawing a ragged whimper from her that made something primal growl in victory within him.

After a few breathless moments, whistles, applause, and catcalls reached their ears, their older friends at the pavilion having a perfect view of them.

Mal broke off gently, laughing low and sensual and sending his blood racing. He managed to laugh too, still breathless and on fire. He touched his forehead to hers, wrapping his arms around her tightly with a long overdue sigh of relief.

The noise from the pavilion faded, and Mal suddenly pulled back with a groan.

"What?" he asked in surprise, keeping his arms locked around her.

"I have to go back to the Hen House tonight," she moaned, making a face. "And you have to go to Stag Night."

He'd forgotten all about that, which showed how important it was. He shook his head. "I don't care. I'm staying right here with you."

Hunter leaned in and kissed her again, gentling his touch and doing his level best to tempt her into staying. She curled a hand around his neck, toying with his hair, and he faintly wondered just who was doing the tempting now.

She eventually forced herself away from him, stepping out of his hold, and let the night breeze come between them. "You have to," she scolded, sounding winded, much to his delight. "And I have to. If it were anybody else, I wouldn't care, but it's Tom and Jenna. We have to," she repeated firmly.

And he knew she was right. He put his hands on his hips and tried his best to calm his breathing, giving her a crooked smile. "You are going to drive me crazy, you know that?"

She tilted her head impishly. "In a good way?"

"The best," he assured her.

She gave him a curtsy and smiled, holding out her hand. "Walk me back?"

His grin spread, and he took her hand, kissed it, then tugged her against him for one brief, searing kiss. "Fine," he growled, chuckling at her sudden panting. "But if I'm grumpy tomorrow, I'm blaming you."

Mal shuddered and released a tiny moan, making him laugh again. He intertwined their fingers again and slowly, very slowly, they walked out of the water and toward the Hen House.

Chapter Fifteen

She was going to be late to the breakfast, but she couldn't exactly be mad about that. Technically, it didn't start until nine, and it was only ten to. But considering she was the photographer, she should have been there way before now to take pictures of the spreads and everything else. Hopefully, Taryn and Dan were on top of things and had started already.

It wasn't exactly her fault she would be late, either.

She'd been forced into regaling Caroline with her stories from last night, every nitty gritty detail, and they'd stayed up too late, talking as if they were teenagers. Then this morning, she'd woken up early and gone for a stroll along the beach, no camera, just her in her rolled-up jeans, barefoot in the water again, arms folded over her flapping flannel. She'd enjoyed the peace and the serenity of the brilliant morning, while echoes of the night before played in her head.

Hunter loved her. Was that even possible? They were worlds apart, and yet in this magical place, they'd become closer than she'd ever been with anyone, including some family members. He'd taught her to dream things and open her eyes for a better look at herself.

She loved who she was with him.

Wasn't that the whole idea of love?

She hadn't told him she loved him, technically. She'd have to do that at some point, when the time was right. She did love him, there was no question, and surely he had to know, considering she'd told him it wasn't one-sided.

But, as Caroline put it last night, nothing in love is certain.

She'd gone back to the house after her walk, but something caught her attention: Jenna sneaking out of the back patio door, hair down, in a simple T-shirt and yoga pants, grinning at something Mal couldn't see. She moved for a better look just as Jenna dashed off the patio and Tom caught her in his arms, holding her tightly, her feet dangling.

He just held her for a moment, then slowly let her down. They cupped each other's faces, talking softly, both grinning like mad fools. Mal was too far away to hear them, and she was glad for that. It was their wedding day; they deserved a moment of privacy. She waited until they had disengaged themselves a few quick kisses later and Jenna had gone back into the house before doing so herself.

She was instantly attacked by Caroline, who forced her to get in the shower and then set to work on her hair. Between sessions of drying and product and curling, Caroline allowed Mal to get changed, and then pulled out the dress for breakfast. It was a formal occasion, so she'd decided on a designer dress—Alexander McQueen, to be precise. It was a fitted cream dress with an ivory Celtic lace pattern overlay, cap sleeves, and a pencil skirt that would fall below her knees. Best of all, it was a knit dress, so it would hug her minimal curves. Mal balked at the idea of wearing something bridal-looking, but once Caroline assured her that Jenna was wearing mint, it wasn't an issue.

Then Mal tried to suggest it was too much, but Caroline shushed her and said it was at least four years off the runway, so it wasn't even the hot thing anymore. As long as it wasn't trendsetting, Mal could deal with it, apparently. Thankfully, she'd been permitted sensible T-strap pumps that meant at least her feet would be steady, if nothing else was.

Caroline had done a perfect job of her makeup, again, with a natural, yet elegant look that had Mal shaking her head. The hair, on the other hand, would take some getting used to. She'd gone for blowout curls, and it had been mountainous at first. But once Caroline calmed it down, it wasn't half bad. It just took forever.

Mal entered the breakfast room to find it only half filled with bridal party members and various other relations that had apparently just arrived. Jenna and Tom, looking like the perfect combo in a Doublemint commercial, were standing close together and mingling with some of Tom's family. Taryn and Dan were already at work but gave her smiles and thumbs-ups.

She glanced around and smiled at various other people, even Sophie, who seemed to have mellowed out after the bachelorette party. Lucas had been sequestered into conversation with Aunt Joni and gave Mal a pleading look that she pointedly ignored. Aunt Cady and Uncle Drake weren't there yet, and Caroline was just behind her, so she couldn't have been late, really.

The prebreakfast spread of juices and fruit was on a table in the far corner, and the tables were decorated with simple, floral centerpieces. All in all, the room looked great, just a hint of their personal touches and not much else required. That was refreshing, considering the rest of the day would be nothing but finery and details.

She saw Hunter at last, leaning against the terrace railing, watching her. He'd probably seen her the moment she'd come in. And with that look in his eyes, he approved. She approved of him as well, with his white shirt—sleeves rolled, as usual—and tie with a black vest and black slacks. His throat worked on a swallow, and he put a very subtle hand to his chest as if he couldn't breathe.

Mal smiled at him softly and winked.

One corner of his mouth curved up.

"Mal," Jenna said, suddenly beside her. "Would you mind terribly taking some pictures of us before the rest of the people get here?"

Mal smiled at her cousin and agreed, which earned her a tight squeeze.

For the next several minutes, she worked her way around the room, taking requested pictures and generally avoiding interacting with family members she didn't mind being estranged from and strangers she didn't care to meet. She compared notes with Taryn and Dan, and then set to work getting the best shots she could of the tables before everyone sat.

The room filled with more people, all relatives of either Jenna or Tom, and work was plentiful. People were kind and cheerful and very Southern in some cases. If her heart got blessed one more time, she'd be an angel. But it was enjoyable, which surprised her, and she found herself looking forward to the rest of the day.

She spent a pointed amount of time trying to get a good shot of the flowers on the end of one table when Hunter came up beside her, glass of orange juice in hand, with his back turned to the room so it would appear as though he were only looking out at the view of the lake. With the current crowd of the room, it was a fairly good disguise.

"That was quite a way to start a day," he murmured as he sipped the juice.

"How's that?" she replied nonchalantly, turning her camera for a different angle.

"Seeing you look like that. I couldn't decide if I'd just had breakfast or if I was suddenly starving."

A soft grunt of distress hit her throat at the drop in his voice, and she looked down at the display on her camera. "Stop that. I'm working." She turned to get some shots of the room in general.

Hunter stepped closer, his shoulder close enough that if she leaned back, she'd make contact. "I'm grumpy this morning," he muttered.

"Sorry," she quipped unapologetically.

"You should be. It's your fault. I barely slept at all."

She snorted softly and continued taking pictures. "Well, join the club, babe."

He cleared his throat hastily and took another drink. "If you want to keep working this morning, you won't call me that again."

She smirked and half turned so he could see her better, camera still safely raised in front of her face. "Don't like it?"

"That wasn't what I meant. At all."

She should know better than to play with the fire that was Hunter. "Good-friggin-night," she muttered, fiddling with her camera strap.

He hummed a quiet laugh of pride. "How many Mississippis?"

"I will be counting Mississippis all day, you jerk," she scolded, tossing her hair and taking secret pleasure in the way it bounced. "Stop distracting me and go be part of the wedding party. You have to be in some of these."

"So do you."

She gave a small shake of her head. "Later, when the rest of the family not in the party come in. Go."

"You're cranky in the mornings," he muttered.

She shrugged one shoulder, focusing back on the table in front of her. "Only when I can't sleep. That's on you."

He said something softly under his breath and cleared his throat. "If I live through this day…"

"We'll both be grateful," she finished firmly. "Go away."

He turned and discreetly stroked her waist as he set down his glass and moved past her to another table, effectively cutting off her train of thought and having quite the emphatic last word. She moved to the other side of the room as quickly as she could without making a scene, but it was no use. His eyes followed her and eventually, she migrated back in that direction.

Once they were all officially welcomed by Jenna and Tom, with a sweet toast from Tom's father, the food was brought out and set up buffet style. Mal was officially supposed to be done with her photographer duties, so she handed her camera off to Dan and took her place at the table she'd been assigned, with some distant cousins she only had faint recollections of, but they seemed fairly normal.

When it was her table's turn, she went up to the buffet table again, helping herself to the food as if it were perfectly normal for her to be in a designer dress with rich people, eating fancy breakfast food at a wedding at which she was both working and attending.

She was at the fruit salad bowl, scooping some onto her plate, when she felt someone move behind her, and she shifted closer to the table to get out of their way, only for them to follow. A hand rested on her hip briefly.

"Eat up," Hunter murmured as he slowly passed, his voice close to her ear. "You'll need it."

She had no idea how he made generic, honest advice about breakfast sound like an invitation to bed, but she smiled and tried not to make a scene.

"Thanks," she murmured back as he moved on, for all the world looking as though he really did need another napkin from the end of the table and nothing else.

She shook her head, still smiling.

As he'd said, if they lived through this day…

The rest of the day was a mad, frantic mess of things, but Hunter couldn't mind that—not when his best friend was happy and getting married, and not when the woman he loved was everywhere he was today.

Someone, probably Caroline, had forced Mal to change into a different dress for the wedding, and he liked it just as much as the dress she wore at breakfast. He didn't know how she was working in it, with the sensual wrapping and ruching and folds of the champagne bodice that disappeared into a fitted black skirt, let alone the heels that made her legs seem endless. But working she was, and incredibly well.

He had to flick a couple of the guys on the ears as they gawked and made comments about her, but he couldn't say he blamed them. Despite looking like the high-class wedding guest she was, she ordered them around with the authority and efficiency of a drill sergeant, somehow looking calm and collected and just as fresh as if she'd only just arrived. She was flawless, his Mal, and he couldn't mind that others took notice of that, not that she heard any of it. She was in her element and, as such, was completely absorbed by it.

She had taken pictures of the wedding party separately, so as not to throw the world on its ear by having the bride and groom see each other before the wedding. It was an odd arrangement, but seeing as how the wedding was in the afternoon and there wasn't time for all of the pictures between wedding and reception, it would have to do. Guys had gone first, considering the girls would take more time getting ready.

Hunter tried to steal a moment with her, but all he managed was to brush by her again, and for her to say something about how the cream suit looked on him. The specifics were lost on him at the moment, as she was looking at him, but whatever she'd said had made him count Mississippis, and she'd chuckled at that.

He had been unsure initially about the cream suits, considering Tom would be in a gray tux, but now that he saw them all together, with Tom's cream vest and the matching berry-colored ties and boutonnieres, he could safely say that it worked. More than that, it was the least ridiculous monkey suit he'd ever had to wear, and that was a relief.

He shouldn't have been surprised, really, considering it was Tom. He had always been a class act, as evidenced by his Stag Night the night before, which was probably one of the most relaxed events Hunter had ever attended—and certainly the first one where he'd been in bed before three in the morning.

His fully functioning brain today was grateful.

Mal quirked a brow at him from where she sat, officially among the wedding attendees now, with Taryn and Dan floating around as discreetly as possible. He mentally shook himself and returned his attention back to the ceremony currently taking place in front of him. Or, more specifically, in the gazebo to his right.

So far, the ceremony had gone perfectly, no doubt thanks to the hours of practice yesterday, and the girls all looked lovely in their elegant gowns. The mothers of the bride and groom were equally gorgeous, choosing gowns in a similar shade as the bridesmaids, and the flower girls had been shockingly well behaved, as if their lives depended on their perfection.

He and Caroline had, of course, been the best couple down the aisle, playing their parts to perfection. He had his token somber face, and she had smiled brilliantly, shocking everyone present who didn't know that the famous Jenna Hudson had a twin.

Jenna had been stunning, he could objectively say, in her vintage-colored, off-the-shoulder lace gown. She'd opted for a band of ribbon around her trim waist that matched the groomsmen's suits, and no veil, which he understood was a point of some contention among her bridesmaids. But nobody cared about any of that now. Jenna's smile distracted any thought from her dress or hair or flowers or lack of veil.

Hunter had heard Tom's breath catch in his throat when he saw Jenna, and he felt an echo of it in his own. What would Mal look like coming down an aisle toward him?

He tried to focus on the emotional and heartfelt vows of his friends, but his eyes kept drifting over to Mal. Oddly enough, every time they did, she was looking at him as well. It was slightly unnerving, in a ticklish sort of way.

After the fifth time, he heard an irritated sigh from behind him. "Do you want me to serenade you two or…?" Reed muttered out of the side of his mouth.

Hunter cleared his throat softly and forced himself to look back at the service, where the "I dos" were being exchanged.

"I now pronounce you husband and wife," the minister said with a knowing smile, just as a breeze came up and tossed Jenna's dangling curls.

Tom had a fairly suave moment as he reached out and tucked one of the curls behind her ear, then glanced at the minister, who chuckled.

"Yes, Mr. Yardley, you may now kiss your bride."

A cheer went up as Tom gladly did so, not dipping her this time.

Music from the string quartet swelled as Tom and Jenna were presented and started down the aisle. Hunter and a slightly tearful Caroline followed, as did everyone else.

Hunter winked at Mal as he passed her, and she did too, which earned her a knee slapping from the older relative she was sitting next to. He made a mental note to ask her about that later.

The wedding party was shuttled into golf carts and driven to the other places on the resort that Tom and Jenna had selected for pictures, with Mal and her assistants directing. She was all business once again and had even pulled her hair back, which did nothing to lessen her beauty, instead highlighting the delicate bone structure of her face.

Everyone obeyed her implicitly, not arguing her suggestions or points, laughing at her smart quips, and treating her the way they should have been treating her all week. Reed was watching her with too much fascination for Hunter's taste, but he always kept his distance, glancing at Hunter guiltily. She didn't seem fazed at all, assessing their positions and the lighting with skill and artistry, seeing everything all at once. A strand of Grace's hair out of place, a bouquet that needed a quarter turn, a wrinkle in Caroline's skirt… And to her assistants' credit, they didn't need her to tell them in complete sentences what she saw. She only had to begin, and then they could see it too.

She was a brilliant mentor for them.

And a sight to behold.

She didn't need the makeup or designer dresses or fancy hair to be gorgeous, no matter how others were taking notice now. What they didn't realize was that the unspoken quality that had them all entranced and enchanted had nothing to do with how she looked or how she dressed. It was Mal, pure and simple, in all her exquisite loveliness.

"Hunter, you look like a deer in headlights," Mal suddenly barked with a smile. "Pick an expression, will you?"

His eyes narrowed briefly as the rest of the party snickered, and Mal teased him with a quirk of a brow, drawing a slow half smile from him. And so it went, from place to place, quickly and efficiently, without anyone really noticing time at all. A few last photos, and they were dismissed. Hunter checked his watch, and it surprised him. They would get back to the pavilion and reception before the drinks and appetizers for the guests were done, and far before they were scheduled to. The others piled into the carts again and started back down, everyone cheerful and excited and ready for a party after all that formality.

Hunter, however, stood where he was last posed and waited, just for the other carts to start off, and then moseyed over to where Mal and her assistants were having an impromptu meeting.

"Lighting might be tricky at the reception," Mal was saying, "so we'll just play that by ear. Stay as long as you want, but no pressure. We'll get what we can. Early flight tomorrow morning, so don't miss the car."

"Do we really have to leave?" Taryn pouted, adjusting the strap of her black-and-blue gown.

"Taryn stole my question," Hunter complained aloud, putting his hands into his pockets.

All three heads turned toward him in surprise. Taryn and Dan looked at each other, then wordlessly headed for the last cart.

Mal smiled as he approached, squinting up at him in the sunlight. "Hi."

He returned her smile and kissed her. "Hi yourself."

She released a sigh and wiped at her brow. "Boy, am I glad that's over. It's like herding cats."

"You made it look effortless," he praised, wrapping his arm around her waist.

She held his arm in place with her hand. "I had extra motivation to be charming today. Guess it worked."

"It did," he assured her, reaching his other hand around to tug the ponytail down and let her still-curled hair fall free. "There. I like it down."

Mal smiled curiously. "What, so I can do this?" she asked as she tossed her head and let the curls dance and fly.

His heart caught somewhere in his throat. "Yes, exactly like that," he said, touching her jaw and kissing her again.

One of the others honked the horn of the golf cart impatiently. "Party on, guys! Let's go!"

Hunter tried to ignore them. "Do you really have to go tomorrow?" he whispered.

Mal put a hand on his lips and shook her head. "We're not talking about tomorrow right now. It's wedding day. I'm still working, and there is a reception to get to. We'll talk about it later, okay?"

He smiled and heaved a mock-irritated sigh. "Okay, fine. But the owner had better do an impressive job with this reception, or the whole thing will have been a waste of some very rich and famous people."

"Shut up," Mal scolded as they headed for the cart. "I know the owner, and you'll like it."

"Promise?" he asked as he sat on the cart and set his arm on the back of the seat.

Mal sat next to him and leaned into him easily. "Promise. Now cheer up, boss man. The hard part is over. Now we get to party. With Tom and Jenna running the show, I think we're in for a good time."

Chapter Sixteen

A good time it was, and she wasn't just saying that. The staff at Rambling Ridge did a fantastic job turning the lodge and pavilion into a perfect reception venue with the stylish Southern twist that personified Tom and Jenna, and the DJ hadn't had a bad number yet. He played just enough country to satisfy the crowd without overplaying it enough to annoy those guests with more varied tastes. The food was perfection, the guests happy, and the same romantic lighting from Jazz Night gave the whole venue a magical feel.

Giving in to the cliché, Tom and Jenna had chosen to have their first dance to Martina McBride and Pat Monahan's version of Train's "Marry Me," and it should have given Mal plenty of cause to roll her eyes. But somehow, she had no desire to do anything but smile and attempt to get rid of the odd burning sensation in her eyes and throat.

She stood near her family, and Caroline wrapped an arm around her, at which point Uncle Drake did the same with Caroline and Aunt Cady, and Lucas followed suit with his mother. It took Mal even longer to recover from that moment than she would have thought. Despite her best attempts to claim she had no family, it felt as perfect as any family ever could.

Maybe she was done shutting her childhood away. Now that she realized what she had been missing, there was no way she could go back. She was a Hudson, after all—through and through.

Drake and Jenna shared an adorable and laughter-filled dance, and Tom took his mother for a spin on the floor, making her smile and look every bit the wonderful woman Hunter had claimed she was.

Mal found Hunter often over the course of the night, but they didn't spend as much time together as she would have liked. It wasn't possible, with her having to take pictures at times and join in the party, especially with the likes of Aunt Joni and Great Aunt Pearl trying to snatch up whatever gossip they could. She dodged her second cousin Vance, who'd spent too much time in the more rural parts of Kentucky, it seemed. She also caught sight of the infamous stripper from the bachelorette party dancing a little too closely with Alexis. Apparently, there was something going on there.

There was dancing aplenty and just as much singing along to the songs. The only upset of the night was when the DJ played "Rocky Top," and the non-Tennessee fans protested. But considering the bride, everyone else was overruled. There was even one dash of line dancing, which brought her mental Reception Bingo tally up.

Food was constantly being refreshed, and it was a tribute to the best of the South, which delighted everyone except the starving bridesmaids, who made do with the lemon slices from the glasses of water the waiters brought around.

Tables had been set up along the stone courtyard between the pavilion and the beach for those who wanted fresh air away from the dancing or to prop up their feet. From the pavilion, Mal could see couples walking hand in hand along the courtyard and over the lighted walking bridge. She sighed and hoped that soon things would be calm enough for her to slip away with Hunter for a few moments. She couldn't leave before Jenna and Tom made their grand, theatrical exit, but that didn't mean she had to be present for everything.

She made her way back into the lodge to take the stairs to the upper level, thinking she could get some interesting angles from there. She'd long lost track of Taryn and Dan, and considering they'd all had to turn in phones, she probably wouldn't be able to track them down until they left tomorrow. She couldn't think about that right now. It was too unsettling.

She found a few people in the quieter upper room, one of whom was Grace, who smiled and waved as Mal approached and moved aside so Mal could get her shots. She saw Hunter on one side of the pavilion, grinning and chatting with Tom's brothers, having removed his jacket and loosened his tie some time ago. He looked just as perfect as ever, but somehow less untouchable. And that made her smile.

A leggy, blonde girl approached the group and hugged them all, including Hunter, and all three smiled at her as she talked animatedly. She had a perfect figure, fit enough to be an athlete, curvy enough to be a Victoria's Secret model, and her dress flattered everything about her. She could have been made from money and custom designed for any of the guys there.

She matched everyone else here. And none of the guys were taking their eyes off of her. Mal didn't like her one bit.

"Hey, Grace? Who's the girl down there with Dave and Trent?" she asked in a would-be nonchalant voice, pretending to take pictures of the rest of the group. "I don't recognize her."

Grace came over and looked, adjusting her beaded strap. "Oh, I wondered if she might show up. That's Emma Halliday. She's a Vanderbilt cousin," she added in a stage whisper.

Of course she was.

"Awesome," Mal tried, going for enthusiastic. "She knows the Yardleys?"

"She knows all of them," Grace said, tapping the window absently. "Since childhood, I guess. She and Hunter went steady a couple of times on and off since high school. Got pretty serious like three years ago."

Mal stiffened and managed to pass it off as craning her neck and stretching. "Oh yeah? How serious?"

Grace gave her a look. "Uh, Hunter had a ring. Never got around to giving it to her. She decided she wanted to go into the Peace Corps or teach English in Indonesia or study male models in Italy—maybe all of the above. Bad break, I heard, but they'd been friends so long, it became fairly amicable after a few months. She always wanted to go back to him but didn't know if he'd take her back. And Hunter had never had a girl this serious before, so…" She looked back at the group with a small frown. "I haven't seen her in years. I thought she was dating a baseball player."

The way she was flirting with the gang, Mal doubted she was dating anyone, but she certainly had plans to. She wasn't focused on the group in general. She had eyes only for Hunter.

And he wasn't looking anywhere else.

Grace eventually wandered off while Mal kept watching, and she grew more and more uneasy the more Hunter smiled. Then Emma whispered something in his ear, and he frowned but nodded and took her arm, leading her away from the music and off the pavilion. Mal followed along the windows of the upper room and saw them go down the stone steps toward the beach.

They talked for a few minutes, and Hunter's expression didn't change at all. He kept his arms folded loosely, listening as intensely as he ever did, while Emma's hands moved and flailed with her words. Mal wasn't close enough to read lips, and the lighting was awful, but she felt her heart jump into her throat when Hunter's arms unfolded and his hands went to his hips. His head lowered, and he nodded just once.

Then, for whatever reason, Emma started crying. Mal saw Hunter's shoulders move on a sigh, and he pulled Emma into a tight embrace. He stroked her hair, murmured in her ear, and smiled when she hugged him back and buried her face into his shoulder. And then he laughed.

Mal clamped her lips together, wondering if she were going to be sick or fall over or scream. None of those things happened, but her eyes filled with tears the longer they held each other. Emma smiled, and so did Hunter before they disappeared, presumably in the direction of the dance floor.

Together.

Mal stared at nothing, but the place Hunter and Emma had been lingered in her mind, and in the haze of her unfocused vision.

That was a picture of a perfect couple—perfectly situated, perfectly matched, and perfectly superior. That was Hunter's path, and Mal had been stupid enough to think that the fancy, rich man with the gorgeous looks was serious about the photographer. He must have been bored stiff with no Vanderbilt cousin fiancée on his arm.

Well, he could have her.

Mal made her way down the stairs, her tears somehow staying contained, and hesitated between going back to the pavilion to make her excuses to her family or just leaving.

Just then, a slow song started up from the reception, and her mind played out a horrifying scenario of Hunter leading Miss Emma

Halliday, the one that got away, onto the dance floor and slowly swaying with her, maybe even dipping his head to kiss her shoulder.

A strangled cry escaped her, and her feet carried her toward the door at the front of the lodge.

"Mal?"

She screeched low in her throat, her tears welling over, but she stopped at Caroline's voice.

"Grace came to get me. What's up?"

Mal shook her head, not turning around.

Caroline was suddenly in front of her, grabbing her arms and peering into her face. "Oh, honey."

Mal looked up at the ceiling, willing the tears back, but they wouldn't go.

"Who am I killing, babe? I'm all fired up. Just name the son of a—"

"Hunter," Mal managed, praying it was the last time she'd ever have to say his name.

Caroline stopped at once, eyes wide. "Seriously? What did he do?"

"I can't." Mal hiccupped, swiping at her face. "I can't."

"Okay," Caroline soothed, pulling her in for a tight hug that Mal returned, which only made Caroline hold tighter. "Okay. You need to go?"

Mal nodded against her.

"Go," Caroline urged, pushing back and smiling. "I'll talk to Mama. We'll come see you in Denver soon, okay?"

Mal nodded, wiping at her eyes, then handed her camera off. "Can you get the grand finale? You know how to work this?"

Caroline nodded, taking it from her. "Point and shoot, right?"

"It's a camera, not a Colt .45," Mal muttered, her chest aching from restraining her cries.

"Same idea," her cousin said with a wink. She leaned in and kissed her cheek. "Go, Mal. Love you."

Mal nodded, unable to say anything else, went to the counter to pick up her phone, and left the building. She'd only gone about four feet when she heard her name again, this time from Jenna. She turned and saw the beautiful bride coming toward her with a brilliant smile.

"Mal, are you leaving?" Jenna asked, looking concerned.

Mal forced a smile. "Headache," she said sadly. "I was gonna try to get some sleep before my flight tomorrow."

Jenna smiled and shook her head. "Silly, you can't leave without saying goodbye to me." She hugged Mal tightly. "It means so much to me that you came. It wouldn't have been the same without you. When we get back, can I come see you?"

"Of course," Mal choked out. "You can come see the pictures in person."

Jenna pulled back. "No, silly, I want to see you. Let's do lunch. Is that okay?"

Mal looked at her cousin for a long moment, considering everything that had changed for her in the last few weeks because of this woman. She'd found her family again, remembered what she had lost, and discovered what her life had been missing that she'd never realized: love.

Maybe this trip wasn't a total loss after all.

"Yeah," she squeaked, letting her emotions show. "Yeah, that'd be great."

Jenna grinned, hugged her again, and returned to the reception.

Mal shoved her phone into her handbag, never turning it on, and headed for the carts. Her tears flowed freely, her ribs aching with the need to cry loudly into a pillow, and her fingers twitched sporadically into claws. She needed to get away from this place, from the memories, from him... from the entire fantasy she had been living for the past week.

The ridiculous notion that she belonged here.

Or with him.

A kid in a golf cart offered to drive her back to her house, and she let him, unable to keep from watching the lake, where fireworks honoring the bride and groom were being shot off from the tour boat.

How could everything change in an instant? How could Hunter claim to love her and then go back to the woman who'd refused him before?

Easy, she reminded herself. She was his type. Hadn't Grace said they dated off and on? It wasn't hard to go back to someone you once loved so much you were ready to marry them, particularly if you'd never stopped loving them.

Poor, gullible Mallory Hudson, thinking Prince Charming actually liked the servant girl.

She had the cart driver wait for her while she dashed into the house and grabbed everything that belonged to her. She wouldn't put it past Hunter to try to find her, play his part one more time, and she wouldn't fall into that trap again. Well, she probably would, but then she'd hate herself later and spend too many days on her couch with Fritos and Häagen-Dazs.

Suitcase in hand, she glanced around the tiny cottage once more, a jolt of regret and nostalgia hitting her gut like a ton of bricks. None of it was real. Not this cottage, not this place—nothing. She sniffed back a fresh wave of tears, went back to her buddy in the golf cart, and had him drive her down to the cabin where Taryn and Dan were staying.

She let herself in and set the suitcase in the corner, kicking off her shoes. The house was quiet and dark, which was perfect. She sat down on the couch, hiccupping sobs making their way out of her at last.

A few minutes later, the sliding glass door opened, and a giggling Taryn and Dan entered, both in swimsuits, and kissing each other with far too much familiarity to be drunk. They caught sight of her after a moment and stopped dead, the only sound the water dripping off their hair and bodies.

"Hey," Mal said simply, her voice raw and filled with tears.

"Hiya, boss," Dan answered with false innocence.

"Hey, boss," Taryn replied glumly.

Mal swallowed and gestured between them. "What's, uh, what's this?"

Her assistants looked at each other, and Dan shrugged. "Well, after you set us up in your office back in December, we sort of—"

"This has been going on from the beginning?" Mal interrupted, her head spinning with the mess of it all.

They looked uneasy, and both scratched the back of their heads in synchrony. "We weren't sure if you had a fraternization policy," Dan admitted.

"Dan's really a lot better than he looks," Taryn admitted with a wrinkle of her nose.

Dan snorted and nudged her hip. "Gee, thanks, babe."

"Shut up. You know you were drooling over Caroline," Taryn said with a roll of her eyes.

"And you didn't have every guy here on your drool wall?" he shot back.

"Caroline's got an Aussie rugby player," Mal managed, their banter too much for her to take right now. "Name's Ryan, very serious."

"Shoot," Dan said, smiling.

Taryn, on the other hand, stared at Mal closely. "Boss? You look like crap."

Mal tried to laugh, play it off, but her quivering jaw and watering eyes wouldn't let her. "Can I… stay here tonight? And can we leave early?"

Taryn's brows shot up. "Yeah. Whatever you need. We're all packed and ready. Do you wanna go now?"

Mal was touched at the offer but shook her head. "No, we need to sleep. No calls, though. I'm not here, you understand?"

They both nodded. "I kind of like not having my phone," Taryn admitted. "I didn't even turn it back on."

"I did," Dan said, turning a light on. "But I'm not answering it. Are we… going to get a certain angry guy banging on our door?"

Mal shrugged and covered her eyes. "I don't know," she cried, breaking down at last.

Taryn wrapped a towel around her suit and sat down next to Mal, pulling her close and rubbing her arm. "Okay, okay, how about Dan goes and makes us some hot chocolate, huh?"

Dan moved into the kitchen at once, already working on it.

Mal sniffled and shook her head. "I want a shower," she croaked, getting up. "And then… herbal tea."

She caught the startled look between the two of them but couldn't bring herself to care. She staggered into the nearest bathroom and stepped out of the dress and into the shower, where her sobs could drown in the echoes of the streams of water pummeling the tile.

The next morning, after miraculously catching an earlier flight and safely landing in Chicago for a layover, Mal finally turned on her phone.

Five missed calls, two voicemails, and seven missed texts—all from Hunter. Three of the calls, one voicemail, and six texts were from last night.

Hey, you have your phone yet?

You're not here. Where are you?

Not funny, honey.

Mal, I'm not kidding. Where are you?

Baby, I'm freaking out. I just went to the house, and you're gone. Where are you?

Pick up your phone, or so help me...

And then just one from this morning.

I love you.

She swallowed hard while reading them, imagining his face, his smile, his furrowed brow. She could hear him saying those things, the subtle inflections in his tone, the intensity of his words, every nuance and facet as familiar to her as breathing.

Caroline was right; he had worked her over. And done a very thorough job of it.

She glanced over at the Starbucks, where Taryn and Dan were waiting for their orders, and played the first voicemail, closing her eyes.

"Mal, I can't find you, baby. You disappeared. I need to see you. You're not answering my texts, and I don't even know if you're getting them. Did you leave your phone somewhere again? Did Sophie say something? I'm going crazy, honey. Call me. I love you."

Mal hit delete before she could talk herself out of it.

She stared at her phone, wanting someone to pull it out of her hand and throw it away, wanting to listen to this morning's voicemail, wanting to never hear his voice again, wanting...

"Mallory, it's five in the morning, and I miss you. I know you've already gone to the airport, and as much as I want to, I can't chase you down. You don't want that. I don't know what happened last night or why you didn't answer me or call me back, and honestly, I don't care. I love you. Please call me. Bye."

Mal deleted it again, drained and unable to cry anymore after doing so all night. She leaned her head back against the awkward airport chair and inhaled and exhaled painfully.

"Did you clean the camera that Caroline dropped off?"

"Of course I cleaned it. How much of a novice do you think I am?"

"Did you sniff it first? For that last whiff of her sultry perfume?"

Someone snorted, and then they stopped.

"How is it possible that you look worse now than you did seven minutes ago?" Dan asked as he sat down on one side of her.

"Are you freaking kidding me, Daniel? Shut up and hand me the muffin." Taryn reached over Mal and sat down on the other side. "Mal, you turned your phone on, didn't you?"

Mal swallowed but didn't answer.

"Where is your phone?" Taryn asked with a sigh. "Where is… Oh, I see. Okay, Dan, you're on phone duty. Turn it off, leave it on, play Angry Birds, I don't care. But you monitor that thing, and Mal doesn't get it back unless we trust the person on the other end. Got it?"

"Yep."

They didn't say anything for a long time, and Mal almost dozed off when she heard a phone vibrate. She jerked with a gasp and looked at Dan.

He looked at her phone, then met her eyes and pocketed it.

She groaned and shut her eyes tightly.

"He came by last night, late, after we'd all gone to bed," Taryn murmured as she sipped her coffee. "Jerry told me about it this morning. He told him he hadn't seen you, but Dan and I hadn't come back to the house yet. He bought it."

"Thanks," Mal whispered, sniffing once.

"Wanna talk about it yet?"

"No."

With that one word, the impossible happened. Her eyes filled with tears, and the tightness in her chest broke into a thousand pieces.

Taryn put her hand over Mal's, and Dan put his arm around her shoulder and patted softly.

And together, they waited.

Chapter Seventeen

Two weeks later.

"Taryn! Did you give Ashley the details on the Yellowstone project?"

"Yep, she knows the drill."

Mal nodded, even though Taryn couldn't see it from her desk in the corner. They brought Ashley in three weeks ago to be the assistant and secretary for the studio. She was a smart girl from the local community college, but she had trouble remembering specifics. She was proving to be valuable, though, and had even asked for a rundown of what sort of projects they would or would not do so she could screen calls better.

Ever since the wedding details and photos had been released, calls had been flooding in. It was getting ridiculous. Not that Mal minded being in demand, but she wasn't about to do more celebrity stuff unless it was actually interesting to her.

She'd given Taryn and Dan more freedom and projects of their own, and they were becoming more like partners in the business than anything else. Dan leaned toward more extreme perspective shots—things that required him to skydive and rappel canyons and the like—and they were very impressive. Taryn, on the other hand, was trying her hand at fashion shots, but in unique and artistic ways. Just last week, she'd been working with preliminary pieces for Fashion Week and had done some breathtaking work with lighting and a full moon in a prairie.

Mal was proud of her assistants, although she couldn't really call them that anymore. They had taken up a lot of the workload, once she'd decided to pursue her own projects. Yellowstone, for example, wanted her to come out in the fall to work with them, but she wanted to rework the contract details now that she had more experience in bigger playing fields.

It was an idea she'd had after a quick trip to Maine over the weekend had given her some spectacular pieces she could do something with on her own, not just for publicity. They'd been good enough to give her the rights, which was typical, but immediately sent her searching for a lawyer for the more complicated projects.

The trouble with growing higher in demand was that everything got a little bit harder.

"Did Dan say when he'd be back?" Mal asked in an offhand way as she turned back to her computer and started going over the pictures Jenna had asked for again.

"Three, I think," Taryn said around the pen in her mouth, swishing her chair back and forth so her floral skirt swayed. "Go to lunch. Caroline will shoot you if you miss it."

Mal shuddered and rubbed at the back of her neck. "I really don't know if I can stand the Inquisition again. It was bad enough when Jenna came, and she doesn't know anything."

Taryn made a noncommittal noise but didn't turn to look at her.

That was how things had gone. No mention of Hunter, thank goodness, but everyone knew he still texted and called—not nearly as much anymore, and Mal never returned any of them. But the reminder was painful.

Dan and Taryn had been understanding and supportive, overwhelming her with their response, but the lack of answers or explanation left them in a sort of limbo. They knew not to ask about it and pretended Lake Lure had been just another job, but the sympathy had also faded, which Mal understood. They were on her side, but she hadn't given them anything to be sympathetic about. She knew that if she ever decided to share, they would be all ears and probably have popcorn ready, but until then, it was business as usual.

"Go, Mal," Taryn urged, turning at last. "I'm serious. Aunt Cady got my number somehow, and if she calls me one more time…"

Mal groaned and clicked through a few more pictures. "I'm sorry. She's impossible."

"Yeah, but she's also sending me cobbler, so it's fine." Taryn laughed and went to the fridge they'd put in the back. Mal heard her rummaging around, and then it suddenly stopped.

"Mal," Taryn's voice said slowly, "why are there three pints of Ben and Jerry's in the freezer?"

Mal winced. "For emergencies."

Taryn marched over and stood directly in front of her. "The work freezer?"

Mal shrugged. "Emergencies happen at work, too."

Taryn turned Mal's chair and leaned forward so they were face-to-face, her long, surprisingly tame red bangs falling from behind her ear. "Okay. You don't want to talk about sexy boss man? Fine, I get it. But pull yourself together, woman. You had three days on your couch with nachos, and I said nothing–"

"The breakfast nachos were a really good invention," Mal interrupted stubbornly, folding her arms.

"—and I knew you were buying ice cream like it was melting, but I got that, so I said nothing," Taryn continued. "And then you came back to work and were driven like crazy, and I thought, 'Great! She's back and ready to go!' Don't go back to the boys, Mal. Think of your hips."

Mal gave her a look. "That's what you're most concerned about? My hips?"

Taryn smiled mischievously. "What else would I worry about? You could use some help in other areas, but ice cream is no respecter of body parts."

Mal snorted and covered her mouth, which made Taryn grin and move back to her chair.

"You're a tough cookie, Mal," Taryn said lightly. "Nothing breaks you."

She looked at Taryn for a long moment, wondering if the girl was stupid or just being funny. She had seen Mal in her darkest moment and screened her calls for a full week. She knew Mal had been broken. She was still broken, to be honest, but she was better—much better.

Mal shook her head and went back to her computer, one more group of wedding pictures to look through and mark for retouches before she went off to meet her visiting family.

"Do you want me to do that?" Taryn asked her in a quiet, understanding voice.

Mal shook her head. "No, I've got it. It's just wedding breakfast stuff."

"I got a shot of Sophie sneaking bacon at that one." Taryn sighed, leaning back in her chair. "Some vegan she is."

Mal ought to have laughed, but she couldn't. There on the screen in front of her was Hunter. She was supposed to be seeing Taryn's shots from that day, not hers, but this one she remembered. She'd gone around taking pictures of each table of guests, as Jenna had requested, and she'd taken a few extra shots of the bridal party table. Hunter had leaned closer to Tom, and the two looked as thick as thieves.

Something about Hunter's expression, the hint of a knowing smile, the teasing, adoring light in his eye, the dark stubble even though he'd shaved, all combined to make her go for the extra shots, focusing on him.

And he'd known it.

That expression was all for her.

If only she'd known then that he was playing her, that he'd been leading her on all week, despite what he'd said. She'd felt the warning signs, that it had all been too easy and too impossible, but she'd let him lead her around and around in circles until she was dizzy with the ecstasy of it. She'd known better.

She skipped ahead quickly, clearing her throat and tugging on her vest with one hand, feeling that something about her was off and needed to be set to rights. She smiled faintly at a few shots of her, taking secret pleasure in how good she had looked that day. She'd actually taken more care with her hair and makeup since then, but still nothing to that extent. That wasn't going to happen ever again, unless Caroline traveled with her on every major project.

The next shot appeared on her screen, and her breath suddenly vanished, and her chest seized all at once.

That moment; that wild and breathless five-second moment. It was there.

Mal was at the food table, holding a plate in one hand and the scoop for fruit salad in the other. Hunter was just to her left and behind her, hand on her right hip, his face close to her ear, whispering. Mal was smiling softly and leaning into him.

Neither were looking at the camera, but they didn't need to.

That picture showed two people so in love that the rest of the world had fallen away, stealing a moment for themselves amid the chaos and noise, perfectly content just to be close to each other, coming alive with suddenly blinding brilliancy.

Tears welled up in her eyes, and her throat constricted painfully. "Uh," she tried, choking on the words, "I think I will let you take over." She clicked ahead to the next one and got up, reaching for her purse. "You're right. Caroline will be mad if I'm late. They flew all this way to visit me; I should at least be on time."

"Sounds good," Taryn said, spinning around in her chair. Her eyes flicked to Mal's computer screen, then back at her, her expression suddenly knowing. "One question: was it another girl?"

Mal hesitated, then sighed. "Yeah. Flame from his past."

"Did you know?"

She shook her head, clamping her lips together. "We never talked about past relationships."

"Really?"

"It was only a week," Mal reminded her, the words hitching in her chest. "That's not enough time for anything important."

Taryn gave her an odd look, serene and sad. "I guess not. Have fun at lunch. Bring back breadsticks. I need you to help me with the saturation of the fashion shots before I send those off."

Mal nodded, smiled, and left the studio with a wave at Ashley. Walking the streets of Denver by herself, Mal let herself cry, as she did several times a week when her guard was down. Never sobbing anymore, just sad tears that gently flowed like streams of misery down her cheeks.

How could something not real hurt this much?

Her phone buzzed, and she looked at it.

Hunter.

Wednesday at noon—right on time. Sometimes, she let it ring, wanting him to think she just didn't have her phone nearby and missed the call. Not today. She hit the ignore button and turned her phone off. She wiped her cheeks, forcing a smile on her face as she headed for the restaurant to meet her family.

Hunter sighed and set his phone down on the desk, rubbing his forehead. He knew she was ducking his calls, but this was the first time it had gone to voicemail that fast. Today must be a bad day.

He glanced over at the picture on his desk, as he did multiple times a day. Tom sent it to him after Mal sent them the proofs from the wedding, so it wasn't retouched or anything. It was from the first sunrise shoot, one of the few he'd taken after Mal had tossed him the camera, and it was of her, laughing and standing in the water with the sun behind her.

He was fairly positive Mal had no idea it had been in the proofs. She would never have sent that one on. Taryn or Dan had probably tossed it in, and he was beyond grateful they had. It was in black and white, which seemed to make it that much more special to him.

That was his girl.

His heart ached for a moment, and he leaned back in his chair, rubbing his chest absently. Not a single word from her since the reception, and no one else could tell him anything, either. He'd tried calling every mutual acquaintance, and then her assistants, but they were unfailingly loyal to Mal, much to their credit, and he never got anywhere.

Tom had told him about Jenna's visit with her, and she said Mal looked well—a little skinny, and tired, but she was getting more clients, apparently. That was good; he wanted her to be busy. He wanted her to have work. He wanted…

Well, he wanted her, but that seemed to be more and more of an impossibility with every passing day.

He hoped that with time, she would mellow out of whatever had her so upset, and they would at least be able to talk. He had no idea what he had done to make her hate him suddenly, which made fixing it impossible, and that drove him crazy. He'd priced airfares to Denver more times than he would ever admit, but he knew that wouldn't help anything.

This wasn't a romantic comedy film where the guy chases after the girl and an explanation is put out there, followed by a rekindling of love and a happily ever after. He wished it was that simple. But Mal wasn't a grand gestures kind of girl, and she wasn't a dreamy-eyed romantic. She was a realist and stubborn to the core. If he'd done something to shake her, it would take a lot of time for her to reconsider letting him back in.

It had taken a full week of being with her almost every waking minute of the day for her to admit that she loved him, without technically doing so. A wild and intense week, sure, where they were some of the very few sane people. They stuck together for survival, and his determination and her ambition had seen to it that it continued. He didn't have time and resources like that in the real world. She wasn't under contract with his resort anymore, which was what had forced her to put up with him from the start.

Without that, he had nothing.

He'd told her he loved her so often he'd worn it out. He didn't even say it anymore; there was no use. He'd stopped texting her, and now called only twice a week, just to see if things had changed.

It was time to stop.

He closed his eyes and chewed the inside of his cheek. He'd never been so disappointed to get mail in his life as when the lawyers brought him the disc of pictures from her. Mindlessly, he'd gone through and picked out some for specific purposes and asked the resort manager to order the sizes they needed for placement, then sent the others off to advertising. He didn't know what he'd expected from her when this was done.

He hadn't really expected anything. How could he when expectations weren't getting him anywhere?

The money was hers, and her name was getting out there, which was what he wanted. He made sure his associates with vacation properties and resorts were sent the details of her work, as they always shared good business opportunities with each other. And so far, no one had called him back.

He needed to be careful with his recommendations. If Mal hated him now, for whatever reason, she might not want his connections. And she would really hate being given contracts like it was Christmas.

She wanted to earn them on her own merit, for her work to speak for itself. And he wanted that for her, too. She had worked too hard to be handed things, and she had too much talent for that.

All he needed to do was ensure that her name got around in the right circles. Envy and need would do the rest.

His phone rang, and he answered it. "Hello?"

"Boss man."

His brow furrowed, and he looked at the screen, his eyes going wide at the name. "Dan? How did you get my number?"

"You called me last week, dude."

Hunter barely avoided slapping himself in the head. "Right. And you guys all have my numbers programmed into your phone, right? To avoid them? Probably under a code name?"

"Correct, sir."

"What's the code name?" he asked with a wince, not sure he wanted to know.

"Depends on the person. I can't vouch for anyone else, but in my phone… Red October."

He almost smiled. "I'm a Russian sub?"

"It's ironic. You're trying to defect, and the US isn't communicating with you or going to believe you. And nobody's really sure if they're supposed to help you or blow you up."

Hunter raised a brow and smiled slightly. "That is ironic. Who are you in this scenario?"

"Alec Baldwin."

"You're on my side?" he asked in surprise, jerking in his chair a little.

"Could be. Just hoping I'm not wrong about you, honestly."

"I can handle that," he said with a nod, his tension abating slightly. "And who is Taryn?"

"James Earl Jones." Dan laughed, his voice crackling on static. "She's the higher-up running the show, but she was never here."

"You guys are nuts," Hunter told him, leaning forward and resting his head in one hand.

"Do you want allies or not?"

"Yes."

"Okay, then. I have no idea what the story is. She's not talking, and I'm not asking. She's got this deal coming with Yellowstone for the fall that should set her up nicely. She went to Maine over the weekend and got some nice shots, decided she's going to get way more specific in her terms and the use of whatever she gets."

Hunter nodded, smiling wider. "Smart girl. She's earned her place at that table. Why not use it?"

"Exactly. We've got a lawyer now for the particulars, some ex-boyfriend of hers."

Hunter stiffened and sat up. "What was that?"

"Calm down, boss man. He's married to her college roommate. Mal introduced them, so he owes her for life—not a big deal."

He sat back with a groan of despair and relief, rubbing a hand over his face. "Sorry, it's not my business anyway. I'm just going crazy over here."

"Uh-huh. Anyway, we figured you know people that could get her what she needs contract-wise, stuff that will really interest her."

"You figured right," he said, leaning his head back and looking at the ceiling. "What do you need me to do?"

Again, the line crackled, louder and longer.

"Dan?" Hunter prodded. "Did I lose you?"

"Sorry, I'm coming back from a shoot, and there's a lot of dead zones in the canyon. We're going to send you some pictures we think make a good addition to her existing portfolio. You still have your copy from the negotiations?"

Hunter turned his chair to the bookshelf behind him and pulled the file out. "Yeah, right here."

"Great, so we'll send you stuff, and you get it out there, okay?"

Hunter felt more at ease than he had in weeks, and although it wasn't good by any stretch of his imagination, it was better. "Okay."

"And don't go crazy about it, right? You know how Mal is. People need to want to want her. Your name can't come up at all."

Hunter snorted and pinched the bridge of his nose. "Yeah, I know that, Dan. I'd already figured that out myself."

"Right, right, that's why you're the boss man. Okay, one question, because Taryn will shoot me in the face if I don't bring back some gossip."

Hunter looked at his phone in disbelief, then shook his head.

"I'm afraid to say yes, but go ahead."

"Are you dating anyone?"

Was that supposed to be a sign for him? A hint? Were they digging for clues or doing reconnaissance for Mal? He exhaled slowly, willing to take a leap of faith. "No," he said softly. "No, I am not. Now a question for you, Mr. Brogada."

"Shoot."

He exhaled again briefly. "Do I have a chance?"

Dan was smart enough not to ask what he was talking about. "If the amount of ice cream in our freezer at the studio is any indication, I'm gonna say yeah. That and the fact that we've started listening to jazz now. I think you're good, man. Give it time. We just barely got her back to drinking cocoa again."

Hunter closed his eyes and forced a swallow that actually hurt. "She stopped?"

"Man, girls and their heartbreak is all kinds of messed up. I could write a book, but I'd wind up dead. She's getting there, I promise. We're looking out for her, and the more she works, the better she gets."

"Let's get her some projects she can really sink her teeth into," Hunter suggested with a harsh clearing of his throat.

"That's the plan. Okay, gotta get off before the spies see me talking to you crazy Russians. I'll be in touch." Dan didn't wait for him to say anything else and hung up.

Hunter propped his elbows on the desk and folded his hands in front of his mouth, losing himself in thought and memories. He could give Mal time and space, as much as she needed, but how long would it take? How much could he take?

But as long as those closest to Mal thought there was a chance, he would continue to hope.

His office phone rang, and he answered it after a moment. "McIntyre... Travis, hey, thanks for calling me back. Two questions: Does your brother-in-law still play poker with a VP of the USO, and do you still have your British Columbia properties?"

Chapter Eighteen

Another two weeks later.

"England? Like Prince William England?"

Dan rolled his eyes and snorted. "He's married, Taryn. And a father."

"Yeah, and I'm obsessed with his wife. So what?" She turned back to Mal with an excited current visibly running through her. "When?"

Mal smiled and put her pen behind her ear. "Not for a few months. We're still in the planning stages, but I'll definitely be out there for Remembrance Day in November. Poems about Flanders Fields, poppies, the whole bit."

Taryn gawked, her eyes as wide as her mouth. "I thought you were just doing the project for the USO!"

"So did I. But someone told someone, and I got a call from London about doing the same thing for them. We're all feeling patriotic lately, I guess."

"Unbelievable," Taryn breathed. She sank into a chair, then leaned forward. "Will you see Prince Harry?"

"I thought you wanted Prince William." Dan laughed from his desk.

"I'll take what I can get," Taryn snapped, not looking at him.

Mal grinned and shook her head. "I have no idea. Like I said, still in the planning stages."

"This is going to be huge, Mal," Dan told her, growing serious and sitting up straighter. "Like massively huge."

She couldn't hide the glee she'd been feeling for the last week and a half. "I know. And it's going to be awesome."

"How'd you even get USO anyway?" Taryn asked, reaching for her open Tupperware of veggies and crunching on a carrot stick.

Mal thought back, trying to remember the details. "The call I got from the guy with Canadian properties after he saw the Lake Lure stuff? He knows someone in the USO, and they mentioned a project they were trying to get off the ground and he mentioned me. They liked the portfolio, and we had a video meeting to discuss their vision and what I could do. Honestly, it came together so easily, I thought something was up at first, like maybe Jenna or Tom had flagged them down."

Dan looked surprised and laced his hands behind his head. "Really?"

She nodded, brushing cracker crumbs off her jeans. "But then they started talking about my Rustic Americana project and specific shots there and details about some Lake Lure shots, and I settled a bit. Even if someone did point a finger at me, they like what they see, so who am I to complain?"

"Seriously." Taryn sighed, now munching on celery. "Can I come to England?"

Mal smirked and spun back to her computer screen. "We'll see. If Dr. Durango doesn't mind you guys missing class, we'll talk."

"He won't mind," they said together.

She snorted and went back to editing her Maine shots. It was easy work, but she'd really enjoyed that trip. She made a mental note to visit Maine in every season just to experience it.

With a trip to Canada in August, England in November, and scattered trips across the US in between, she was going to be working nonstop until Christmas. It was going to be a grind, but she could not have been more excited about it. She was getting paid to do the projects she wanted to do, which was all she had ever wanted. She still did some of the smaller jobs on the side to keep those skills from rusting, but big projects on the horizon made everything better.

Reed Summerfield emailed every week with pitches, trying to convert her to some Hollywood stuff, and so far, she'd managed to put him off. He didn't seem to mind, but his ideas were getting better and better. He never said anything that could be construed as flirtatious or suggestive. For Hollywood's biggest playboy, he was surprisingly focused on business with her. And that was almost as tempting as his ideas. But she always said no, though she didn't know why.

"What did Jenna want yesterday?" Taryn asked as she flipped through the latest *People* magazine, swirling her chair slightly so it squeaked.

"A favor," Mal replied with a hint of a smile. "They're having a charity gala for kids with cancer in Chicago in a week and change, and the photographer they hired backed out."

The squeaking stopped, and Mal looked over to see Taryn watching her with a raised brow, her lips twisting.

"What?" Mal asked.

Taryn narrowed her boldly shadowed eyes. "You don't do stuff like that."

Mal shrugged, her cheeks reddening. "Yeah, but it's Jenna. And it's Chicago. And it's for charity, so…"

"Black tie?"

"Yep."

"What are you wearing?"

Mal burst out laughing and shook her head, going back to her computer. "White blouse and pencil skirt. I'm working, not a guest. There's no Designer Day in real life."

"But you got to keep those dresses!"

"No."

Taryn made a noise of disgust. "You're no fun. At least wear some sexy shoes."

"We'll see."

Ashley's voice broke in. "I'm sorry, Miss Hudson?"

Mal sighed and turned to face the girl in the doorway. "Ashley, what did I tell you to call me?"

Ashley's face flushed, and she smiled, tucking a strand of strawberry blonde hair behind her ear. "Sorry. Mal. There's a client for you."

"More fun?" Dan asked with a flash of his grin, chewing on a coffee straw. "Please say we're going somewhere cool."

"Shut up!" Taryn hissed, flipping his hat off his head. "Best behavior unless you don't want to go to England."

Dan glared at her and took the straw out of his mouth. "Just for that, I'm not buying you dinner tonight."

Taryn stuck her tongue out at him, but Mal caught the wink, too. So, they were still together. Interesting. They never discussed it, and as long as the workplace was semi-professional, she really didn't care.

Mal turned back to Ashley, who looked as confused by them as ever. "Who is it? Did they say?"

Ashley looked down at the notepad in her hand. "Audrey McIntyre."

There wasn't a sound in the room. No chair squeaked, no one breathed, and even the fridge in the back stopped humming.

Mal swallowed with difficulty. "Take a message."

Ashley winced and tugged at her denim skirt. "Um, I can't. She's here… like, out front."

If utter silence could go more silent, it did then.

Mal inhaled, exhaled, and leaned back slightly in her chair. She could do this. She'd thought long and hard about Lake Lure and what had happened there, and she'd been wrong before. She wasn't dumb enough, or open enough, to get played like that. It had to have been real—just not real enough.

Whatever hurt he'd caused her, Hunter McIntyre was a good man and wouldn't have jerked her around just for fun. She could claim that all she wanted, but it was a lie. She had been hurt, incredibly so, but the hurt was fading. Reality and acceptance was setting in. He hadn't meant to hurt her; he'd just done what she had expected all along. He'd gone with what fit and where he belonged. And she really couldn't blame him for that.

It still hurt, and she still cried sometimes, but it was okay. She could still remember the details, letting the faint echo of the emotions of them come out, and not hate him. In all honesty, she would never be able to hate him.

Besides, he'd stopped calling altogether now. It was really over. She could move on.

"Mal," Taryn murmured softly, but Mal shook her head and held out a hand.

"Did she say what she wanted?" Mal asked, keeping her voice

level.

Poor Ashley had no idea what was going on and was suddenly nervous. "Um, she had some questions and concerns about the Rambling Ridge Resort pictures."

Ah, so Audrey had a stake in the company too. That made sense. This was business. Business she could handle.

Mal nodded and gave a faint smile. "Okay. Tell her I'll be right out."

Ashley sagged in relief and left the room.

Slowly, Mal got out of her chair and went over to the new mirror in the bathroom. She looked fairly professional today—dark-wash jeans, white tank, and a pale pink shrug, minimal jewelry, decent job on the makeup. Hair was pulled back in a loose, messy bun, but it looked clean enough. She was a photographer, not a CEO. Besides, there was no need to worry about what Audrey McIntyre thought of her.

Right?

She exhaled a short breath, walked back into the office space, avoided looking at Taryn and Dan, both of whom said her name, and headed up to the front of the studio, heart pounding against her ribs.

Audrey McIntyre, as perfect as she had been in photos, sat in one of the waiting chairs, looking out the window, lean legs crossed, gray heels bouncing slightly. She wore a heather gray knee-length dress, Ralph Lauren from the looks of it, and it fit her perfectly. One leg bore a faint but extensive scar that went behind her knee, and Mal's throat caught at the sight.

She wasn't hiding it. She didn't think she needed to.

And she didn't.

"Miss McIntyre," Mal said with a smile, coming more fully into the room.

Audrey turned and grinned, her blue eyes sparkling. "Miss Hudson." She stood and reached out a hand. "It is a pleasure to meet you."

"Call me Mal, please," Mal told her, taking her hand.

Again with the perfect smile. "Then call me Audrey."

Mal nodded, even as her stomach clenched. "Audrey, then. Please sit."

"Actually," Audrey said hesitantly, "would you mind if we went out to talk? I'm starving, and that deli across the street looks really good."

That was an unusual request, but Mal wouldn't insult her by saying no. "Sure, let me grab my purse."

"Don't worry about that," Audrey said with a flick of her hand. "I'll cover you. It's the least I can do."

Mal's arm hairs stood on end. "For what?" she asked, trying not to let the strain of her voice show.

Audrey gave her a look. "One, for agreeing we meet there so I can stuff my face. Two, you had to endure a contract at Lake Lure with my brother calling the shots. I'm fairly certain I owe you lunch, at least."

Mal exhaled in relief, wondering how much of that showed. She forced a light laugh. "Well, if you insist…"

They made their way across the street to the deli, placed their orders, and sat at a table outside.

"I hope this is good," Audrey said as she sat, adjusting the loose cap sleeves of her dress. "But I'd still eat it if it wasn't. I'm famished."

Mal smiled and wondered how Audrey could be so open and easy when her brother wasn't. "It is good," she assured her. "You'll like it. Okay, so you wanted to talk about the Lake Lure pictures?"

Audrey sat up. "Yes. First of all, I saw the proofs, and they were fantastic. I mean, you really got the feel of the place. You can see why it means so much to us, right?"

Mal nodded, smiling at the memories. "I can. Your brother told me a little about your family's history there, and he knew all the best places for me to get shots."

Audrey grinned and ran her fingers through her hair. "Yeah, Hunter's obsessed with it. But since it will keep the resort running just as it is, we let him go crazy there, and he's really good at it."

There really didn't seem to be a need to answer that, so Mal just smiled tightly.

"I did have one thing I need to ask you," Audrey said, turning serious.

A thousand and three warning alarms went off in Mal's head. She forced her face to relax and crossed her ankles. "Oh?"

Audrey nodded once. "All the pictures I saw were of nature and the views and the houses, which are fantastic for the resort, and I'm hanging some in my house." She made a face, as if she wasn't sure if she could actually ask the question. "Do you happen to have any with Hunter in them?"

Mal had chosen that moment to take a drink of her lemonade and subsequently choked. "I'm sorry?" she coughed.

Audrey pressed a hand to her forehead and winced. "I'm sorry. That came out wrong. What I mean is, I am trying to think of what to get him for his birthday in September, and I thought if there were any pictures from your shoot where he's in his favorite place in the world, he might really like that." She gave Mal a desperate, apologetic look. "I am hopeless when it comes to getting him presents and…"

"I'll see what I have," Mal overrode, still coughing.

Audrey smiled. "Thanks." She straightened up even more and said, "Also, I had a concern about the…" She stopped and suddenly slumped back in her chair. "Hang it, I'm done pretending. I didn't come here about the resort photos, although it's not a bad idea to get a picture with Hunter, assuming he sat still long enough for one."

Mal raised her brows in surprise and sat back herself. "You're not?"

Audrey shook her head quickly with a snort. "I have absolutely nothing to do with that place from the business side of things. I think I still have a few shares, but that's an inheritance thing and a technicality at best."

Mal ought to have been upset or concerned or at the very least wary, but instead she felt amused—and a little confused.

"I'm in Seattle," Audrey continued, taking a sip of her water, "and I'm heading down to Florida to spend some time with some girlfriends—adult spring break, if you will. I know, we're nuts, but it is what it is. I had to layover in Denver, and when I heard that, I changed my next flight back a few hours so I could come out and see you."

"Me?" Mal asked in surprise, folding her arms. "Why?"

Audrey shrugged, smiling. "I wasn't kidding when I said I saw the proofs. Those were amazing. Hunter said you were great to work with and would go places in the world, and Hunter never praises anybody. He doesn't even like people, really."

Mal laughed out loud at that. She knew that about Hunter; it was his trademark. It was nice to know he wasn't playing at that, either.

"You wanted to come see if he was lying?" Mal asked, truly smiling at this intriguing woman.

Audrey grinned at her. "Well, Hunter's not really a liar either, Christmas and birthday presents being the exception. Mostly, I just wanted to meet you. I like art, majored in art history, and I'm sort of a curator for various exhibitions in Seattle, so any good connections I can make, I do!"

Mal was shaking her head, unable to stop smiling. "You're trying to soften me up for something, aren't you?"

"Maybe," she said with a shrug. "If my cousin and I happen to have a project for capturing the history and quintessential essence of Seattle through photography, so what?"

Mal threw her head back and laughed, rubbing a hand over her face. "Seriously?"

"Hypothetically," Audrey corrected. "And it could potentially, hypothetically, involve some great food places. If you're a foodie like I am."

With perfect timing, their food arrived, and Audrey's eyes went wide as her sandwich was placed before her.

Mal thanked the waiter, then looked at her companion. "What?" she asked, seeing her expression.

Audrey met her eyes, still looking stunned. "You didn't tell me it was this huge!"

"I did too. I told you to get a half sandwich, but you insisted you were starving."

"I'm gonna die." She took a bite of the sandwich and moaned as she chewed. "Oh, but what a way to go."

"You did what?"

"I went to Denver before I came here. There aren't direct flights from Seattle to Atlanta."

Hunter shoved the heels of his hands against the side of his head and turned to the window, inhaling and exhaling at a frantic pace he tried to control. "That part I got," he ground out, his jaw aching. "Explain yourself."

"Oh," his sister said, as if she didn't know. "I stopped off and had lunch with Mal. I like her a lot. You didn't tell me nearly enough about her."

"Shasta," he hissed, his hands turning into fists.

"What did you say?"

He stopped, squeezed his eyes shut, and sighed. "Nothing."

"No, I heard you. You said 'shasta.' That's not even a word."

"I know."

There was a long pause and then, "I heard Mal say that."

"What?"

"She dropped mustard on her pants at lunch and said that. She said she makes up swear words all the time instead of actually swearing. It was the funniest thing I'd ever heard."

The ache in his chest intensified while the tension in his limbs softened. He cleared his throat and tried to find his gruff persona again. "Why would you stop off and meet with the photographer from the Lake Lure project?" he asked, folding his arms tightly.

Audrey snorted loudly.

He glanced at her and saw her sitting on his couch and kicking her heels off. "What was that for?"

Audrey gave him a look of sheer and utter disbelief. "If you expect me to believe that is all she is to you, then you, dear brother, are a moron of the highest caliber."

He opened his mouth, then closed it. "I never said that was all she was to me," he muttered, leaning against his desk. "But right now, that is all she is."

His sister sighed and tucked her legs under her. "Hunter, you're trying your best to hide everything emotional, and I get it, it makes you vulnerable, but it's me. I heard it in your voice, all the way in Seattle. You love her."

He sighed and unfolded his arms. "Yes."

"So why are you here and she's there?" Audrey asked, leaning her elbow on the armrest. "What happened?"

He shrugged, shaking his head. "I have no idea. I must have done something, but I've been over it thousands of times… I don't know."

Audrey hummed and threaded her fingers through her hair. "You should have seen her jump when I said your name."

"What?" he cried, all systems on the alert again. "Why would you do that?"

His sister's trademark mischievous smile lit her face. "Oh, come on, I had to try it. And it worked. I think I covered it well, though."

"Why would you put her through that?" he barked. "What is wrong with you, Audrey?"

A look that was a little too like their mother's for his comfort flashed in his direction. "Oh, stop. Like I intentionally went to Denver to torment the one who got away from you. I'm not entirely heartless, just a bit defensive of my brother."

"What did you do, Audrey?" he asked her, suddenly exhausted.

"I went to her studio and said I wanted to discuss the Lake Lure project and turned it into lunch." She shrugged unapologetically. "But then I liked her too much to pretend, so I gave it up and talked about Seattle with her. I think I might have convinced her to come do a project for Abby and me, if we ever get it off the ground."

He was surprised by that. "Abby's in on it?"

Audrey gave him a look. "Our little cousin is quite the talented writer, brother dear, if you haven't noticed. I wanted her in on it, and it's not that far for her to come. It's the only way she lets me fly her in and out."

He grunted but said nothing further. Abby was the daughter of his mother's only sister, and she was as stubborn and independent as everyone else he was related to. Despite her impressive skillset, she was holed up in some little town in Oregon, barely making ends meet doing freelance writing and working at a library. They'd offered to help her out financially, but she adamantly refused every attempt.

"Are we still paying the bills for her aunt?" he asked quietly.

She nodded. "Yep. Her dear Aunt June will get everything she needs, and the money Abby thinks she's paying for bills goes right into the trust for her. And the house is covered. I put that money into a fund strictly for repairs and upkeep."

Hunter nodded once. Abby could refuse and be as independent and stubborn as she wanted, but Hunter and Audrey were more stubborn and even more interfering. And she could deal with it.

"And she wants in on your project?" he asked, still dubious.

Audrey tilted her head. "Are we talking about Abby or Mal now?"

Hunter gave her a hard look. His sister was poking at him, and he did not like being poked.

"Abby's all the way in," Audrey said with a roll of her eyes and a sigh. "Very excited and really wants to meet Mal." She smirked at him, then let it fade. "Mal seems pretty game, but she needs more details. We talked about it for quite a while, and she's got some great ideas. She's impressive, Hunter—professionally and personally."

He swallowed with some difficulty. "And then?"

She grinned up at him. "Then we talked about food, and she persuaded me to move to Denver if Seattle gets too old. We talked about all the best places to eat, the best dishes, and some shows on Food Network."

Against his will, he returned her grin, his heart warming just thinking about the conversation between his sister and Mal. "You like her," he said simply.

"I told you I did," Audrey reminded him, gesturing as if he were stupid.

He smirked at her and nudged her knee with his foot. "Yeah, but you mean it."

She tipped her head slightly, her smile growing fond. "Yeah, I mean it. I like her, Hunter. I don't understand why you've hung around Atlanta when you could go to Denver and get her."

He sighed and pushed off the desk to sit beside her on the couch. "It's complicated. She left without a word to me, and I haven't talked to her in four weeks. I've tried, but she won't answer or respond. I can't go invade her personal space. She would hate that."

"I think hate might be too strong a word," Audrey mused, making a face.

He gave her a look. "Don't get my hopes up, kid. I've done what I can to get her name out there so she has work, and I have some allies in her office that keep me updated every now and then. I think, if enough time has done the trick, maybe someday she'll talk to me again. Then I can get somewhere. Or get closure. Whichever."

"Oh, buddy." Audrey sighed heavily, putting a hand on his back and rubbing softly. "You are one tormented soul."

He snorted and raised a brow at her. "Didn't you say I needed to learn to be more patient?"

"I did," she allowed, patting his back. "You are also intense, so you might want to work on that."

He smiled softly but didn't answer that. He'd heard about his intensity, and it had been a source of pride for him. He liked that he was intense and could get somewhere with it. He'd never considered that it might be a negative, that there could be a downside to it. Was his intensity the reason it was taking Mal so long to forgive him?

Would she forget him instead?

"What did she say when you told her you were coming to see me?" he asked softly.

"Oh, I didn't tell her that." Audrey laughed, shaking her head. "No way."

He turned to look at her more fully. "What did you tell her?"

"The truth. That I was going to Florida to see some girlfriends and go to the beach. I had a layover in Denver and changed my flight to see her." She gave him her impish grin again. "I just left out the part where I was stopping to see you for a few days first."

Hunter grinned, wanting to laugh at the irony. "You were never dishonest," he said softly, an echo of former days rushing through his mind.

"Nope. Just not completely forthcoming."

"Semantics."

She shoved at his back with a laugh. "You are such a dork."

He pulled his sister in for a hug, and she leaned her head against his shoulder. "How did she look?" he finally asked, almost holding his breath.

Audrey looked up at him, her eyes searching his for a moment. "Good. She looked good. And I think… I think you might be able to get her back. She wouldn't have agreed to see me if she hated you, right?"

He hugged his sister tighter. "I don't know, Audrey. I just don't know."

Chapter Nineteen

A week and change later.

The Hancock building was one place Mal could honestly say she'd never been before, and it seemed a shame at this moment. They were at the top of the building in the new 360 Chicago, and the surrounding Chicago skyline and scenery were breathtaking in the fading light of sunset. What was once glorious transformed into something magical when the night came and the city lights were all aglow. She'd never been that much of a city girl, but that view might have convinced her.

She came early, as arranged, to get a fair number of pictures before the guests arrived and the room became overcrowded, and it was a good thing she did. There was so much to see and take in that she barely got it done before the guests had arrived. It would be impossible to get it all, but she could try.

The room was gorgeous with its view alone, but the decorations tonight set it at a completely different level. The lights were tinged gold, and all the table decorations and place settings were golden themed, in honor of pediatric cancer awareness. Elegant and tasteful floral arrangements were scattered about the room and on tables, and the whole place seemed to sparkle.

Jenna and Tom greeted her at once, looking just as blissful and happy as the day they got married. Jenna was a vision in a royal blue mermaid gown with a sweetheart bodice covered with a sheer and elaborately detailed neckline and cap sleeves. With her hair in a loose chignon and gold details and jewelry, she looked like a vibrant goddess or queen of some spectacular and imaginary kingdom far, far away. Mal told her as much.

Jenna laughed, kissed her cheek, and then winked. "Not entirely a goddess, sweetie," she murmured and then turned to show her that the gown was backless. On some people, it would probably have been shocking, but on Jenna, it was perfect. She kept herself so fit that it almost made sense for her to show off her back.

Mal smiled and shook her head. "This is amazing," she said gesturing to the room around them.

Jenna's smile would have lit the room on its own. "I'm so excited. I can't believe how well it turned out. The room only sits about a hundred comfortably, so we had a donation battle, and only those who donated the most could come. It's barbaric, I know, but everyone else is coming to a much bigger event at the Field Museum in a month. Come to that one too, won't you?"

Mal grinned, which made Jenna take her hand and give her a teasing look.

"Come on, Mal," she drawled playfully. "You know you want to."

She laughed and gave her cousin a look. "Of course, I want to, Jenna. Let me know the dates and times, and I'll check. I'm supposed to go to British Columbia next month to work a resort shoot."

Jenna raised a brow slowly. "Travis Bradford's place?"

Mal nodded, surprised. "How'd you know?"

"He's the biggest name there. Gorgeous resort. You'll love it. If there's a conflict, let me know. Travis owes Tom a favor. We can switch him around if we need to."

"Does everybody do what you want?" Mal asked her cousin with a laugh.

"Pretty much," Tom said, appearing at Jenna's side, looking dapper in a classic black tux. He kissed Jenna's cheek, then did the same with Mal. "Hi, Mal. You look great!"

Mal laughed and looked down at herself briefly. She hadn't been kidding when she'd told Taryn what she'd wear—white blouse, high waist black pencil skirt, with a simply detailed ribbon belt at the top for emphasis, and her hair done up in a French twist, with diamond stud earrings and a silver heart necklace. Simple, elegant, but ultimately, professional.

Particularly with the camera around her neck.

"Thanks, Tom," she said with a wry grin. "Not quite black tie, but I'm working."

Tom winked at her. "You look fantastic. And if you'll look around the room, you'll see that you look better than most of the women here. And with those shoes, kiddo, you're almost average height!"

Mal rolled her eyes and looked to the ceiling but smiled all the same.

"You're wearing the Christian Louboutins!" Jenna squealed, turning Mal to see them better.

"Of course," Mal said simply. "I have nowhere else to wear them, and they matched."

Jenna gave her a look. "They're black pumps, Mallory. They match just about everything." She looked down at the shoes again. "I love those on you."

"They were a very generous gift, Jenna," Mal said, taking her hand again. "Particularly when I wasn't in the wedding party."

Jenna waved that off. "You're my favorite; that means you get the presents too. I don't care what the other girls said about your choice. I firmly believe every woman needs a sexy pair of black pumps. They do amazing things for your legs, and they are always in style."

Mal smiled and sighed as more people filtered in. "I guess you guys better get to it. Host and hostess, after all."

Jenna wrinkled her nose up. "Guess so. I hope this works, you know? I want to make a difference here. After Emily…" Her throat worked, and she looked up at the ceiling to blink the tears away.

Mal squeezed her hand tightly. "I know," she murmured, remembering their second cousin, who'd been more of a sister to them both and a best friend in childhood. "I was just thinking about her. I thought about that fantastic children's choir at her funeral service, remember?"

Jenna smiled broadly. "Such cute kids. I think they still have that choir down in Memphis." Her eyes suddenly brightened, and she turned to Tom. "Can we get them for the event next month at the museum? That would be amazing!"

Tom sighed and took Jenna's arm. "We'll talk about it, babe. Let's do this one first, okay?" He looked back at Mal. "Brunch tomorrow, Mal. No excuses, no exceptions. We'll call you."

She smiled and waved as they left, then went back to her job.

A small group of musicians in one corner of the room started playing, and Mal's heart leaped to her throat as they started playing light jazz. She listened to jazz almost all the time now, but hearing it live was something else entirely.

She swallowed hard and captured what she could of the evening. The guests, the food, the decorations, the musicians—everything all wrapped together. Faintly, it occurred to her to wonder how much money was in this room with her, and that made her smile. A few couples started dancing near the musicians, and Mal moved in that direction to take pictures of them.

Jenna and Tom worked the room expertly, making it a point to speak to everyone, which wasn't hard, as everyone wanted to speak to them. They had grown even more popular after their wedding than they had been before, which was quite an accomplishment. True to form, they smiled and laughed the entire time, took a brief break in socializing to dance, and were never more than ten feet from each other all evening.

If anybody thought their marriage was all for show and publicity, they wouldn't think so if they saw them tonight. It was almost too intimate to watch, and Mal's throat burned at the sight. She ventured out onto the stretch out of the building, and the night air felt wonderfully cool against her flushed skin. From inside, she could hear the jazz ensemble start playing "It Never Entered My Mind," and she leaned her head back, closing her eyes as she remembered that dance. Had she ever felt that beautiful or loved?

No, of course she hadn't.

No one had ever made her feel what Hunter had.

She inhaled slowly, letting the fresh air fill her, and then went back inside, professional face on once more. Jenna and Tom introduced her to a number of people, never once bringing up their relationship, but overflowing with praise and reference. She collected so many cards and promises to call that she couldn't remember half of them. At this rate, next year would fill up quickly, too.

For all her pride at wanting to make it on her own, there were some doors she wouldn't be able to get through without help from her family and their connections.

As the evening wore on, Mal grew more and more tired, the glow of the evening fading as she found herself missing someone who belonged here, who probably ought to have been here…

Someone who just might have forgotten her, thanks to her pride.

Insecurity was a crippling weakness, and stubbornness made recovering from it excruciating.

Maybe she should have called him back, just once. Maybe, if he were still calling her, she would have answered this time. If she still felt this way, maybe he—

She shook her head quickly, forcing the thought out. There was no use in maybes and what ifs. What was done was done, and she was going to have to live with her stupidity.

She got Jenna and Tom's attention and signaled she was leaving, which earned her a wave and a blown kiss. She got her bag and coat from the bag check, situated her camera snugly, and started the long elevator ride down. She was staying at a hotel nearby, and she would have brunch with Tom and Jenna in the morning, get the details of their next event, and then head back to Denver.

There was a lot of work to do, and more to come. Life was good… or something.

She pushed open the door of the Hancock building, just as a breeze came through, courtesy of the Windy City's tricks, and she smiled to herself as that troublesome lock of hair dislodged itself again. She tucked it back, readjusted her coat on her arm, and started toward the street to get a cab.

She looked up and stopped dead in her tracks.

A cab was already in front of the building, but that wasn't what stopped her.

It was the man leaning against the cab.

Hunter.

In a formal black tux, collar open, tie undone. He stared at her hungrily, as if she were dessert.

"Hunter," she gasped, losing sensation in her lower extremities. She swallowed and tried to remember how to breathe. "What are you doing here?"

"Waiting for you."

She almost threw herself at him right then and there, but there seemed to be a miscommunication between her brain and what used to be her legs. Hunter had that effect on her. He would always have that effect on her.

His voice, that low, almost rough timbre that had once scorched her lungs, set them aflame again. His eyes never moved from her face, and even with his casual pose against the cab, she could see a coiled tension that set her on edge.

She swallowed several times. "You're wearing a tux," she managed, blurting it out stupidly.

He nodded slowly. "Yep."

"You hate tuxes," she murmured, more controlled this time.

Again came the nod. "Yep."

She smiled, the familiarity so natural, and his difficulty with taking bait entertaining. "Why are you wearing a tux?" she asked automatically.

"Oh, I've just been to a gala," he said as if this were just a simple conversation.

Mal's breath caught. "You hate galas."

There was a slight tilt to his head as he heard that catch, and somehow, his gaze was more intense. "Yep. But I heard the photographer was amazing, and I had to come and see for myself. It was a black-tie thing, so…"

He'd been here. The whole time. She'd gone over the entire room. How could she have missed him?

He'd come for her. He wanted to see her.

"You look good," she murmured, looking him over briefly, though she would much rather have spent a long time doing it.

He shook his head slightly, and something about his expression made her hurt. "Not as good as you."

"Please," she protested, snorting softly. "I'm a mess." As if to emphasize that, her bangs dislodged again, and she shoved them back quickly.

"You're beautiful," Hunter said at once, his tone and eyes warm, and a quiet sigh escaped him. "I've missed you."

Mal looked at him for a long moment, drinking in the sight of him, letting the warmth race through her. "I've missed you, too," she whispered.

He shifted his weight, still leaning against the cab, that tightness in his body more pronounced. "Then why don't you pick up when I call?" he asked, his chest heaving. "Why are you hiding from me?"

Tears sprang to her eyes. "I thought…" she tried, her voice more of a croak. She cleared her throat. "I thought we were done."

"What in the world gave you that impression?" he demanded, shoving his hands into his pockets. "I'm not done with you. I'll never be done with you."

She staggered to the side, staring at him in shock. "What?"

"Did you not understand what I was saying at Lake Lure?" Hunter asked slowly, shaking his head again. "That I'm in love with you? That it took less than a week for me to realize that what my life was missing was you?"

Mal's tears started down her cheeks slowly. "I saw you with Emma," she managed, her tone far less accusing than she thought it would be when she said these words. "You hugged her and…"

"Of course I did," Hunter said, his tone gentler. "She and I have been friends since we were kids. She wanted to get back together, and I told her there would be no getting back together because I had found my one and only. She was sad, but she got it. She's fine. And I'd be fine too, if my one and only weren't doing her best to avoid me."

Mal had the most intense desire to cover her face with her hands, but she couldn't feel them. "I was scared," she admitted, swallowing back more tears and staring at him in agony. "I always knew you belonged with someone like her, and I was reaching for the stars. I knew I'd never be good enough for your world—"

"Shut up."

"What?" she hiccupped, going suddenly cold.

"Shut up," he said again. He shook his head, sighing heavily. "Don't you get it? You are my world." He swallowed, and she watched his throat work in wonder. "I love you. You are what I've always wanted, and I'm tired of trying to get you to see it. Tell me what I have to do, Mallory Hudson. Because I will do anything you say if it means I get you at the end of the day. That's all I want. Just you."

Something inside of Mal burst like the grand finale fireworks at the Fourth of July. The saxophone solo from "Baker Street" was playing in her head, and she could suddenly breathe for the first time since Lake Lure. Her lungs expanded with freedom, and she dropped her bag and coat, her feet moving at twice their usual stride to get to him.

She reached for his face and pulled his mouth to hers, nearly crying again at the relief of feeling his lips on hers. She kissed him as she had never kissed him before, with fervent abandon and reckless passion. She inhaled sharply when his arms seized around her waist and lifted her against him so only her toes were touching the ground. His slow moan of satisfaction matched hers, and she broke contact briefly, running her lips along his breathlessly.

"I love you," she breathed, her lower lip grazing the skin of his chin with her words.

Suddenly, her back was against the cab, and Hunter loomed over her, pressing her back against the metal frame, his mouth a frenzy against hers. She slid one arm under his jacket while the other surged into his hair, earning her a rough growl of approval that she swallowed with delight.

He devoured her, slowly and steadily, his hands pulling at her waist and her hair, her fingers pressing into his back, tensing almost rhythmically against the taut muscle straining beneath his shirt.

There was no way of knowing how long they kissed, and she didn't care. Even the cab driver seemed perfectly content to let them go as long as they wanted. There was no hurry. They had all the time in the world, and no one was going anywhere. Eventually, the deep kisses faded into soft, breathless grazing of lips against each other and panted breaths on cheeks and throats.

"I'm so sorry, Hunter," Mal whispered, stroking his cheek and jaw gently. "I'm so sorry."

He kissed her again in response, infinitely tender, clearly in no rush to hear any apologies from her.

"The cab won't wait," Mal eventually stammered out, taking at least four breaths to manage the effort.

Hunter chuckled and nuzzled her throat. "Sure it will. I paid the driver a lot to do whatever we wanted. He's fine."

He was missing the point. Mal didn't want to stay here against the cab forever. She slid her hand from his hair to his throat and played with the open collar. "Fine," she said with a defiant stare as she met his eyes, their noses almost touching. "I won't wait."

A slow, simmering grin crossed Hunter's face. "Now that's more like it." He gave her an assessing look. "You didn't eat all night. Hungry?"

"Starving," she said bluntly, enjoying the double meaning in that.

He closed his eyes as if praying. "Mallory."

"I love you," she said again, reaching up to touch his face. "And I'd love a pizza."

He kissed her quickly, as if relieved she had stopped teasing him. "I love you, too. Pizza it is. Now, get in the cab, woman. I have a lot of time to make up for." He reached behind her, making her yelp as his surprisingly warm hand brushed her hip, and opened the door.

She slid into the seat, reaching out her hand for him. Hunter grabbed her coat and bag, shoved them into the space between the front seat and theirs, and slammed the door shut, taking her hand and lacing their fingers.

The cabbie was already grinning as he turned to look at them, thumbing his cap back. "Where to?" he asked in a not-at-all-innocent voice. "I thought I heard something about pizza, but…"

Hunter looked at Mal. She brought her finger to her mouth and ran it over her bottom lip softly. "One Mississippi…" she whispered slowly.

Hunter groaned and hauled her into his lap. "Oh, just drive around for a while. We'll figure it out later." And then his lips were on hers again, her hands clamped around the back of his head, and his latched around her hips and back.

The cabbie chuckled, pulled away from the curb, and slowly turned up the radio, his head absently moving along to the beat of Barry White as they ventured off into the Chicago night.

And apparently, there were some acceptable excuses for missing brunch the next day.

Epilogue

"Hunter! Where did you put the cereal?"

"Baby, I didn't stock the kitchen. I called ahead."

"You know how I feel about that!"

"There wasn't time, love! If you remember, I was with you the entire time you were doing the Farmlands piece for what's-his-name, and we came here together. When would I have been able to stock the kitchen?"

Mal grumbled under her breath and began opening random cabinets in the kitchen. It wasn't as though she really expected him to do his own shopping for the house when they hadn't really planned out the trip extensively. It had been a whim of his to get away, considering things had been so insane with his job and her contracts, and heading back to Lake Lure had seemed like the perfect answer.

"You did tell them to get Froot Loops, right? And not the generic kind?" she called out as she opened another cupboard.

She heard Hunter laugh. "Yes, Mallory, I did. I know better than that."

"Good," she grunted, though it really wouldn't make much difference if she couldn't actually find the cereal. Then, miraculously, it was there in front of her, though she was positive she'd already looked there.

"Whatever," she muttered, reaching for a bowl that somehow was in the same place the bowls had always been, despite the food getting changed around. She opened the cereal and poured it in, shaking her head.

"Wait." Hunter suddenly popped his head into the kitchen and gave her a wry look. "You're hungry?"

She turned and leaned against the counter, taking a handful of the dry Froot Loops. "Yeah. Why?" she asked as she tossed them in her mouth.

"Why?" Hunter repeated, chuckling and coming farther into the room, sliding his hands into his fitted jeans. "Because you were sick this morning, and on the plane too. You were green the entire way through the airport and most of the drive in."

Mal tried to raise a brow but didn't have his skill of moving one at a time. "I don't travel well."

He knew better than that, and a sly, too-attractive smile crossed his lips. "Liar. You travel amazingly well, as evidenced by the turbulence we had on the way into London last year. I can count on one hand the number of trips we've taken where you have been anything less than perfect."

She shrugged and moved to the fridge for the milk. "I was queasy last night, you know that. And today, I delivered."

Hunter blocked the fridge and smiled even more. "And now you're hungry?"

Mal looked up at him, torn between irritation, amusement, and more than a little attraction. It was the usual conflict of feelings where he was concerned, and she still hadn't fully adjusted. "Yes," she told him. "I am."

He shrugged and folded his arms. "Pay the toll."

She snorted once. "For the milk? I didn't know there was one."

"There's a toll for everything, babe. Come on." He gestured with his hand.

Mal rolled her eyes and went up on tiptoe, kissing his cheek.

He glared at her. "That wasn't what I meant."

"You weren't very specific," she said unapologetically, shrugging.

He lowered his chin, his eyes turning a dark and serious shade. "Pay a real toll, wife."

As always, the word sent a thrill down her spine that lit up her toes and made her feet curve with a ticklish tension. She went up on tiptoe again and closed the small distance between them, sliding her hands up his chest and around his neck.

"A real toll, husband?" she murmured, nudging her nose against his. "That could be anywhere from seventy-five cents to two dollars and ten cents. What exactly did you have in mind?"

His hands wrapped around her waist, one tucking into her back pocket as he nuzzled against her lips. "I'm sure you'll catch on."

"I'm usually pretty good at that," she whispered, yelping softly when his teeth grazed her jaw.

"The best," he told her, the words muffled as his lips dragged across hers.

Mal moaned without warning and pressed his lips more firmly to hers, wishing she could arch up farther still to have more of him. Hunter held her more securely, lifting her until she couldn't feel the floor beneath her at all. Not that she was paying attention to such minor details when her husband was kissing her like that. He turned her to the counter, pressing her against it as he leaned more fully into her, his kisses making Mal's head swim.

A trill of a phone going off interrupted the would-be memorable liaison, and they paused, lips touching, panting, sense nowhere in sight. The ringing continued, sounding like a phone from the sixties and twice as annoying.

Mal pulled back, stroking Hunter's neck. "Are you going to get that?"

He kept his eyes on hers, leaning forward to kiss her again. "Wait."

Wait? No way. She was going to keep kissing him, annoying ringing or not, and she kissed him back in the most encouraging way she could to let him know that. He caught on, and the ringing stopped.

And then the ringing started again.

Mal groaned and firmly put her hands on her husband's shoulders. "Go make that stop," she ordered, pushing him away.

Hunter laughed and pointed at her. "Stay there," he shot back as he moved to the phone on the counter.

"No way," she said, hopping down. "The fridge is free, and I can have cereal now."

"Mallory McIntyre," he growled as he picked up the phone.

"You get back over there by the count of five, or…"

Mal waved the milk jug at him and skipped back to her bowl of cereal.

"So much trouble," he muttered, pressing the answer button on the phone. "Hello? Audrey! Hey, you!"

Mal waved at the phone brightly, pouring the milk now, and Hunter nodded at her with a wink.

"Mal says hi." He paused. "Audrey's blowing you kisses."

"Good," Mal said, taking a big bite. "Someone should."

Hunter widened his eyes in warning, smiling in a way that spelled a fun sort of trouble for later.

"Really? That's an interesting project. You sure it's him?" Hunter didn't sound particularly pleased about whatever it was, which sent Mal's curiosity into a frenzy. She cocked her head at him.

He frowned but shook his head. "I don't like it, but it sounds like a good chance for her. Let me know, all right? We'll see you next weekend in Utah, right? Yeah, Park City. All right. Love you."

"Bye, Auds!" Mal bellowed.

Hunter sighed, shaking his head. "You got that, right? 'Kay. Bye." He tossed the phone on the counter, then looked at Mal again, smiling.

"What?" Mal asked, cradling her cereal closer.

"Have I ever told you how much I love the way you look in flannel?" he mused, his tone relatively innocent, even if the words tickled everywhere.

Mal blushed and took another bite. "Not really, no."

"I do." He slowly started around the island toward her. "I love you in flannel."

Mal swallowed before she was ready, purely out of instinct. "Just in flannel? That's good to know."

Hunter chuckled in a low, warm tone, his eyes still on her.

"Wait," Mal warned. "Wait. Cereal in hand. Lemme finish."

"Hurry," he suggested.

She pointedly took another bite, which he approved with a nod. "What did Audrey want?"

That shut him down, and his posture eased at once. "Oh. Abby's got a new gig. Believe it or not, she's going to interview Reed

Summerfield.”

Mal grinned at that. “No way, really?”

“Why does that make you happy?” he asked, his tone tense. “He’s a partier and a playboy, Hollywood royalty.”

“Yes, I know,” she replied, rolling her eyes again. “He’s also decently nice when he’s not being that, and he still emails me project pitches.”

“Does he?” Hunter growled.

Mal scolded him with a look. “Down, boy. He’s perfectly professional, even by your standards. And it would be a good op for Abby. Everyone will buy it. When is it?”

“To be determined,” Hunter said, his tone and expression returning to normal. “Reed is very busy.”

“No doubt he is.” Mal took another bite of cereal and sighed, looking out of the kitchen to the pictures on the wall.

One of their wedding pictures was front and center, and it was her favorite shot. Taryn and Dan had taken them, and though they hadn’t been her assistants anymore, they had insisted on doing it for them. Not wanting to recreate Jenna and Tom’s wedding in any way, they’d kept things small and intimate. They had married on his parents’ estate, though she was the only one who called it that.

“It’s just a house,” they all said.

The word house would refer to half of the place, but not the whole of it. Very estate-like, especially with the garden and fountain in the back. Still, it had been perfect—simple, elegant, and without any fuss—and everyone important to them had been there.

And now, just five months later…

“Mallory.”

She jerked to look at Hunter, the milk in her bowl sloshing onto her thumb. “What?”

Hunter smiled warmly. “You’re drifting. You okay?”

Mal’s stomach clenched, and she chewed on the inside of her lip for a moment.

Well, when the time was right…

She carefully set the cereal down on the counter behind her, then turned back to face Hunter, folding her arms. “Actually, no.”

“No?” Hunter asked at once, his eyes raking her over. “What’s wrong? Are you sick again? You shouldn't have dairy so soon after, you know."

Mal laughed to herself and shook her head, taking a few steps forward. "No, I'm not going to be sick again. At least, not right now. Probably a lot more for a few weeks. You've been getting up early for the past little bit, so you've missed my usual morning bouts, but I'm told it's all pretty normal."

"What's normal?" His eyes were wide and confused, completely clueless as to what was coming.

Mal paused, cherishing the anticipation even as fear licked at her. "I was late, and I never am, so I wondered, but then I started feeling off, so I was pretty sure…"

"Mal, baby, stop playing."

She smiled at him and moved even closer, though there was still a good foot between them. "I took a test, Hunter. And I went to the clinic before we left." She bit her lip, then exhaled. "I'm pregnant."

Hunter blinked once, then again. "Pregnant."

Mal nodded, just once. "Pregnant."

Nothing happened for a moment, then Hunter started laughing. Softly at first, then a disjointed chuckling, and then it rolled into deep belly laughs that shook him until he had to brace his hands on his knees.

Mal watched him, wondering when he was going to say something, but grinning at his laughter all the same. "This better be good laughter, husband, because I'm not going to be laughing once we get to the end–"

Hunter cut her off with a triumphant kiss that told her everything she needed to know and more. "Yes, baby," he whispered against her lips when he let her breathe, cupping her face. "Yes! I've wanted a family with you from day one. Nothing could make me happier. Are you okay? Are you excited? Scared?" He pulled back and ran a hand over her hair. "Are you scared, babe?"

"All of the above," Mal admitted, gripping his shirt in her hand. "I didn't know we'd start so soon, and my career is just taking off–"

"We'll make it work," he overrode, shaking his head and nodding at the same time. "We'll make all of this work. It won't mess anything up. It'll just make us more creative." He smiled and kissed her hard.

"I will wear the baby in a carrier at the office any time you need me to, I promise."

Mal bumped her nose against his chin, giggling. "I might let you." She sighed and looked up into his eyes. "I wasn't sure I wanted this until you. And I wasn't sure when I wanted it even then. But now it's here, and… I want your baby, Hunter. I want our baby. Because it's ours."

Hunter leaned down, touching his brow to hers and closing his eyes. "I love you, Mal. So much."

Mal hummed and reached up for the back of his neck. "I love you too, babe. And so does our baby."

He grinned at that, then kissed her again.

And it was something to remember.

About the Author

Growing up, Rebecca Connolly wanted to be Elizabeth Bennett, Mary Poppins, or British royalty, so it came as a great shock when she discovered she was an American girl from the Midwest. She started making up stories when she was young, and thanks to a rampant imagination and a fairly consistent stream of hot chocolate, ice cream, and cookie dough, she's kept at it. She loves a good love story, and a good swoon, and tries to share that with her readers. She still lives in the Midwest, has two degrees in non-writing fields, and dreams of one day having a cottage of her own in her beloved British Isles.

Rebecca is a huge fan of period dramas and currently writes in the Regency era, though she refuses to rule any other time period out. You just never know where the imagination will take you, and she'll write whatever story comes to her whenever it's set! There is always a story to tell, and she wants to tell them all!

You can find out more at www.rebeccaconnolly.com.